BIRTHPYRE

And he remembered . . .

An outline in black against the darkness of the room. Cowled, within the folds of shadow, a face, glowing with the pale light of a funeral shroud. The cruel gash of mouth, twisted hideously into a grin that burned itself indelibly into his memory: a grin that had smiled at the taste of charred human flesh, a mouth that had drunk hot, pumping blood. And the eyes, empty receding caverns. Yet not empty . . . not empty . . . within them a vision of squirming victims impaled on sacrificial stakes, their skin licked greedily by flames like dagger-points.

And all the while that hideous mocking smile. Until a hand came out from within the shadow, leprous, black talons reaching out toward him, toward his eyes . . .

LARRY BRAND

BIRTHPYRE

AVON
PUBLISHERS OF BARD, CAMELOT AND DISCUS BOOKS

BIRTHPYRE is an original publication of Avon Books.
This work has never before appeared in book form.

AVON BOOKS
A division of
The Hearst Corporation
959 Eighth Avenue
New York, New York 10019

First Avon Printing, November, 1980

AVON TRADEMARK REG. U.S. PAT. OFF. AND IN
OTHER COUNTRIES, MARCA REGISTRADA, HECHO EN
U.S.A.

Printed in the U.S.A.

for my grandparents

Acknowledgments

I would like to express my gratitude to the following for their help, in many ways, in the writing of this book: Tom Wotherspoon, Rob Glaser, William Ngai M.D., Chuck Ashbaugh, Liz Derby, Eddy C. Dyer, Bob Gorga, and Ken Johnson; I would also like to thank the two editors with whom I have had the luck to work on my first book, Nancy Neiman and Richard Sewell, for their insight and willing help along the way. My very special thanks to Richard Fireman, for his precise intellect, his boundless patience, his care, and his painstaking job of Firemanization.

Prologue

A glimmer of light, morning's refraction, splits the future day, soft thunder crowds the horizon, building.

Then all is motion, spinning, electric dance: out of the void.

Eternity is split, as Heaven and Earth are split.

And in the freedom of nascent day, forms swirl into creation, mutating away from the larger body, shaping self, drawing essence from the sway of primal forces, until. . . .

The miracle occurs: within the field is design, within the body light. Separation. Infinite possibilities. . . .

Life.

City of Gold.

Passed down, an inheritance: the many in the one, here. Crystalline, the growth is natural.

The light is fresh, colors bright: eyes have not yet fallen into the sleep that will remove the subtler tones, only to allow their return over the vast space of years. There is unity of senses, a sea of life. Continuity. . . .

Knowledge and being are one.

(But there will come a time: prepare.)

A new separation, a new knowledge. Power, a force of will. And with it, a loss. Man comes under the *sway of the finite. The course is drawn. We select our fate, accept its confines, choose to be determined.*

(And dark shapes climb through the atmosphere as though on wings.)

The new vision slices like a knife, so smoothly you feel nothing: it passes cleanly between nerve endings; no pain. Yet.

But there is a future of victims: their screams reach us, reach back across the abyss, as flames melt skin, as steel pierces flesh. . . .

I see, can see it still, will know. We will remember.

For memory is all.

The Ancient's hand was finely formed, worthy of a Renaissance sculptor, the soft blue veins were visible, suggesting the subtle rises in the marble of a statue. He pointed to the structure, his eyes smiling, though with a touch of sadness. There is no doubt that he possessed great wisdom. His fingers, so delicate, grazed mine. I looked up, into his eyes. (I believe they changed color, according to his humor.) A teacher I had as a boy, not so long ago. Ah, there will come a time, he told me then, tells me still, there will come a time. . . .

Alone, alone in one, alone in all: there is no warmth here, no light. Death will cry out in the streets, blood will flow, sobs will be heard. . . .

Evil Ones, black spitting reptilian eyes. There is something within struggling to escape, to break through the skin and spread its ashes over the land.

Smoke of death will rise to the sky.

(We will strike you down, end your world, split the lines by which you see. Righteous Old Ones, we will defile your corpses. The world is ours.

He will be ours.)

Creatures of the night, they will turn from the

day, flee to the depths. They will find a home in the darkness. Waiting. . . .

(Dark below, dark among us. Whenever two gather in our name . . .)

They will watch us as the sacrificial blades fall; They will watch as victims are impaled on wooden stakes;

They will watch as children are thrown, alive and screaming onto the vast crematory fire.

Already a new thunder: the Earth rebels. For the power has become twisted.

There is no escape. Only a hope. The preparations have been made, the task accomplished. The possibility will survive, protected from the fire, the ice.

And it begins.

The raging. . . .

The wind and seas rise up, turning against man. The mountains erupt against the power, the will. The earth splits, oozing lava like gouts of thickened blood, to flow into the risen waters and explode at their cold touch.

The fire builds toward the sky, which lowers a shroud of ash and rock. A sea of flames swirls in the windstorm, cracking stone and melting flesh. The Earth splits, and again. . . .

The smoke of death will obscure the sky for a thousand years.

There is calm in this place.

Silence rings a pure sweet tone, cold, eternal, as deep within the earth the possibility of future life endures.

The waters' withdrawal has left the land fertile, though no longer able to reflect the night's six thousand shining eyes as they fade imperceptibly into blue. . . .

Morning.

The sun bright and fierce, the air still and crystal-clear over the soft flat dunes stretching across the desert floor toward the distant rocky foothills.

The man, middle-aged and tired, carrying a bloated canvas sack over one shoulder, walks along the single dirt road, heading toward his village. He walks slowly, without taking his eyes from the road; he has made this trip a thousand times.

He stops for a few seconds to wipe his brow with a dirty handkerchief, looking without interest over the wasteland. He sighs deeply and resumes walking.

A sharp glint of gold, sparking to his eye.

He stops, squinting into the hazy red-whiteness of the sand. He shields his eyes from the glare of the sun, but sees nothing. Muttering, as if angry with himself for the waste of time, he leaves the road, walking into the desert to look for the source.

After an hour's searching he begins to turn back.

But again a flash strikes his eye. This time from just beyond a sand dune a few yards in front of him. He continues up the slope.

And stops, transfixed.

The sack drops from his shoulder. His eyes widen, as though about to burst his skin. His lips begin to quiver, perhaps with the broken forms of an ancient prayer.

Slowly, he drops to his knees.

Part One

shrinking to a point. And at the same time he stood

Part One

*

THE WIND THAT had swept the desert had been the worst in many years, a hot, scouring breath that singed the lungs and wasted the few spots of arable land. It had gathered strength quickly, at first a mere whistling in the night (the wailing of an ancient beast, some of the old men of the village had said), then rising up like a black cape drawn across the sky. For six days it had reigned, driving inhabitants into their mud-brick houses and threatening to strip the earth of its skin and reveal its dark underlayer. But just as suddenly it had subsided, leaving a fluid tranquility in its wake, and again allowing the village children to be seen outdoors.

The lives of the villagers had returned quickly to the routines of antiquity, even with the sudden incursion of Western visitors. The great wind—as it would become known—and its strange discovery had, perhaps, been the beginning of something new, something they did not yet fully understand, but, with the patience of an ancient people, were willing to accept.

Not far from the small village, the streets of the Old City began to fill with its human tribes as if in response to some dark, chemical stirring in the blood. A varied pattern emerged, different every day, every sundown, depending on the day of week, time of year, and which of the many holy celebrations was in progress. And yet, the component parts were

17

always the same, the rush of sound and color pulsing forth with the inertial momentum of five thousand years: on one of the broad stone streets a large wooden door squeaked shut, pushing back until next morning the scents of various meats, some fresh, others already decaying; farther up the street a small dark man hastily swept the sidewalk in front of his establishment, pushing some straws under the door, cursing some minor incident, a half-forgotten slight; on Suo Khan Ez-Zeit a family of Hassidim marched along, men in front, women following with a certain automatic pride, talking animatedly; and at the gates the beggars, some blind, some faking blindness, resumed positions at the more strategic spots, curling their features into the grimaces most likely to produce results from the tourists entering the Old City for the evening meal. And as the day's energies shifted from business to home, and the women began preparing meals for returning husbands, and the urgency waned from even the streetsellers' voices, through the streets a sigh could almost be heard, a subliminal moan of neither agony nor tedium, but acknowledgment of another day's passing, another subtle death. It swept along easily, crossing squares and spires, penetrating flesh and stone alike: the voicing of a distant reflection, precipitating to form the tiny circlet of sweat on each man's brow at the end of the workday. And yet the air, as always, was still tinged with a residue of anticipation: it was the city.

John Alric sat quietly in the far corner of the tent, writing hand resting on the cluttered folding table in front of him. He watched the green canvas walls shift back and forth in rhythm, now expanding, now contracting the tent's volume, breathing in response to the breezes outside. The loose entrance flap allowed an occasional small gust to enter, sometimes to inflict considerable damage to the array of papers, photographs, and index cards on the table's surface.

Words had always come easily to Alric, flowing effortlessly from his hand, as if it were the tool of some higher inspiration. But today he found them incomprehensibly heavy, and apparently irretrievable by any effort of will.

Reflexively, he glanced over at a paperback book that lay at the far corner of the table. It had taken him only four months to write. Almost nostalgically, he recalled the early experiments that had led to his first tentative speculations, little more than musings. The book had been successful, though (or perhaps *because*, he often felt) it had lacked the scientific rigor he, himself, would have liked to have seen.

Again the tent sighed. Alric tapped his pen against the edge of the table. The developments over the past several months had brought him, as well as colleagues from various disciplines, into a dazed, yet somehow expectant, state of confusion. There had been so little time available to assimilate the new information, and, as always, much sorting had had to take place: the realities had had to be sifted from the many crackpot or merely misguided notions concerning the recent find.

When it had become known that something remarkable had been discovered in the desert not far from Jerusalem, he had received the news with excitement. The possibility of an unexpected archaeological find proving the deathblow to a pet theory had been secondary, clearly overbalanced by the promise of the knowledge to be gained; no place for vanity in the life of a scientist. Moreover, he reminded himself, he was confident that his theories would be substantiated, rather than discredited. Surely he had been convincing on that talk show, he now thought—visualizing his own face, always somewhat foreign on the television screen—as he had cogently answered the interviewer's question.

(There was always the matter of the golden apex. Was it solid gold? How far down did the structure go? And of course, and above all, *why?* And the familiar material had had to be gotten through, the old guard given their due. There were always the questions about the Great Pyramid of Cheops, the monumental achievement of the pyramid-building age—though its connection with this most recent find was, at best, tenuous. Yes, brick ramps could have been built along the sides and raised gradually as the construction grew higher. Yes, the stones had been quarried in the Mokattam Mountains, carried to barges with the use of sleds and rollers, placed with the use of wooden cranes, pulleys, ropes. . . . Such were the predominating theories. He had heard himself answer smoothly, coolly taking note that it got easier each time.)

And now, perhaps, the many months of research would culminate in a final test. An act of nature, a chance occurrence, six thousand miles from his home, had pressed down upon him with the strongest pressure of materiality: the testing ground was here.

He remembered standing from his chair in the den and walking through the open door to the living room, drawn there by the fluid voice of the television commentator. So calm that voice had been, so reasonable, so *objective.* "*Archaeologists report finding, in the Judean desert . . .*" The words had seemed to spark from the television speaker, jumping directly into Alric's brain. He had searched the walls of the room, unconsciously expecting to find something out of place, something changed. "*. . . an unusual artifact. . . .*"

Yes, the testing ground.

And now Alric searched the walls of his tent, again the physical evidences of his new-found recognition reminding him of the almost casual chain of events that had led to his involvement. It had, in fact, seemed a windfall, as, perhaps, things often were under such circumstances (though he couldn't help wondering how much his father's reputation in the field had contributed to his appointment). Someone at the university had suggested that, since his latest research, the most promising and scientifically credible in the field, was progressing so well (two published articles that month), he be put in charge of the excavation and study, along with, of course, an older man, perhaps the noted archaeologist Chandler. The course of events had seemed to have been drawn from without; greater forces had been at work. He had not had to vie for the opportunity, but had accepted it with growing anticipation.

"An unusual find in the Judean desert. . . ." Alric had almost felt that the commentator had been speaking directly to him.

And how clearly he could remember his first sight, so unlike other first views of anticipated objects, never as fulfilling as expected. A golden tip, protruding through the sand. . . . It had looked almost new, remarkable, considering its possible age. A reminder, perhaps, that not *all* things change.

A golden tip, no taller than a man. Yet he had been struck dumb.

It had been several years earlier that Alric had become interested in the question of "pyramid power"—at the time, a rather peculiar interest for a theoretical physicist. But certain reports concerning the properties attributed to pyramids had caught his attention, and he had become intrigued with the possibility that there was a group of phenomena that acted outside the bounds of everyday experience—in ways, perhaps, similar to those encountered in relativistic effects. The material regarding the properties of pyramids grew more extensive every day, though little of it bore the stamp of scientific credibility. As was to be expected, the claims vastly outweighed the evidence, and before long the reports ran the gamut from the mundane to the miraculous. One consistent claim, however, was that any pyramid built to the same proportions as the Great Pyramid of Cheops, and placed along the north-south axis, would have the ability to mummify meat and preserve food— that, in fact, it was the pyramid shape alone that was responsible for the process of mummification. Another interesting—if unsubstantiated—idea was posited by a man receiving a patent for a "razor-blade-sharpening device"—consisting of simply a small styrofoam pyramid. The "inventor" believed that the crystalline structure of the edge of a razor blade became realigned when placed within the "energy field" of a pyramid, hypothesizing that there might be a relationship between the pyramidal shape and the physical processes going on within it.

In the main, it was idle speculation by individuals with far more imagination than scientific rigor, and, in the atmosphere of pseudoscientific dilettantism of those years, the authorities at the university had been reluctant to allow Alric research time and funds on anything that even obscurely hinted at occultism. So he had begun his research at home, constructing crude pyramids of cardboard and wood. When his work had begun to yield interesting, if not yet clear, results, and grants had become feasible, he had begun the construction of larger and more sophisticated models made from a variety of materials, including wood, glass, fiberglass, and plastic sheetings. Several pyramids had been constructed with various metals, some of which seemed to interfere with the electromagnetic properties of the phenomena, increasing certain effects, decreasing others.

Within the different pyramids Alric had placed a variety of items, for periods of time from a few minutes to several weeks. The results had not always proved significant, but after several months of testing a weak yet defined pattern had emerged: old coins and jewelry seemed to lose much of their layer of tarnish after being placed inside a pyramid; meat and eggs dehydrated and mummified rather than decayed; polluted water became purified within a few days; milk remained fresh for days at room temperature, then produced a yogurt-like substance; plants tended to grow faster and healthier inside a pyramid.

Encouraged by these results, Alric had decided to test the pyramid's alleged powers on human subjects. Ads had been taken out in the school newspaper, and soon students from the university had volunteered to take part in the experiments. With the understanding that any results would, by their nature, be subjective, Alric had conducted experiments in which persons had remained inside pyramids for periods of time ranging from several minutes to several hours. Many of the subjects had claimed easier relaxation, peacefulness, enhanced ability to meditate, and even a feeling of rejuvenation, and the healing process for minor injuries, cuts, burns, etc., seemed to have been speeded up within the space of a pyramid.

Regarding the factors responsible for these effects —Alric had written at the beginning of the section devoted to his speculations—there had been nothing conclusive to report, though several avenues of approach had presented themselves. Could there be, Alric had mused, a relationship between energy and the spaces bounded by certain shapes? Did the possibility exist that there were energy resonances occurring in space which were subject to functional rather than mechanical laws, and to which the pyramid shape was particularly receptive? Alric had gone on to stress that he was a long way from anything that would have represented conclusive evidence to the scientific community, the findings indicating, at that point, only possibilities.

Nothing conclusive. . . .

But Alric had, in fact, believed he'd detected a possible link, a clue tying together the various phenomena: in each of the experiments a process was either slowed down (the decaying of food, souring of milk, etc.) or speeded up (plant growth, healing, etc.) Therein, perhaps, lay the key.

What had struck Alric as the most interesting avenue of approach was the possibility that the time frame was in some way altered within the space of the pyramid, causing all physical processes inside it to change relative to the external perception of time. Throwing off the blinders of human perceptors—attuned to the "limit case" reality of three dimensions and unable to encompass the supra-reality of space-time, a fourth direction of space— was it not possible that the pyramid in some way created a tear in the continuum, a tiny area where the structure of time as we knew it was radically altered?

And now in the Judean desert time had yielded yet another mystery. Alric sat back in his seat and allowed the collage of words, images and events of the past several months to filter through his mind, hoping to find coherence, or at least substance, to create form out of the tangle of interrelated events: they had to point somewhere. He reached for the book at the far end of the table and opened it to a page near the end—the section concerning the building of the pyramids—and smiled slightly as he read his own words—words which each passing hour might bring closer to vindication or obsolescence.

To understand the significance of the pyramids, he had written, one did not have to look to "visitors from the stars"; the answers lay within the range of human experience, and pointed to the vital heritage of mankind. All of our current ideas about the development of civilization were founded on an unquestioned belief in the evolutionary process, based on certain assumptions which were taken for granted but never proved. It should be remembered, he had stressed, that the great majority of popular legends, myths, and folk beliefs contained in them accounts of an earlier age of man, during which he had possessed a knowledge far superior to that of his descendants. The idea of a linear, upward process of evolution, that which was called "progress," was really a minority viewpoint when looked at within the context of civilization as a whole.

In his book he had gone on to list the many "proofs" offered by the "gods from outer space" theorists: the recurrent themes in ancient folklore of "gods" with magical powers, among them the gift of flight; the astounding accuracy of ancient calendars and astronomical observations; the maps of Piri Reis and others—including accurate details of the then-unknown continent of Antarctica; and the stunning engineering achievements of archaic cultures, including the Great Idol of Tiahuanaco, the prehistoric calendar at Stonehenge—and, of course, the pyramids. How much more plausible was the idea that the ancient civilizations of man—the Egyptians, in particular—had possessed a scientific knowledge that present man was only beginning to rediscover? Secrets of universal forces, seen as through a hazy dream by the alchemists, glimpsed at and translated into mathematical formulae by Einstein and Heisenberg—were these in reality the first discovery of man, moreover, his birthright, lost with his expulsion from the Garden?

He looked up from the book and leaned back in his chair. *Heisenberg.* The name still coursed through his body like a purifying rain. It had sparked the birth of the scientist in him. Or rather, the coming of age. It had been his first year at college; a world had opened up to him within the pages of a physics textbook. He remembered the poorly lit dormitory room, the bed covered with books, his clothes strewn haphazardly about. Heisenberg. He could see himself as a student, his fingers almost trembling on the page . . . and for an instant it had appeared that the letters, so black and clear upon the paper, had flitted briefly, engaged in an unknown and ancient dance, returning quickly to their assumed postures, as if to stay his alarm. But it had been too late; the motion had been detected. He could never return.

He now turned back to his own book, and continued reading about the pyramid builders, who, perhaps, through their monumental structures, had sought to endow their descendants, at their eventual coming of age, with the secret, the birthright. . . .

"The author's a bit stuffy, don't you think?" said a voice from the entrance of the tent.

Alric looked up from the book and smiled broadly at his wife. "I wish you'd knock before entering."

Diana Alric's eyes shone in the pale green light of the tent. "I did," she said, twisting in the soft canvas entrance flap to show him. "Didn't you hear?"

She stood by the entrance, casually resting a hand on her hip, her long dark hair moving slightly on the small air currents. She walked over to Alric and sat in his lap, her arm across his shoulder.

"Where have you been?" he asked.

"Just out for a stroll in the desert," she said, pushing a stray lock of hair from his forehead. "Did you know there were snakes around here?"

"Of course," he smiled. "This place used to be the Garden of Eden, didn't you know?"

She cupped her hand in front of her. "Care for an apple?" she asked, proffering him the imaginary fruit.

"Thanks just the same."

Diana stood and walked back to the entrance. She pulled back the flap and tied it off in the corner of the tent, allowing a triangle of sunlight inside.

Alric picked up his pen, leaned back to the table, and began writing.

She looked over at him. "Are you going to stay in here all day?"

He did not look up. "I'm going to the site in a little while," he said absently. "They're pretty far along."

Diana nodded soberly. "I know."

She walked over to one of the two folding cots across from the worktable, sat down, and reached for a magazine lying on the floor. Idly, she flipped through the pages, then tossed it back down.

Alric looked over at her. She didn't notice him watching her, but sighed deeply, her eyes fixed on a random spot on the tent's ceiling.

"Are you sorry you came here?" he asked, after a few minutes.

Her head moved imperceptibly in his direction, cocked slightly in curiosity. "What?"

"I told you there wouldn't be much for you here."

"You're here," she said, now returning his gaze.

He nodded, slowly, as if not quite satisfied with her answer.

"And besides," she continued, "it's a change from New York. I mean, you don't see any snakes in Central Park. Or any camels. . . ."

Alric smiled. "You haven't seen any camels *here*, either."

"But I could if I wanted to," she said, half-seriously. "Really. There's a camel auction in Beersheba every Thursday. Ahmad told me."

"He's a fund of information, isn't he?" said Alric, turning back to the table. The mention of the guide's name had reminded him of the work to be done.

"I like him," said Diana, again reaching for the magazine.

From outside they heard the sound of a jeep approaching quickly and coming to a stop, followed immediately by its door being slammed shut.

"Carl back already?" wondered Diana.

Before Alric could respond, a young Arab workman appeared through the entrance, visibly excited.

"Dr. Alric!" he blurted, unconsciously brushing sand from his clothes onto the floor of the tent.

Alric looked up at the small, dark man.

"We've found the entrance!"

Alric's body reacted first; he half rose from his seat. "I thought it would be another day or two."

"Apparently it is not as deep as we had assumed. Dr. Chandler said you would want to see right away."

"Thank you, Khalid," said Alric, standing.

Diana stood as well, and her eyes met Alric's, the intensity in them unmistakable.

The *entrance*. . . .

They had been in the desert for three months, every handful of sand bringing them closer. Now he had to rein his excitement and calmly accept the fruits of their efforts. Objectivity, dispassion, were all-important. But his mind reeled: soon they would be inside the structure. . . .

The three walked quickly through the tent's opening. Outside, the descending sun cast the small camp in dark colors. A few Arab workmen were in the vicinity of the two fifteen- by twenty-foot tents. Nearby was a small, unlit campfire. They walked to the open-topped jeep and got in, Khalid behind the wheel. Alric took a deep breath and gazed out through the windshield, as the jeep began to kick up sand, heading farther into the desert. Yes, the entrance, he thought, and with it perhaps some answers. The theories and speculations had been many, as was always the case in the absence of hard fact. But not until they could enter the structure, see its treasures, read its messages from the past, not until they could examine its artifacts with the knowledge and tools at their disposal, would anything be proved. Anticipation was a warm feeling that bathed Alric as he looked up and saw the small hill obscuring vision of the site. The jeep rounded the hill, slowed, and stopped, and the three climbed out, walking the remaining few yards.

Alric stood once more before the pyramid.

Sunlight glinted sharply off the capstone, and Alric hesitated briefly, his eyes accustoming themselves, as if to a strange light. As it was each time he viewed the structure, a shock ran through his blood as he stood at the high end of the narrow wooden ramp leading down to the base. The pyramid stood before him, gleaming, polished stone, pointing authoritatively, inexorably, heavenward: the mark left by an ancient race, hewn with such precision that a casual stroke against one of its edges would break the skin. Its surface, polished to a deep shine, reflected the setting sun, hinting at the magnificence of its crown. And his eyes twitched briefly as they approached that upper height: the capstone cased in solid gold. Alric searched the structure, each time as if the first, struggling to decipher its history, to find the key to its existence.

When, on a clear morning three months ago, an unknown villager had told assembled relatives and neighbors of his discovery, it had led to a chain reaction that had created in academic circles a fevered pitch rivaled only by the unearthing of the Rosetta Stone and the discovery of the Dead Sea Scrolls. He had told, in excited tones and with much gesturing, of how, while walking along a desert road, he had been momentarily blinded by a brilliant flash of light. He had searched for almost an hour for the source, until, almost at the point of believing he had imagined the flash, he had seen, from just beyond a sand dune a few yards in front of him, a tiny shaft of light. He had climbed the dune—and there had been awestruck, his legs no longer able to support his weight. For before him, in the depression between two sand dunes, had stood a pyramid of gold, rising to a man's height, and gleaming magnificently in the sunlight.

The small research team sent to supervise excavation of the site had soon discovered, with the use of sounding equipment, that what the villager had found had been merely the golden capstone of a pyramid some sixty feet in height. The apex of gold —in fact, a pyramid atop a pyramid—had, perhaps, not been unprecedented. Some scholars had long postulated that the missing top section of the Great Pyramid of Cheops—stolen during the long, dark intervening centuries—had been made of gold: a scaled-down model of the pyramid itself, the entirety mirroring the essence of life process. In their view, the Great Pyramid was a metaphor for the natural laws of growth, the golden apex symbolizing the seed, catching the vital spark from the sun, and igniting the body with the sacred fire of life.

Whatever the theory's basis in fact, the capstone of the Great Pyramid had been lost to history, and much was left to speculation. Similarly, its sides of polished limestone had been removed, stripped away in the thirteenth century to rebuild large portions of Egypt destroyed by earthquake. But here in the Judean desert, buried—and thus protected from the necessities and greed of men—stood a structure as uncorrupted as it had been on the day its construction had been completed.

Alric and Diana made their way down the wooden ramp which ran along the inside of a crater of excavated sand. At the bottom they found Dr. Carl Chandler amid a group of Arab workmen, explaining, with much gesticulation, exactly how something must be done. He was a middle-aged man, always somewhat ponderous-looking in his baggy khaki shorts. His cheeks were red and puffed under black horn-rims, giving him a perpetually out-of-breath look. He noticed Alric, and, with a brief motion of his hand, indicated to the workmen that the conversation had ended. He walked quickly over.

"Come have a look," he said, and went to the pyramid's wall and knelt in the sand, indicating to Alric to do the same. When Alric was beside him, Chandler pointed to a hairline crevice, about two feet long, just above the level of the sand. "That's it," he said.

Alric looked down in surprise, then back at Chandler. "It's exposed. . . ?"

Chandler returned the look, saying nothing.

"What do you mean?" asked Diana.

"The entrances of pyramids were usually covered by the casing stone," said Alric. "We assumed we'd have to find it with sounding equipment."

He ran a finger along the crevice, then looked back at Chandler, immediately catching the look in the older man's eyes. "What the matter, Carl?" he asked.

Chandler hesitated. He tapped the cool surface of the stone entrance. "It's *also* on the wrong side," he said.

"I don't understand."

"Virtually all of the known Egyptian pyramids have their entrances on the north side. This one's facing east."

"Is it *that* unusual?"

"It's not just that. . . ." said Chandler. "Several things have been bothering me."

"What do you mean, Carl?"

"John," said the older man, his voice growing grave, "we knew this was old . . ." He hesitated before continuing. "But I think it's pre-Egyptian."

Alric said nothing, his eyes locked with Chandler's. *Pre*-Egyptian . . . ? The working theory had been that an offshoot of Egyptian civilization, perhaps during, but more probably after, the great pyramid-building epoch, had migrated northward, for reasons unknown, bringing with it the elements of the culture. Carbon dating had suggested an older date, but archaeologists had been skeptical, utilizing the customary objection to controversial findings: disputed association, the uncertain connection between local fossil remains and the artifact.

"I've been thinking about it for some time now," continued Chandler, "and certain things just don't fit. The masonry is unlike any I've seen at Egyptian sites. Or anywhere else, for that matter. And the sides . . ." He shook his head. "The angles forming them are exactly the same. I mean *exactly*. I've never come across anything like it . . ."

"*How* old, Carl?" asked Alric, quietly.

Chandler looked meaningfully into Alric's eyes. "I'd say six thousand years, at the very least."

Alric began to respond, the objection apparent in his face, but Chandler continued quickly. "If it were any less than that, there would have to be a clear overlap with the Egyptians, in terms of style." Again he hesitated. "I'm inclined to think the original carbon estimate might not be far off."

"But that would mean—"

Chandler nodded. "A civilization of which nothing is known, of which no record remains. A civilization older than, but perhaps as advanced as, the Egyptians, that vanished without a trace." He paused, as though to allow his words to settle. "Until now," he finished.

Alric's hand rested against the flat surface of the pyramid. His fingers tingled. If Chandler was right . . . He shook his head slightly, as if to remind himself of the necessity to separate the possible, or even the probable, from the proven. Knowledge had to be gained incrementally, and nothing could be taken for granted, nothing accepted without proof. But the one question spun around in his head like an accelerating vortex.

If not the Egyptians, who?

He looked into Chandler's eyes, as if to convey his thoughts.

The older man returned his gaze, and nodded slowly. "Yes," he said, "I know."

Alric motioned toward the crevice in the pyramid. "How long before they'll have it cleared away?"

Chandler called one of the workmen over to him. They exchanged a few words in Arabic, then Chandler turned back to Alric. "He says by tomorrow morning."

"Good," said Alric.

Then, quietly, to himself, "Good."

The streets of the Old City pulsed with the pressure of the human wave. The energy, absent just an hour ago, had begun to rise again, as though another notch had been reached, a new part of the cycle begun: the evening time was sweeping in. The eyes of the many tourists were alert as they flitted around, seeking out a suitable eating place, searching for an auspicious find in one of the trinket shops that did their best business at night, or perhaps simply taking in the flow of color and motion of a foreign place.

Alric, Diana, and Chandler sat in the outdoor section of a small restaurant not far from the Damascus Gate, their senses following various bits of activity along Al-Wad. Within their enclave, the three were separated from the rest of the world, removed by their passivity, their spectatorship. In the street before them, a heavy American woman bustled her two children ahead of her, whining in a language that now sounded strange to them; from farther up the street wafted the acrid odors of a smoking salon, wherein Arabs drew long, contemplating breaths from water pipes, as their fingers moved along the backgammon board with blurring speed; in the distance a streetseller's voice could be heard over the general confusion of sounds, calling plaintively to no one in particular.

The usually talkative Dr. Chandler sat quietly and looked down at the pita bread, stacked evenly in the center of the table. He toyed absently with his fork.

"You feel it, too," said Alric, noticing the older man's strange mood.

Chandler looked up through horn-rims, then back down at the bread. "I suppose it's hard not to feel a bit strange," he said. "When one has devoted one's life to the study of a science, and then a find of this magnitude comes up. . . ." He finished with a shrug.

For a moment Chandler sat silent again, his thoughts turned inward. He recalled the years of his apprenticeship, working at several of the ancient sites of the Middle East, when, as a young scientist, the discovery, the breakthrough had always seemed imminent; the conclusive proof had always seemed to be in the next pile of statistics, that corroborative microfossil in the next handful of sand. He could still visualize the ragged cardboard data folders which each day had grown mysteriously thicker, as if by magic; could still feel the ancient dust that had filled his lungs as he would gently tap clean the surface of an artifact, and the calloused knees, worn to insensibility as his fingers had groped through mounds of dirt, seeking archaeological treasure. And now here it was, presented to him. It seemed the fulfillment of a life's dream. He recalled descriptions of the discovery of the tomb of Tutankhamen, as the archaeologist Howard Carter, nagged by a persistent inner voice, watched as workmen cleared the last of sixteen ancient steps leading to the sealed door; as his eyes marveled at the clear inscription of the seal of the boy pharaoh; as, with unsteady hands, he made a small breach in the upper corner of the second door, lit a candle, and held it by the hole; as, trembling with expectation, he peered through the opening, feeling the easy rush of warm air escaping from the chamber; and as he stood, dumbstruck, while his eyes conferred form on the dark patches within. After an eternity, the man behind him had asked, "Can you see anything?" Slowly, the archaeologist had responded. "Yes," he had said, his voice tremulous. "Wonderful things." And now the desert had yielded yet another enigma. Now was Chandler's turn. He would wake up tomorrow morning as if it were an ordinary day, as if the world would not have changed by its end. He would again stand before the pyramid. Tomorrow, just a few months after its gold tip had been revealed, its boundaries would be breached, and its inner walls would again resonate with the vibrations of human voices.

"This is really going to topple some theories, I suppose," said Alric, watching for Chandler's reaction.

Chandler looked up again. "You think there's that much vanity in archaeology?"

Alric nodded, smiling.

"Well, you're right," said Chandler, now smiling as well. Then, returning the chide, but meaning it, "But then we *all* might see some theories go down the tubes."

Alric put up his hands in mock capitulation.

"Come on, Carl," said Diana. "This has got to be the most important thing in your life. And not just because of any theories."

"In *my* life? My dear, this may well prove to be one of the most important discoveries in the history of archaeology."

The waitress came and placed their meal before

them, sliding dishes and glasses off the serving tray with swift, practiced movements, then scurrying quickly back into the kitchen.

Chandler tentatively stabbed at a piece of meat, then put down his fork and tore off a piece of pita bread. He couldn't help smiling internally at Alric's earlier remark, remembering the unceasing interdisciplinary disputes—sparked by personalities as often as evidence—following the discovery of the Dead Sea Scrolls. Careers had been made and broken, almost whimsically, it had seemed, and selective blindness had played its customary part, allowing interpretations to be subtly persuaded along the paths amenable to a given theory. And how many theories there had been! But now, with this latest find, most serious scholars had remained conservative, if not downright laconic, regarding their views. Perhaps the small pyramid would speak for itself.

Tomorrow. . . .

Chandler frowned, finally finding a piece of meat with his fork. He turned to Alric, suddenly eager to change the subject.

"By the way," he began, chewing the meat methodically, "when are you going to see that Michaels fellow again?"

Now was Alric's turn to frown. The mention of Michaels's name reminded him of his other quest in this country, and suddenly he realized that he had been putting off his next—and perhaps last—meeting with the man. And he understood why: if there was nothing to be learned here, then there was nowhere else to go. . . .

"I should drop by his office sometime this week," he said quietly. "He might have something for me."

Diana watched Alric silently, seeming to share his concern.

"Nothing so far?" asked Chandler.

"He said sometimes it can take months. And even then, nothing may turn up."

36

"Well," said Chandler, "it's been over thirty years."

"I know. But being here, I had to at least try. I may not have the chance again. I'd like to find out what I can."

"Their records go back that far?"

"Some do."

Chandler nodded.

The restaurant was beginning to grow crowded. Alric watched the single harried waitress scoot from table to table, neatly balancing a tray filled with several orders. His frown deepened as he thought back to himself as a young boy, standing in the hallway of his house, waiting with the inevitable question, his throat dry, his face troubled . . . until the click of the turning lock had told him that the door was about to open. The words had fallen from his mouth like drops of mercury, beading up on the floor to embarrass him with their presence. His mother had looked up. She had not been surprised to see him standing there. She had nodded slowly, to herself. She had known this day would come. . . .

Alric felt his throat growing dry. He raised a hand to signal the waitress, but, out of sympathy for the woman, stopped his motion. Instead, he drew in a deep breath of the cooling night air.

The three Americans walked slowly along Suo Khan Ez-Zeit, still, after three months, looking about the ancient streets, still finding new sources of interest in the Old City. They were, it seemed to Alric, more attentive tonight, more observant of the textures and turnings of the city. It was as though a burden had been lifted, or a veil dropped. And Alric thought he understood the reason: the pyramid was now accessible; tomorrow they would enter it, would finally cross the boundary between imagination and fact. And, expectation and nervous tension having reached their peak, they were suddenly pervaded by a strange calm, the final respite before the real work would begin. Their serenity allowed them to see the Old City in sharp focus, for perhaps the first time: the city proclaimed by King David to be the capital of the Jewish nation; the city whose streets Jesus had walked; the city which housed the Dome of the Rock. They saw the home of three religions, the city which had endured countless sieges and partial destructions, had risen from the ashes five times, and had changed hands at least twenty-six. There was endless variation within its walls; each day a million themes were replayed. It was a city where an instant could flower into an eternity, and a thousand years could pass in the closing of an eye.

They paused briefly at a shop while Chandler bought a hundred-gram slice of halvah. "Been here twelve weeks, and already I'm addicted to the stuff," he said, offering a piece to Alric and Diana.

Alric smiled and accepted the offering, returning quickly to his thoughts. Even with the soothing peace they were experiencing, and this fresh awakening to the Old City, he was aware of a disturbing feeling, nagging at the limit of his awareness—and whenever he caught Chandler's eye, he sensed it in the older man as well. The great antiquity of the pyramid. It was compelling—and he couldn't help recalling the reports of the ancient historians who had claimed that the Egyptians were themselves the degenerated branch of an earlier civilization, lost to time. Alric thought back to his youth, and his first intimations of a golden past. The books had spoken of legendary peoples, magic, alchemy. His eyes had widened at tales of supermen, flying saucers, the miraculous. But, even in the magical exuberance of pre-adolescence, the pull of materiality had always brought him back, gravitated him toward the line. Yes, to be rigorous, objective—to be *scientific*. And there was enough there, within the confines of matter (the electron flits, says Heisenberg, black on white on black, two places at once, no places at once; it can go either way, it can always go either way). The infinite existed, no need for children's fantasies, or for the more recent "gods from outer space." The infinite existed. Had one of its facets appeared in the Judean desert? And would the scientific method bear out his intuitive, unvoiced search? He felt himself getting closer, but, for now, let his thoughts rest.

Tomorrow. . . .

At the next corner they slowed as they passed a small trinket shop. Several shelves ran along the inside of the window, displaying antique oil lamps, rings, and coins in various stages of corrosion.

The Arab shopkeeper stood in the doorway. As the Americans passed, he touched Alric's shoulder and held out a small ring. "Fix a price! Fix a price!" he called.

Alric turned to the man and smiled. "No, thank you."

As though he had not heard, the man persisted. "Fifty pounds. Just fifty pounds. Good price."

"It's only a few dollars," whispered Diana.

Alric looked at the ring, a simple metal band. "I'll give you ten," he said.

The shopkeeper looked hurt. "Forty. It's very old."

"How old?"

"Five hundred years."

Alric winked at Diana and Chandler, then looked back at the shopkeeper. "I need something older."

The man considered. "I make mistake," he said, suddenly angry with himself. "Two thousand years old. Twenty pounds."

Alric smiled again. "Ten pounds."

The shopkeeper, now indignant, made a motion of refusal.

Alric shrugged and turned to walk away.

"Ten pounds!" the man called after him.

Alric returned and gave the man ten pounds. With an unconvincing expression of anger and hurt, the man handed the ring to him.

The three continued walking. Alric showed the ring to Chandler. "Two thousand years old," he said.

Chandler studied the band. "They drop them in sulphuric acid," he said, handing the ring back to Alric. "Instant age."

Diana took the ring from Alric. She rolled it playfully in her palm, then slipped it on a finger. She smiled. "Believe what you will, but I say it belonged to a pharaoh."

They continued to the Damascus Gate, and climbed the stone ramp leading out of the Old City. A few old beggars, sitting along the walls of the ramp, watched them as they passed, walking the remaining few yards to the jeep.

That night Diana joined Alric in a stroll through the desert. On milder nights it had become his custom to take long walks before going to sleep. He would try to let his mind—cluttered with each day's new material, new assessments, new possibilities—go blank, become as vacant as the vast, surrounding dome. In places where rock-strewn terrain gave way to pillowy expanses of sand, he would remove his shoes, tie the laces together, and sling them over his shoulder. It was so easy to let go of thoughts that way—or, rather, to think within the more natural rhythms of the body.

It was a comfortable night, cool and clear; a mild breeze sifted through their hair and refreshed their faces. They walked quietly, hand in hand, and it seemed to bring to life in Alric's mind the times they would walk through New York's Central Park on summer afternoons, and he would watch Diana, studying her profile as if for the first time, the full lips, deep red under the mild slope of her nose, the eyes bright, watching the ground serenely, but attentively, perhaps searching for a squirrel to follow in its nervous hunt for food. And if she would notice him watching her, her eyes would jump to catch him, sparking mutual laughter. He could almost see the blue of the lake, the water still, its mirror surface true, seeming to touch the mind and reawaken times when there had been more to see than to say. How long ago had it been?

He turned to Diana. "You want to hear something funny?"

"What?"

"I'm scared."

She turned to him, smiling gently. "That's not so funny."

He slowed his pace slightly. "It all seems so . . . easy."

"What do you mean?"

"I don't know exactly." He looked away, ran a hand through his hair, looked back at Diana. "Did you ever stop to think about this whole thing? I mean, why me? Why was I selected for this project, given this opportunity? I'm not even an archaeologist."

She smiled. "Because you're a 'brilliant young physicist with unorthodox ideas concerning the nature of pyramids.' See, I've been reading your book jackets."

He had to smile as well. She always seemed to be able to pull him from his darker moods before he'd sunk too deep. "Why else do you think I married you?" he asked.

"And I always thought it was my cooking."

He put his arms around her. "Wrong," he said, bending his head to kiss her.

She put her arms around his waist, pulling him toward her. She wanted to envelop him when his doubts assailed him, wanted to offer him easy respite. She would tell him with her eyes that all was well, but she always felt that her unspoken assurances were not fully accepted; in some ways he always seemed alone. She could only keep repeating her offer of sanctuary.

They continued walking, arm in arm, their vision aided by the nearly full moon. Around them they could make out an occasional cactus or bramble bush sticking up from the desert floor; a low uneven darkness on the horizon indicated where the foothills began.

Alric narrowed his eyes, as if trying to discern vague shapes in the distance. He still couldn't shake the feeling, like a dull ache, nagging, yet impossible to pinpoint. He couldn't put it into words, it was just a kind of . . . uncertainty. He frowned. Like, perhaps, the uncertainty of his last visit to that doctor, the specialist, with his gray office and gray desk . . . but no, better to think back to the park, warm afternoons, safe memories. But, even there, hadn't there been that feeling, ill-defined and fleeting? That uncertainty? He would be standing before the lake thinking back to times before he had stood in that gray doctor's office to learn of the findings which would have so much bearing on his future, times before he would shrink from the words that threatened to entomb him, turn him to stone, times before he would have to banish that white-haired doctor to some level below consciousness, in a vain attempt to impose his will upon matter. He would stand at the edge of the lake, looking out over its glassy tranquility. But then the reflected skyline would seem to shimmer, then fade, and he would have the icy feeling that there was something behind him, always behind him, he would sense it, but wouldn't be able to turn . . . a sudden web of fear would threaten to ensnare him as a shadowy figure hovered at the periphery of his awareness, and he wouldn't know if it was there, with him in the bright sunlight, or if he was asleep having a nightmare, like the ones that had started recently, the ones so real that he would wake up cold and sweating and wondering which was the dream and which the reality . . . and on some deep unclear level he would wonder if this was his past or his future hovering behind him like a figure shrouded in black, closer still . . . and he would know that his mouth was opening in a cry but that nothing was coming out . . . *don't let it come* . . . closer still, can almost touch it, can almost feel the fire, feel the cold . . . *don't* . . . the head cowled in shadow, and the face—no, not a face, no face, sick whiteness, pasty, death shroud, funeral whiteness . . . and closer still, black gashes where mouth should be, where eyes should be . . . closer. . . .

They had walked in silence, arms linked, for some minutes when Alric stopped so suddenly that Diana's momentum swung her around to face him. She looked up and into his eyes, crystal blue in daylight, now glistening violet in the starlight, half forcing, half supplicating their way into her own soft brown ones. He dropped slowly to his knees and buried his face in her belly. She dropped down to face him, and, embracing, they toppled easily sidewards to the ground.

The desert snake watched quietly, carefully; unmoving, its two small eyes peered out from within a low mound of sand. It watched the two figures, less than ten yards distant, as the shapes converged, separated, grew into each other, became one dark mass against the sky's faint glow along the horizon.

It waited in silence.

Unblinking, it watched.

*

ALRIC'S EYES OPENED after only a few hours' sleep. The blue dome of sky greeted him less harshly than he'd expected; his instinctive hand-to-brow gesture had been unnecessary. For a moment he watched the large red disk of the sun move perceptibly upward, revealing its motion clearly as it passed the sharp line of the horizon. Somewhat disturbing, he thought, this obvious demonstration of the quick passage of time. He looked over at Diana and touched her arm to wake her, then stood and stretched his limbs.

"What time is it?" she mumbled through half-sleep.

"It's dawn."

She opened her eyes slowly, allowing daylight to filter in a little at a time. As she began to sit up, Alric crouched down in front of her, putting his hands on her shoulders. He looked into her eyes, his face intense, yet unsettled.

She returned his look, smiling, though her face remained serious. She stood up and looked around, as if trying to reorient herself in the barren stretch. Then, from behind him, she slipped her arms around his waist and pulled herself to him, turning her face so that the side of her head rested against his back. Her expression was intent, concentrated; she could have been an eavesdropper, with head pressed up against a wall, listening for incriminating sounds from beyond. Alric, his face impassive, rested his

44

hands on hers. They stood silent for a few moments, then turned to make their way back to camp.

When they arrived, Chandler and their Arab guide, Ahmad, were already sitting by the small campfire, sipping black coffee from paper cups. They turned to the new arrivals.

"Good morning!" called Ahmad, standing. "Did you sleep well?"

"Very well, thank you," answered Alric, brushing some sand from his hair and smiling at the Arab.

He liked Ahmad. The villager had proved indispensable to the Americans, serving as guide, interpreter, and jack-of-all-trades. Educated in England, the dark, slender man had returned to his homeland in the hope of integrating the knowledge of a technological society with the ancient wisdom of the desert people. When the pyramid had been discovered, it had been he who had informed the New City's Archaeological Society, which in turn had contacted the Americans, who had helped in the financing of the excavation, and provided the heavy digging equipment necessary.

"Nights in the desert can be very beautiful," he said, holding out cups of coffee to Alric and Diana.

Alric downed the hot coffee in two gulps, then threw the cup into the fire. He watched the flames furiously devour this new morsel, vaporizing the remaining drops of dark liquid inside. He turned to Chandler. "Is it clear yet?"

Chandler nodded. "As soon as we're ready."

"Then we're ready," said Alric, turning toward the jeep.

In a few minutes the four stood at the high end of the wooden ramp leading down to the pyramid. For a moment they just looked down at the ancient structure, its polished walls glistening in the morning sun.

Alric squinted as the glare from the pyramid's golden tip hit his eyes—but he stood watching, allowing the light inside, as if to illuminate the mystery of

45

the body standing before him. And gradually, almost imperceptibly, the other figures around him began to fade from his vision, their outlines shimmering like desert mirages. He was alone, he felt. *Before him, so clear ... the Ancient's hand ... there is a vague tingling. ...* He opened his eyes, not realizing he had closed them. And slowly—though perhaps it took only an instant—he saw the world darken, the colors lose their life. He searched briefly for the sun, finding nothing. The sky and ground darkened until they were one continuous realm of black—except for the small central triangle of gold. *So clear, so clear it stands ... take a step, remember ... gold, brilliant ... take a step. ...* Then a vibration, a motion of air, and he was freed from the dark world. Again he found that his eyes had been closed.

"This is the one," Ahmad had said, stirring Alric to the present. "The first one."

Alric looked at Ahmad, then back down at the pyramid.

"Well," he said, "I guess it's time."

They walked down the wooden ramp and stopped at the base of the pyramid. A small rectangle had been cleared away, and several boards placed to form a flat surface for the working area. In the wall of the pyramid the entrance was now fully exposed: a small, square door, about two feet on a side; in the center was a cylinder, about five inches in diameter and rising an inch from the surface. No other markings were in evidence. Alric touched the cylinder with a finger, then looked at Chandler.

Chandler shrugged. "No idea." He, too, touched the cylinder, then ran a hand along the edge of the door. It was flush with the wall's surface.

Hefting the crowbar he'd brought for the purpose, Alric crouched down and attempted to force it into the hairline crevice where the door and outer wall met. He hit the curved end of the crowbar several

times with the flat of his hand, but could not suc-
ceed in inserting the sharp end.

He took a deep breath, relaxing his body. He
turned to Chandler. "Do you think we'll have to use
a drill?"

"I wonder . . ." said Chandler, stepping between
Alric and the door, adding with a smile, "Maybe we
should ring before entering." He knelt on the platform before the door. Then, with both palms, he
firmly pushed at the cylinder. "Give me a hand here,
John," he said.

Alric knelt by him and put his right palm on the
cylinder, also applying pressure. Slowly, the cylinder
retreated into the door until it was even with the
surface.

"Now try it," said Chandler.

Again Alric attempted to insert the crowbar, while
Chandler and Ahmad placed their hands on the door,
applying pressure sideways.

"That's it!" said Alric suddenly. "I felt it move!"

"Just a crack, now. Open it just a crack," said
Chandler. "Allow the gases to escape slowly."

The door slid slightly to the right.

"That's enough!" said Chandler, already turning to
his rucksack. He hastily fumbled through its contents, spilling an occasional item out onto the
platform or nearby sand. After a few seconds he
retrieved a small stump of candle, which he lit and
placed near the crack in the doorway to check for
poisonous gases. The flame wavered in the escaping
air, but did not go out. When it stopped moving he
directed Alric to reinsert the crowbar.

Slowly, the door slid open.

"Must be on some sort of balance mechanism,"
said Chandler. "The cylinder serves as a locking
device."

A thin tunnel of blackness stretched before them.

The end, thought Alric, gazing into the darkness.
The past three months seemed to congeal inside him,

shrinking to a point. And at the same time his mind almost rebelled against the ease with which access had been gained—as if the Mysteries should not yield so freely. *And a touch of familiarity in the smooth surface of the opening door . . . sliding softly, tunnel of blackness, the way is clear, forced. . . .*

Ahmad touched Alric's arm, after what seemed eons. "Doctor," he said, without removing his own eyes from the opening, "as head of this party, it is your honor to be the first to enter. It is your right."

Alric hesitated, looked into the guide's dark face, the eyes reflective of generations of desert dwellers. After a moment he took hold of Ahmad's arm. "No, Ahmad," he said. "It's not my right. It's yours." The words had escaped him, had surprised him.

Diana and Chandler exchanged glances, but the guide just smiled and bent toward the opening. But he, too, hesitated before entering. He closed his eyes, and his lips moved for a second as he knelt in the sand. Then, with a brief skyward flick of his opening eyes, he crouched down and wriggled through the pyramid's entrance.

Alric followed him into a narrow corridor. It seemed just wide enough to accommodate Ahmad's slender frame, and Alric was momentarily concerned with whether the larger Chandler would fit. Just beyond the entrance the tunnel became cylindrical and so constrictive that they were forced to crawl, both shoulders touching the sides. It seemed inclined at a slight downward angle.

After about twelve feet the tunnel became level and widened, permitting them to continue on all fours. At this point Alric looked back to find Diana right behind him and coming into the wider section of tunnel. Behind her was Chandler, struggling and squirming, but successful, nonetheless, in negotiating the narrow stretch.

After another few feet, Ahmad called back, "It's okay here. I can stand up."

The three Americans followed him into the next section, a hall about twelve feet long with a six-foot ceiling. This last part was inclined slightly upward. At its end, Ahmad's flashlight revealed another stone door, this one normal size.

As they approached, they found that it, too, had a small cylinder rising from the center. Alric stretched a hand to it, but stopped all motion as the cool stone met his skin. He turned slightly, half facing Chandler.

"It all seems so easy," he said.

In the complete silence of the corridor his words seemed to hang suspended, sounding tinny, the faintest modulation apparent. He was momentarily embarrassed by his voice, his words, as if they had been a poor choice.

The older man just nodded, mechanically, it seemed. "Yes," he said, "I know." But his thoughts were already focused on the room beyond, his eyes imagining the possibilities on the other side of the door. He was seeing, through Howard Carter's eyes, the vision of Tutankhamen's tomb, the golden couches and gilded throne, the large black statues, alabaster vases, and intricate shrines, the shadows of strange animals' heads shifting eerily on the walls, the golden snake silently watching from an open shrine, as the two royal sentries stood mute guard over the treasure, themselves clothed in gold, protected by the sacred cobra upon their foreheads.

Alric watched the cylinder retreat soundlessly into the door as his hand applied even pressure. The door slid open easily. He walked past the threshold, the others following closely.

Inside the chamber, they stopped cold.

Apart from a low stone pedestal, upon which sat a small gold pyramid, the chamber was empty.

Empty. . . .

Alric and Chandler turned reflexively to each other, their heads moving simultaneously, like two parts of some larger, malformed beast. And each set of questioning eyes found no answer in the other. They stood bewildered, their footsteps echoing in the empty chamber, while their unvoiced expectations escaped quickly, unnoticed, like the silent rush of air when the pyramid had been breached. No riches of knowledge within, only another riddle. Another door opened, another mystery found—a pyramid within a pyramid, a question within a question.

"Tomb robbers?" asked Alric, when at length he'd found his voice.

Alric's question roused Chandler. He lowered his flashlight's beam and carefully examined the floor. He knelt, at one point, and felt the surface with his hand. "No," he said, after a few seconds. "The floor is smooth and unscratched, which would preclude anything heavy, such as a sarcophagus, from having been dragged out."

"And if anyone had taken everything else," added Diana, "why would he have left the gold pyramid?"

"You expected treasure?" said Ahmad, smiling. "The pyramid is the treasure."

Alric looked curiously at the guide for a moment, wondering if he had meant the gold model or the pyramid itself. He walked over to the model. It was about eighteen inches high, and rested on a three-foot-high stand built into the floor. The square base of the pyramid was of the same dimensions as the top of the stand, but offset at a forty-five degree angle from the highly polished surface of the pedestal. Near the top of the stand, on each of the four sides, Alric found a sign etched in the stone: on the side facing east was a circle an inch in diameter; on the northern side was a five-pointed star; the western face bore a crescent of somewhat smaller radius than the circle; and the southern side showed a thick, vertical lens shape, about three-quarters of an inch wide.

"What do you make of these, Carl?" he called to

Chandler, who had begun inspecting the walls of the chamber for inscriptions, finding nothing.

The archaeologist came to the pedestal and bent down to examine each figure in turn. He then pulled out a pen and pad and copied the signs. "I don't know," he said, straightening and dropping the pad into his shirt pocket. "Have to give it some thought."

Carefully, Alric lifted the pyramid from its stand. Again he looked at Chandler. "It's too light," he said.

"What do you mean?"

"It must be hollow."

Chandler reached for the model. "Let's have a look."

The two searched the exterior of the small pyramid for a moment, slowly turning it on its axis, examining the edges carefully.

"There don't appear to be any openings," said Chandler. Then he adjusted his glasses, looking closer at the model in the weak light. "But look at this."

Just above the base, finely etched in the smooth gold, were the same four symbols as on the stand. Alric looked at the signs, then replaced the pyramid so that, no longer offset, its sides corresponded to the sides of the pedestal.

Diana ran a finger along the cool, flat surface of the pyramid. "Look at the colors in here," she said, noticing the back of her hand.

The four gathered by the model and examined each other's clothes and skin tones. The colors seemed more intense than normal.

"I wonder what causes it," said Diana.

"Turn off your flashlights for a second," said Alric after a moment. "I want to see something."

The lamplight extinguished, they could still see one another clearly. A cool, bluish light permeated the chamber, seeming to exude from the stone bowels of the pyramid itself. Then, as if by transference, their skin, too, seemed to emit a pale light, giving a slight shimmer to their outlines.

"The walls must be made of some phosphorescent material," guessed Chandler. "I'll try and get a sample." He reached into his pocket for his knife, but Alric restrained his arm.

"No," said Alric, a bit loudly.

The others looked at him.

He smiled self-consciously. "Why don't we do that tomorrow? I'm feeling a bit claustrophobic."

Chandler studied Alric for a second before answering. "All right," he said, nodding tentatively. Then, motioning with his head toward the model pyramid, "What are we going to do about that?"

"The museum's closed today," said Alric, considering. "It'll be safe here overnight. I'll drive it into town tomorrow morning."

"You and Diana still planning on spending the night in here?" asked Chandler, with a hint of irony.

Alric, untouched by the older man's faint amusement, looked over at Diana, who smiled assent.

"Yes," he said. "We are."

The market's tangled web of voices left Alric uncaught; still an observer, he passed under its lure a free man. To his right an old woman prodded suspiciously with gnarled fingers at a fruitseller's wares. She had no teeth, and a few strands of gray hair hung across her face, escaping the confines of a black linen kerchief. Unknown to her, a small insect struggled frantically to extricate itself from the wiry strands.

Alric had decided on a brief walking tour of the Old City before meeting Diana and Chandler for lunch. Too little time had been available for anything apart from the excavation, and he felt the need to learn what he could about these people whose ancestors had left so many secrets buried in the sand. Now he found himself in a large outdoor market, immersed in myriad unfamiliar smells, flashes of color for which he could find no name, and the guttural shouts of bickering Arabs, willing combatants in an ancient game.

But the noise grew quickly oppressive and, seeking to escape the market's late afternoon bustle, he turned into a narrow, uncrowded street. The change was abrupt: in a few seconds he found himself alone, protected from the bedlam as if separated from it by the body of the earth. He continued walking, surprised by the sudden silence and enjoying it. It was peaceful, warming, mesmeric; he thought of the past, walks through the park, warm afternoons . . . and suddenly, his mind drifting, he once more saw himself standing before a large, neatly arranged metal desk; outside, gray rain lightly touched the window.

"Low count," the white-haired doctor had said.

"Could we ever . . . ?"

"It is possible. But very unlikely, I'm afraid." A pause. "I'm sorry."

He had nodded slowly. Appropriate, he had thought. I never had a father, either.

From somewhere there was the sound of children's laughter.

A warm gust of air returned Alric to the present, momentarily disoriented, as if caught in an eddy of time. He stopped and looked around him. The empty stone windows seemed to stare back at him, like unnamed gravestones, returning his gaze, defiant reminders that he existed only for a while, but they remained—the city remained.

A touch of high-pitched laughter from nearby, and Alric freed himself completely. The flights were becoming more frequent, he noted detachedly. He continued down the street and turned a corner. A group of young boys had been playing, but on his approach stopped and ran to him. The smallest, a boy of no more than six, held out a thin hand.

"Some money, Mister?" he asked, in well-practiced tones.

Alric reached into his pocket for a coin, but seeing this, the other boys sprang toward him, pushing the small boy back and onto the ground. They pawed at Alric, yelping like a pack of dogs, until he reached into his pocket and pulled out a handful of coins, throwing them far down the street, sending the boys, cursing, in pursuit. He then picked up the first boy and pressed a large coin into his hand. The boy pocketed the money, then turned to join his companions in their treasure hunt. Alric shook his head, smiling. It occurred to him that he had never even seen the boy's eyes.

He turned away and continued walking. At the end of the block, he made his third right turn, this one onto a partially ruined street leading back toward the broad avenue on which the restaurant was located.

A quick motion, a peripheral blur off to the side caught his attention—a scrap of age-browned robe, a shock of tangled white hair, disappearing into an alley.

Curious, he turned back and walked to the beginning of the narrow passage running between the ruins of two buildings. Fragments of concrete and broken glass lined the ground. There was no sign of anyone. Had he imagined it?

He took a step into the alley.

A dark mass hurtled into his visual field, and before he could react, the blow knocked him breathless, a stinging pain tore at his stomach and chest. The huge black alleycat had sprung from the darkness of a nearby window, its hind claws digging into the flesh above his belt, its fangs inches from his face. Alric jerked his head back as the cat took a vicious swipe at his eyes. With a painful wrenching motion he tore the animal from his chest, trying to hold it away from his face. The cat bit at his hands, burying its teeth into the soft, fleshy area between thumb and forefinger. Alric stifled a scream as he ripped the cat away with his other hand and flung it to the ground. The pain knifed from his hand to his shoulder; for an instant his mind threatened to blacken. On the ground, the cat backed away slowly, arching its back and hissing malevolently. It appeared about to strike again, but Alric picked up a board from a nearby pile of rubble, ready to bring it down on the animal's head. The cat continued to back away, then turned and leaped through another window of the deserted building.

Alric took a few deep breaths, then slowly backed out of the alley. When he was back in the street, he finally dropped the board to the ground, leaning heavily against the wall of a building. The warmth of the sun was reassuring, its light broken and muted on the pavement; in the distance he heard sounds that he recognized as having human origin. In a moment he headed toward the broad avenue at the end of the street.

Chandler winced at the loud conversation of the four Americans seated a few tables away. He adjusted his chair, wooden and uncomfortable, so that his belly touched the edge of the table. Diana sat next to him, looking out onto the thousand-year-old street. They were sipping iced tea in the outdoor section of the restaurant when Alric joined them. He sat down heavily.

Diana smiled at him, her eyes bright. "Have a nice walk?"

"I was over by the outdoor market. Interesting place." He had decided to say nothing about the cat.

She nodded. "I've been there."

"Madhouse, if you ask me," grumped Chandler.

She took a sip of her tea, then looked back at Alric. "John, Carl has an interesting theory on the pyramid."

Alric began to turn to Chandler, but Diana, reaching over to hold his hand, saw the deep gashes.

"John! What happened to your hand?"

Alric looked down at his hand, himself just noticing the crusting blood.

"It's nothing," he said, almost embarrassedly. "I tangled with an unfriendly cat."

"A cat?"

Alric shrugged.

Chandler examined the wound. "Looks pretty nasty," he said. "You'd better have it cleaned."

"It's nothing. Really." Then, anxious to be relieved of the topic, "Diana said something about a theory on the pyramid?"

"Well," said Chandler, quickly forgetting Alric's wounded hand, "it's hardly a theory yet. I've just been telling Diana about the Great Pyramid of Cheops. Though I don't know if it's something we can apply to our pyramid."

"What's that?"

"I've been toying with the possibility that there might be something inherent in the structure of the pyramid."

Alric nodded slowly. "Like astronomical and mathematical data?" he offered.

"Yes, but not necessarily just data," said Chandler. "For example, in the early nineteen-hundreds some Egyptologists believed that the Great Pyramid might be a physical representation of the prophetic history of Man. They compared the physical features, particularly passageways and chambers, to the prophecies of the Bible."

Alric nodded. "The parable in stone idea."

"Exactly." Chandler was warming to his topic. "Telling of the mass of humanity proceeding down the Descending Passage toward darkness and evil." He gestured vigorously, hands following the imaginary patterns. "Then, with the advent of Christianity, the evil are cast down into the Pit"—his left hand thundering down to the tabletop—"whereas those who have accepted Truth move up the Ascending Passage"—traced through the air by his right hand—"toward the Grand Gallery." A pause for dramatic emphasis. "Then humanity must proceed through the Antechamber of Chaos, before finally reaching the King's Chamber, representing the Second Coming." He finished with both hands clasped in front of his face.

Alric smiled. "Quite a tale."

Chandler nodded, then frowned. "Only problem is," he said, "the Great Pyramid is quite complex, a veritable Rorschach in stone. One can read pretty much what one wants into its structure. But our pyramid is so damned simple."

Diana said, "Well, I think the idea's fascinating."

"Fascinating is not always scientific," said Chandler.

"Always the scientist," she said, smiling.

Chandler shrugged, reddening.

"What about the signs on the little pyramid?" she asked.

"Can't say for sure yet. But I'd guess the circle and crescent represent the sun and moon; that much seems pretty clear."

"And the star?" asked Alric.

"The five-pointed star is a traditional representation of Man," said Chandler. "But I didn't think the symbol went back that far. And as to the other figure, the lens shape, I have no idea."

Alric said nothing. He sat still, his mind sifting through the myriad possibilities that lay before him like a strange mutating webwork, changing shape before his eyes could grow accustomed—his thoughts constantly returning to the question of *purpose*. Had the pyramid served, as Chandler had speculated, as a kind of prophecy in stone and gold? Or, as some archaeologists had theorized about the Great Pyramid of Cheops, was it the bearer of a forgotten wis-

dom, designed to survive some cataclysm and preserve its secrets for the future? And if so, what had
its builders, predating even the Egyptians, incorpo-
rated into their structure? What message had they
sought to convey across the space of years? Their
mysterious gold-topped pyramid had survived them,
survived their civilization and countless others—
would perhaps survive Alric's. What had been their
intent? Or—and Alric could not exclude the possibility—had it been a mere symbol, the discarded and
forgotten relic of a dead religion, buried by a con-
quering people, despised by a new nation with different customs and foreign gods? The answers would
not unfold of themselves, Alric knew; he would have
to draw them into the light, force them from the
dark corners in which they lay hidden. He shook his
head briefly, as if shaking off a vague fear, a remnant
of an uneasy sleep.

Next to him Diana, too, sat silent. She peered out
onto Al-Wad as if half expecting that enlightenment
was about to turn the corner and come into view.
After a moment her eyes narrowed slightly. She
pointed to the other side of the street. "Isn't that
Ahmad?"

Alric turned to look. The guide stood at the corner,
in conversation with two men. "Yes, I think it is."

"Why don't you ask him to join us?"

Alric hesitated for a second, then stood up from
his seat and waved briefly to attract Ahmad's attention. The guide noticed the gesture and smiled. He
nodded in Alric's direction, then said a few more
words to his companions and crossed the street to
the restaurant. Alric motioned to him to take the
empty seat.

"We've just been discussing the pyramid," said
Diana, happy to see the guide.

Ahmad smiled. "I see. And have you reached any
conclusions?"

"Not yet, I'm afraid," said Chandler.

"It is quite an enigma," agreed Ahmad.

Chandler turned to Alric. "John, you haven't told us if you have any ideas."

For some reason Alric no longer seemed eager to discuss the subject. "Well," he began, somewhat reluctantly, "if there's anything we've learned in our experiments, it's that there's something about pyramids that aids in preservation, that tends to slow down the process of decay."

"But what could they have been trying to preserve?" asked Diana. "Except for the gold model, the pyramid is empty."

Alric frowned. "I don't know."

At this point the waitress came to their table, placing before them, in haphazard manner, an array of dishes, some hot and steaming, others cold or at room temperature, leaving the patrons to divine for themselves which order was which. As she turned to hurry back into the kitchen, Ahmad ordered a beer.

He then turned to Alric. "Tell me, Doctor," he said, "what do you think of the nature of time?"

Alric was taken aback by the question. The guide had seemed to read his mind. He smiled. "How much time have you got?" he asked. "Never ask a physicist about the nature of time."

"Why is that?"

"The discoveries at the beginning of this century have destroyed every common sense idea connected with time."

"Please elaborate," urged the guide.

Alric continued, his interest growing. "We can no longer look at time as an absolute, independent of external factors, such as velocity or gravity. We can't make clear distinctions between space and time, but rather look at the space-time continuum."

"Ah," smiled the guide, "Dr. Einstein."

"Yes," replied Alric, smiling at the Arab's range of knowledge, "Dr. Einstein. And because of Einstein, and others, we now understand time as a dimension in space, offset in a direction imperceptible to us and perpendicular to the three physical dimensions. It's a limitation of our senses that forces us to perceive three-dimensionally. The universe isn't constructed according to our biases."

Yes, the discoveries at the beginning of this century. . . . A universe envisioned by Riemann, formulated by Einstein, intuited by Plato and Pythagoras, parabled by Jesus. *Time.* The fundamental mystery—the root from which all other mysteries grow. Alric's mind seized upon scattered phrases, shadows of thoughts; his beam of attention scanned the silhouette of a four-dimensional field, reaching for many concepts, holding onto none. Word-images flipped along, illuminated haphazardly, giving the appearance of motion.

Ahmad considered Alric's words, then spoke. "Forgive me for smiling, Doctor, but, with all due respect to your science, my people have always held with a more . . . intuitive understanding."

Chandler momentarily set down his knife and fork, glancing at Ahmad over the rims of his glasses.

The guide continued. "You see, the magic of the desert lies in its changelessness. In other places nature changes the face of the land every season. Even where the larger features—the lakes, forests, and mountains—remain the same, the outer cover is always changing. The grass, leaves, plants, are constantly born. But in the desert, the sand and stones are the same that have been for thousands of years. The same that were seen by the builders of the pyramids, and the same that were commanded by the pharaohs. It instills in us quite a different perspective." He was silent for a moment, allowing his words to settle like the dust scraped from a timeless artifact.

It was true, reflected Alric; they had all felt it at times. Out in the desert, away from all evidence of civilization, surrounded by an immensity of cold perfection, unchanging, unknowable. It was a feeling they could not have put into words, sometimes a mild tingling sensation, sometimes powerful, heady —a longing. Was it the muted evocation of eternity? he wondered. Or a summoning? He studied the dark man, in many ways so unlike his fellow villagers. When the Americans had set up camp a few miles from the small hamlet, they had been greeted warmly, almost deferentially. But they had always sensed there was something else behind the dark eyes of the inhabitants, something faintly amused. It was not so much that they were interlopers in a foreign place, but, perhaps, that they were newcomers to the game of civilization. They always felt terribly *young* around the villagers. But Ahmad was different. Perhaps it was his Western education.

After a while, Ahmad asked, "Doctor, have you ever heard of the Akashic Record?"

Alric shook his head. "No, I don't think so."

Chandler said, "It's some sort of racial memory, isn't it?"

"Like Jung's 'collective unconscious'?" asked Alric.

"Something like it," said Ahmad. "The Akashic Record is said to be a thread that runs along the timeline. On it are imprinted all the events in the history of time, both past and future."

"From the Sanskrit, isn't it?" asked Chandler.

"Yes. And the belief is that at certain times a man may be allowed to view a portion of the Record. He may see the points at which he has touched it, and where he will do so again."

Alric tried to recall an idea he had once come across. Ahmad's words had had a ring of familiarity. Had it been something he'd read?

The guide continued. "Perhaps that was the original purpose of the pyramids. To form an oasis of sorts, a place where the rules of our limited world-picture no longer hold. A place where the universe stands exposed as it is, free of the binds of our—as you call it—three-dimensional perception."

"Sounds like mysticism to me," murmured Chandler.

At Chandler's words, Alric looked up. He sensed a familiar argument in the offing, one which had been played out a number of times during their association. Chandler would carry into battle the standard of the "scientific method" and the ultimate objectivity of the universe, whereas he, Alric, would opt for that principle of a higher science, the supreme god of nature, uncertainty. He leaned back and smiled. He had grown to like and respect the older man over the past several months, but seldom could resist the temptation to enter into philosophical debate. "A little dose of intuitiveness never hurt science," he said, trying to get a rise out of the archaeologist.

"Neither has hard work," countered Chandler.

"Hard work without intuition is merely technology. Science is dependent on creative thought and speculation."

"And speculation without corroborative evidence is *idle* speculation," said Chandler, now visibly annoyed. "It is the job of science to be objective."

Alric shrugged. "All right, agreed. But there's no way to be *completely* objective. And that's true of everything in science. Relativity and uncertainty demonstrate that a scientist can no longer study a system without taking himself into account as a part of that system."

"I'm afraid this is getting a bit too abstract for a simple peasant like me," said Ahmad, smiling.

"Make that two peasants," said Diana.

"Sorry," said Alric. "I tend to get carried away."

"I know," agreed Diana.

They laughed, Chandler as well, saying, "I don't know what I'd do for exercise if it weren't for our occasional bouts."

Ahmad leaned back and lit a cigar. He drew deeply, then turned back to Alric. "And how was your walking tour?"

"Fine," answered Alric, distractedly. Then, interest returning to his voice, "I thought I saw a strange old man earlier. Long, tousled white hair, tattered robe. . . ."

"Where were you?" asked Ahmad.

"Not far from the open market."

Ahmad nodded. "Perhaps it was the Blind Man."

Alric looked quizzically at the guide.

"He lives in the ruins," explained Ahmad, "the area of the Old City not yet excavated. But occasionally he is seen in the streets in the vicinity. He has been here for at least a generation, and those who remember say he was ancient even then."

Alric nodded slowly, as if hearing a familiar tale. Then, without knowing why, he asked, "Was he blind from birth?"

"No. The story is that he plucked out his own eyes in self-punishment for some unknown crime."

Diana winced at the grisly mention, but Ahmad smiled. "I doubt it's true, though," he said.

"How does he live?" asked Alric.

The guide shrugged. "Who knows?" Then, as if in afterthought, he said, "Some say he is the Eternal Wanderer of medieval legend, condemned to walk the earth forever, undying, yet unable to rest, in punishment for not permitting Jesus to rest on his doorstep while en route to Calvary."

"Is that what you believe?" asked Diana, raising an eyebrow in curiosity.

"I am not religious," said Ahmad, with a smile.

As a boy he would sit under an improvised tent of baseball bat and sheet, fingers leafing through the pages of a well-worn book. There had been revelations there, facts of great import. The flashlight's irregular circle of light would disclose this miracle, then the next; it had seemed too simple to be true. There had been so much to learn. But the batteries had been new and leak-proof, and the house had been quiet, and his fingers had followed the lines of words, as if to reinforce their content: *"There are nine planets in our solar system, the smallest of which. . . ."* This was the foretaste, it had seemed to say; greater things would come. And next the flashlight's beam would reflect the captured light of a hundred billion suns, and the page would explode in the young boy's mind, exciting the circuitry of nerves, imprinting images on his brain as if it had been a photographic plate. *"There are a hundred billion suns in our galaxy. . . ."*

Alric's eyes scanned the night sky, as if searching among its six thousand visible stars for one in particular; it was a habit acquired in childhood, born with the scientist in him. The desert sky seemed to return his gaze, its dome greeting the newcomers solemnly, it appeared to him, but not without the subtle humor born of age tempered with wisdom.

Diana walked alongside him, began to point as a meteor cut a brilliant arc across a few degrees of sky, but, realizing that he had noticed it, stopped her motion.

The dark shape of the pyramid grew quickly as they approached. Soon they reached the wooden ramp and descended to the base of the pyramid. They passed quickly through the lengths of tunnel, and once more stood before the small gold pyramid inside the larger one's only chamber.

Silently, they stood holding each other, looking at the model as if expecting it to unfold its secrets at any moment. It glowed softly in the pale blue light of the pyramid's interior. Alric began to turn away, but Diana put her hand gently on his arm.

"Listen," she said.

"What—?" began Alric.

She put a finger to his lips. "Just listen."

He cocked his head slightly, tensing his neck muscles as though to aid his hearing. Nothing. What did she mean?

Then he heard it.

In the distance a ringing, like a chorus of muted church bells, echoing softly around them. A pleasant sound, resonating mildly in their heads, producing a faint tingling at the base of their spines. Then growing louder, clarifying, beginning to take shape. They exchanged curious glances.

"What do you suppose it is?" asked Diana.

Alric shook his head.

The ringing continued to grow louder—suddenly, painfully loud. Alric saw Diana's face tense in fear, as she brought her hands up to cover her ears.

"What *is* it?" she moaned, as he, too, tried to protect his ears.

But just as suddenly as it had begun, the noise subsided. And was gone.

They both relaxed, already somewhat embarrassed and amused at their quick fright.

"That was *strange*," said Diana, letting go a deep breath.

Alric nodded, his eyes on the model pyramid, remembering several reports he had come across telling of the mysterious "voice of the pyramid," noted by several investigators of the Great Pyramid—the strange, resonating echoes inside the Grand Gallery, or, even more bizarre, the description of a researcher who had stood atop the Great Pyramid, watching in disbelief as sparks had emanated from the upraised fingers of his Arab guide, to the accompaniment of a distant ringing sound. But no one had yet reported the ringing to have reached painful intensity. Alric let the question drop for now, making a mental note to mention it to Chandler in the morning.

He walked to the model and ran a finger along its edge. The gold was cool, flawless; his finger tingled at its touch. And once more his mind reeled at its implications. Untold millennia ago this pyramid had been placed here. By whom? And *why?* He bent slightly to look at the inscriptions. They were clear, perfect, engraved by a master's hand. His fingers traced the four signs, one by one. He closed his eyes: a blind man, trying to decipher a foreign braille.

Behind him, Diana stretched a thick double sleeping bag across the floor in front of the model. She smoothed it out, then removed her clothes and slipped between the soft folds.

"Coming to bed?" she asked.

He turned and took a step toward her, then sat down beside her and took off his clothes. He lifted the top cover of the sleeping bag, saw her smooth, white body clearly outlined on the dark material below. She shivered slightly when the cover was withdrawn. He looked at her a moment, then gently rested his hand on her belly. She quivered at his touch, then reached up and held his shoulder, pulling him toward her. In the cool air they wrapped themselves, cocoonlike, in the sleeping bag.

She looked up and saw his eyes, a clear crystal blue in the strange light. She reached a hand to touch his face as he slipped his arms under her back and held her tightly.

"I wish we could have a baby," she whispered, immediately regretting it.

This time he didn't wince, but merely pressed his body to hers. He closed his eyes.

The man sits at the edge of the stream, his feet resting on the slick surface of a submerged stone. His mind's eye traces the water's path from its origin, high on the wooded hill, to the point where it now soothes his toes. Many times he has followed the stream around trees and behind boulders to the narrow rock crevice through which it flows. Though, even as a boy, his body lean and tough, he could never squeeze through the gap to find the source.

He glances upward. Above him, bits of sky filter through the webwork of leaves, dappling the ground and casting diffuse light into the water. He cannot see the sun, but senses it is growing late.

He rises slowly and turns to start down the hill. He is expected elsewhere. From his vantage point the City opens before him, being seen the thousandth time as if for the first. The streets glisten, alive with activity, projecting, wavelike, to and from the center. Movement is multifaceted, yet integrated. And in that golden center great blocks of stone float effortlessly over the heads of the Wisemen. Everyone is engaged in a project of enormous import.

He reaches the bottom of the slope, and walks through the gates, where he is no longer in view of the construction. The air, as always, is warm and dry. He stops by a fountain and dips cupped hands below the water's surface. He sees himself, his crystal blue eyes, inside the water for an instant—and he hesitates. A strange, brief feeling tingles inside him as he withdraws his hands to drink, watching the water's mirror-surface return quickly to tranquility, as though forgiving of his trespass, incurious of his presence. He continues toward the construction site. He is of prime importance.

So well, so easily, the work progresses; but he senses that it will not always be so. In a part of his mind he sees that one day there will be a hundred thousand men at a place called Gizeh, replacing the handful of Wisemen here. They will groan as heavy ropes cut into their collarbones, as the blocks of stone, feather light under the Wisemen's spell, move imperceptibly along on wooden rollers. And in the quarries of what will be known as the Mokattam Mountains, men will bore holes into the stone, then drive wooden stakes inside, soaking them with water to expand and split the rock. He closes his eyes for an instant and is once more in the City. Things are better here.

But today the faces of his people seem strange. Something weighs upon them. They smile or nod when they see him, but he senses something new behind their eyes. Something different. He shakes off a feeling of uncertainty, pushes back a vague sensation of displacement.

(And there, around the next corner, waiting. . . .)

He stops.

For a brief second, he felt it. . . .

He wants to continue walking, but the feeling grows. Along with a coldness in the pit of his stomach. And now he can feel tiny beads of sweat forming on his back, tingling in the suddenly cold breeze.

He begins to take a step forward, but again stops.

(Waiting, twisted leer, ancient flesh, deep brows overhanging—)

His brain ignites in a blinding instant of knowledge, and he almost cries out against its brilliance.

And then he's running, desperately, his footsteps on the stone street resounding in his head. The people around him are startled, watching him with fright, as he runs madly through the streets. And a face, shrouded, yet darkly familiar, smiles through the crowd. . . .

The earth is rotating under his feet at the same rate as his steps, and it's like running the wrong way on the moving ramp at the airport. (Airport?) The word suddenly smashes through the fabric of his timesense. (I understand air. I understand port. But airport??)

Running wildly, he stumbles, falls to his knees. A man bends to help him, but he shrinks away, regains his feet and continues running. Passersby look on in bewilderment.

A face, shrouded, yet darkly familiar. . . .

A shattered scream, a blinding pain—
And falling, falling. . . .

Another world, another time, black sheath of sky,
swollen orb of moon, cold fire. . . .
Severed watching.
The girl has been walking, alone, a nighttime stroll
in the desert, stars above, icy, uncaring eyes, until. . . .
Hands coming up from behind, around her mouth,
around her throat. Muffled, helpless screams . . . and
then—
The rite. . . .
Men with strange, haunted looks, cold, hard eyes,
faces like skulls, hollow masks . . . but fervent, be-
lieving. They have gathered from the dark corners
of the world—for the summoning is about to begin.
The time is at hand.
And They must come forth. . . .
When the blue-eyed man opens his eyes, he is al-
most blinded by the glacial brilliance of the full
moon suspended before him. He looks around, dis-
oriented, sees the gentle slopes of sand reaching out
in all directions, the distant rocky hills, vaguely fa-
miliar . . . and then the slowly moving shapes of the
men, engaged in the ancient ritual.
Slowly the images grow in clarity, his mind's eye
filling the gaps in his vision. Soon he understands.
And his eyes widen in horror.
He begins to move forward, desperate to try to
stop the atrocity, but feels a hand on his arm, re-
straining him. He turns toward the dark figure stand-
ing beside him, the face obscured within its pale
hood. The man indicates for him to be still.
The blue-eyed man looks back at the site, the
strange, dark figures dancing in sinuous movements,
vaguely obscene, around the prone shape.
And again the blades are raised . . . and driven
downward in merciless, tearing arcs.
Again and again.

The dark man nudges him. "Look," he whispers. "The seeker of Eluth. He hasn't the stomach for the execution of his beliefs." He gestures to one of the men taking part in the ceremony.

The man's face looms large before Alric, even at this distance. It is sensitive, suggesting a man of thought—horrified at the proceedings. Under the cold light of the moon the eyes shine, like bits of polished stone. . . . And in the left one there is an impurity—a small, star-shaped fleck of gold just beneath the pupil.

Alric wants to scream, but at the same time sees himself wanting to scream. It is no longer the time for screaming. Knowledge strikes him with the force of a thunderbolt, but is forgotten in the instant of awakening, leaving him with no more than a mild tingling at the base of his spine.

*

ALRIC OPENED HIS eyes. With a vague numbness he lifted his head a few inches from the floor. The small chamber looked exactly as it had the night before, but he knew it must be morning. Next to him, Diana slept peacefully, curled fetally on her side, her hair a dark shroud around her face.

He allowed a few seconds for the quickened blood to re-energize his body, then carefully extricated himself from both Diana and the sleeping bag, and reached for his pants. The hard touch of the belt buckle against his knuckle crisply brought to his awareness a coldness in his limbs, and he rubbed his hands together briskly. As he pulled the pants over his legs, a soft glint off to his left sparkled in the corner of his eye. He turned toward the model pyramid.

And stopped.

He sat as he was, transfixed, the coldness spreading from his hands and feet through his body like a wildfire touched off in a dry forest. Only his mind was alive, burning; and at length it prevailed upon his body to respond. He stood, slowly, as if afraid that any sudden motion would destroy the tentative reality of what he saw. He walked over to the pyramid.

The gold model stood atop its pedestal as he had yesterday replaced it—but all four sides had unfolded, petal-like, on unseen hinges in its base.

Questions flared into his mind before he had time
to catalog them. His hand reached for the pyramid
without conscious intent, acting only as the body's
messenger, seeking to confirm the tangibility of the
object.

And it *was* real. It *was* there before him, inno-
cently arrogant, unknowing—or uncaring—of his
stupefaction. His thoughts of the previous day (had
it been only twenty-four hours?) echoed in his brain.
*A pyramid within a pyramid, a question within a
question.*

And the opened model held inside it the seed of
yet another mystery: in the center of the base was
a miniature pedestal, the top of which formed a tiny
silver cup. And inside were five oval-shaped objects.

His hand was almost trembling as he removed one
of the ovoids. He held it between thumb and forefinger and brought it up before his eyes as if looking through a slide. It was made of a light, trans-
lucent substance.

"Good morning," said Diana, from a half-risen
position on the floor behind him.

The sudden sound of her voice startled him briefly,
but he didn't remove his gaze from the pyramid and
its strange contents. "Come look at this," he said,
without turning.

She stood slowly, letting go of the remnants of
sleep, and walked over to him. She looked at the
small bead-like object in his hand, then over at the
pyramid.

"These were inside it," he said, still without turning to her.

"How did you get it open?"

"I didn't. It was like this when I woke up."

"I don't understand."

"Neither do I."

She took one of the ovoids from the small cup.
"What are they?"

"No idea."

She rolled the object in her palm, studying it as if it were an unusual insect. She looked up at him again. "What could have caused the pyramid to open?" she asked, handing the object back to him.

"I don't know." Then, halfheartedly, "Maybe something to do with the way I repositioned it. . . ."

She thought for a moment. "Or maybe the ringing. . . ."

"What?" He looked at her for the first time.

"Yes, remember? That ringing we heard last night."

"What do you mean?"

"You know. Like one of those high-frequency locks on garage doors."

He nodded quickly, understanding. "Yes, of course. The ringing could have set up some kind of resonance inside it." He paused, smiled, grateful for the possibility of a logical explanation. "There might be air channels built into the pyramid itself, and when the wind outside reaches just the right velocity, a reverberation occurs, and is matched by the locking mechanism in the small pyramid."

"But why now? After thousands of years?"

"The builders could have planned it that way. The air channels could have been blocked and connected to the chamber door in such a way that only when the door was opened would they be freed." He grinned. "Thanks. You're brilliant."

She smiled, studying her fingernails with mock pride.

He held her shoulders and kissed her briefly on the lips. "I don't know how I ever got through college physics without you."

"You did all right, from what I hear," she teased.

He cleared his throat. "Yes, well. . . ."

She stood on tiptoe and kissed him lightly on the corner of the mouth. "Well, I guess it's time we packed up and left this motel. Great accommodations, but a lousy view. And no color TV."

He nodded soberly, as though her remarks had been without humor, then turned back toward the pyramid. He tore a sheet of paper from his pocket notebook, folding it into a small envelope and dropping the five beads inside, then picked up his shirt from the floor and slipped the envelope into the pocket.

Behind him, Diana had slipped into her jeans and was buttoning her workshirt. An uncertain look creased her brow as she looked over at him. He stood still, studying the small pyramid. From her position she could see his jaw muscles moving slightly, sending a mild ripple down the side of his face. He was always so preoccupied lately; it was unlike him.

She knelt down and began folding the sleeping bag into a manageable bundle. "I'm sorry about last night," she said quietly.

"What about?" he asked, without turning.

"You know. About mentioning the baby. I said that I wouldn't, and I'm sorry."

"Already forgotten," he said, still facing the pyramid.

She nodded slowly, to herself. Perhaps she was making too much of it. But there had been something strange in his eye this time, something different; changed. Or was she just imagining it? Certainly she could understand the weight of the project pressing on him. But still. . . .

In a moment he turned to her. "Ready?"

"Uh-huh. Are you taking the pyramid to the museum today?"

He nodded. "I'd feel safer if it were there. There's no point in leaving it here any longer."

He lifted the model from its stand and cradled it in his arms. Its sides outstretched, it was awkward to carry, but he didn't want to risk closing it up again. They began making their way through the tunnels.

By the time they had reached the entrance, the small pyramid seemed to have doubled in weight. Yesterday, when they had first found it, it had seemed surprisingly light; now, the farther it was taken from the chamber, the heavier it seemed. His muscles straining, Alric pushed it through the small, square entrance door before him, setting it down easily on the flat working area outside. Then he climbed out, turning and reaching a hand back to Diana to help her through the opening. They both stood on the small wooden platform, shielding their eyes from the diffuse glare of the sky.

"It seems so bright already," she said. "I wonder what time it is."

"Still pretty early," he guessed, noticing the elongated triangular shadow cast by the pyramid.

He bent to pick up the model, then moved slowly up the ramp and to the jeep. He gently deposited it in the passenger seat, then walked around to the driver's seat while Diana climbed into the back.

In a few minutes they arrived at the campsite. Chandler was crouching by the campfire with a pot of coffee.

"Just in time for breakfast!" he called, straightening with a grunt.

"Good morning, Carl!" Diana called back, as she and Alric stepped out of the jeep.

"Have a good night's sleep?"

"Come look at this, Carl," said Alric, standing by the jeep.

"What?"

"The pyramid opened last night."

"What. . . ?"

"The model. I found it like this when we woke up this morning." He gestured to the passenger seat. "Have a look."

Chandler walked over to the jeep and looked inside. His neck quivered slightly with an aborted motion back to Alric, but his eyes predominated, forcing him to stay with this latest surprise, gleaming now in the morning sun.

Alric said, "There are hinges in the base allowing the sides to fold downward."

Finally, Chandler turned back to him.

Alric shook his head slowly, shrugged.

"But how. . . ?"

Alric told him about the sound they had heard last night, and how it might account for the phenomenon. The older man listened carefully, nodding occasionally; he seemed to glance over at Diana at the mention of the strange noise, perhaps for corroboration.

Then he shook his head slowly, a man in confusion. "Well, it should be easy enough to check out. If there are any air channels leading to the chamber, we can find them. But as to why. . . ." His voice died in a weak shrug.

"Show him the beads, John," said Diana.

Not understanding, Alric turned to her.

"The beads," she repeated. "The ones you found inside it."

"Of course," he nodded, turning back to Chandler. He pulled the envelope from his pocket. "These were inside the little cup." He dropped one of the ovoids into Chandler's hand. "What do you make of it?"

Chandler rolled the object between thumb and forefinger. "Never seen anything like it. Certainly not pearl. And it's too light to be made of stone." He looked back at Alric. "You say they were in the cup?"

Alric nodded.

"Mind if I hold on to this for now?"

Alric hesitated briefly at the rhetorical question, then put the envelope with the remaining objects back into his pocket. "No, of course not."

He walked back around to the driver's side of the jeep. "I'm going to the New City to bring the pyramid to the museum. The curator is expecting me."

He turned back to Chandler. "Unless, of course, you'd like to study it further."

Chandler shrugged vaguely. "Nothing more I can do with it at this point. It's to the books now for me."

Alric nodded, climbing into the jeep.

. . . a hand on his arm, restraining him. . . .

"Aren't you going to have some breakfast with us first?" asked Diana, curious at his haste.

Alric looked at her as if she had spoken a foreign language.

"Aren't you hungry?" she asked. "I'm famished."

"I'll have something in town," he said finally. He seemed hesitant. He reached a hand to the ignition key.

. . . the dark man nudges him. . . .

He stopped the motion, his face unsettled. He looked back at Chandler. "Carl?"

The archaeologist looked up.

"Have you ever heard the term 'Eluth'?"

Chandler squinted at him. " 'Eluth'?"

Alric nodded, uncertainly.

"Can't say as I have," said Chandler, shaking his head. "In reference to what?"

"I'm . . . not sure."

Chandler and Diana exchanged looks, but the confusion on Alric's face faded quickly. He smiled, as he turned the ignition key.

"It isn't important." Then he added, "I'm going to see Dan Michaels later on. I should be back in a couple of hours."

By the time Alric reached the New City, the sun had halfway reached its zenith. It shone in a clear, warm sky, and seemed to have purified the air, giving it the clean taste of the desert. The traffic was heavy, but not New York, and he looked out from the open jeep, watching the citizens flood the streets as if only to experience the fresh day.

He parked the jeep by the curb in front of the museum, got out, and walked around to the passenger side, reaching in for the small pyramid.

Then he noticed his hand.

The area between his thumb and first knuckle, bitten savagely yesterday by the alley cat, had almost completely healed. Under a thin layer of scab he could feel the new skin, fresh and resilient. There was no pain when he moved his fingers. What should have taken days had occurred overnight. In the pyramid.

He looked down at the model, and it shone up at him, sides unfolded like open arms; a posture of welcome, perhaps? But no, he reflected, they seemed to reach out coldly, under the warmth of the sun; coldly, with the alien touch of frozen fire.

He leaned in and lifted it from the seat, then turned toward the museum entrance. A brief darkness passed over his eyes, a small cloud. He thought for a second, then set the model back down. Carefully, he folded up the sides, so that it was as it had been when they had found it. The sides held in the upright position. He then removed the pyramid from the jeep and turned to climb the wide stone steps leading to the main entrance.

The marble coolness of the museum's interior brought pleasant relief from the growing heat of the morning. Alric remembered the museum well from his earlier visits with the curator. He had spent several hours strolling down the long corridors and looking through the display rooms, making cursory surveys of the art and culture of many long-dead civilizations. But now he turned down the first hall to his right and quickly found the curator's office. The door was open.

A thin, elderly man looked up from behind a large, old wooden desk. "Ah, Dr. Alric," he said pleasantly, his eyes immediately falling to the pyramid. He spoke softly, with a mild accent.

Alric smiled. "Where can I put this?" he asked, glancing around the room. "It's pretty heavy."

"Here, let me help you," said the curator, standing and walking over to him.

"No, it's all right. Just tell me where to set it down."

The older man walked back to his desk and hastily cleared a portion of the top, heedless of the several papers accidentally swept to the floor. He pointed to the newly vacated area. "Right here will be fine for now. I'll have the attendant put it in a case in just a moment."

Alric set the pyramid down easily on the desk's surface. He stood back and shook his arms briskly, aware of a lingering numbness.

The curator touched the pyramid gingerly, with mild trepidation it seemed, as if it were a fragile object grown brittle with age. "Just beautiful," he whispered. "One is reminded of the Egyptians, and the golden objects they would place in tombs, in order that the gold—the 'flesh of the gods' derived from the sun, as they believed—would preserve, in the deceased, the eternal spark of life."

"The alchemists believed that gold symbolized the highest spiritual development attainable by man," said Alric.

"Indeed," nodded the curator. "Indeed." He walked back around the desk. "If you could wait just a moment, Dr. Alric," he said, going through a drawer, "I'll fill out a receipt form for you." He found the proper sheet, then seated himself. "This is a most unusual artifact, really," he said, hastily filling out the form. "A pyramid within a pyramid."

Alric nodded, though the curator was looking down at the paper. A sudden gust of surprisingly cool air entered through the open window, unsettling several of the pages now lying on the floor. The curator absently pushed back a wisp of white hair dislodged by the breeze.

"Have you any idea what its purpose was?" he asked.

"Not yet, I'm afraid."

"Most unusual," he repeated, checking over the receipt.

He handed the form to Alric as he stood, and the two men walked to the door. In the hall, the curator summoned one of the two guards standing by the main entrance. When the man was beside him, he pointed to the pyramid. The guard lifted the model, and the three men left the room, walking down the first long corridor.

In a moment they arrived at a nearly vacant display room. It was a small chamber, a cubicle of no more than twelve feet on a side, containing two exhibit cases: a small empty glass receptacle near the middle of the room, no doubt meant for the pyramid, and an upright glass-fronted cabinet set against the near wall, housing three shelves of artifacts.

While the curator fumbled among his many keys, Alric studied the larger case, not remembering having seen it before.

The bottom shelf held several pieces of ornamental beadwork, some gathered together in intricate fanlike webs suggestive of the splendor of a golden age, others strung in single strands, with slender blue cylinders of lapis lazuli separated after each fifth or sixth one by a small chunk of carnelian. On the middle shelf a bronze lion crouched, perpetually ready to spring, jaws wide, claws digging into the marble of the base, perhaps standing guard over the royal necklaces that lay to either side, displaying leaves of gold so delicate and finely detailed that they could have been real, frozen in mid-growth by the touch of some earlier Midas.

But it was at the top shelf that his gaze stopped. Before him, at eye level, stood two foot-high statues of the purest black, unlabeled and alone on the shelf, peering out from hollow eye sockets that receded into the depths. There was something unformed about the figures, with their soft curves; something embryonic. Their surfaces were smooth, flawless, yet they did not seem to reflect the room's light; rather they drew it toward them, into them, they devoured it, letting not even the mildest glimmer escape. But it was the faces which held Alric's fascination: the mouths, cut smoothly yet sharply into the stone, the lips curving slightly upward and inward in an obscure smile; the foreheads, bulging forward, then arching back easily toward the void; the noses, mere indentations in the stone—and, above all, the eyes, those deep, hollow caverns, seeming to grow larger than the statues themselves, larger than the room, drawing in the casual viewer, requiring vigilance to keep from being swallowed up in their emptiness. It would have been so easy to be pulled into those caverns, so easy. . . .

"And here is its new home," said the curator, opening the door to the small case and directing the guard to gently place the pyramid inside.

Alric turned to them, an unformed question quickly eluding him. He nodded hesitantly to the old man, who smiled in return, checking the security of the glass door, then dropped the key ring into his jacket pocket.

"I cannot tell you how much we appreciate the opportunity to view and study this artifact, Dr. Alric," he said. "Needless to say, it will be at your disposal at any time." He took Alric's arm as the three men left the small chamber.

Alric allowed himself a brief backward glance, and saw the pyramid, *his* pyramid, sitting there, again closed and secretive, now under the strange, watchful eyes of the two small statues.

At the door to the curator's office the two men shook hands.

"Thank you for everything," said Alric.

"And I thank you, Dr. Alric," said the curator,

pressing his hand warmly. "And do tell Dr. Chandler to drop by."

Alric nodded and watched the older man turn and walk back into his office.

Thoughtfully, he headed toward the entrance.

A strange quiet had descended on the village.

The few stores were closed, as they were at the religious times, and the gentle commerce that proceeded in small villages where inhabitants knew each other was gone, as if spirited away and buried in the sand. It was as though all human activity had been summarily banished. The town was settled in its peace; a newly risen ghost town, or a village frozen in time.

In the dusty clearing between the canteen and general store, a child's toy sparkled in the bright sunlight, set down, it seemed, only a moment ago by some toddler who had been carted off to his midday nap; the creaky wooden bench that had stood in front of the canteen for a generation was vacant, as it was on only the hottest of summer days; and even the somber whoosh of an occasional passing car was absent: the single dirt road running through the small village was untraveled, had been for the past day or two.

Only in the ancient mud-brick dwellings were there signs of life.

Silent preparations were being made.

He had been a young boy when the questions had first materialized, the inevitable child's questions, put forth with innocent curiosity—and never receiving answers. Now he was a man, and the intervening years seemed to have condensed to a point. He walked along the brightly lit corridor of the Bureau building, already feeling the tension, the ambivalence he always felt before meeting with Dan Michaels. Today, though, it was greater, a physical pressure that twisted him in two directions at once—for this would doubtless be his last visit here of an official nature; and perhaps the last dead end in his search. The American government had been able to offer little help; the University records had been incomplete. He could see no other avenue of hope. He realized now why he had avoided a trip here for years, having to admit the necessity to keep one channel open, one possibility intact. But the discovery in the desert had brought him here, and this last step could no longer be put off. He might not have the chance again.

He turned away from his thoughts, trying not to get too hopeful—it had been, after all, a long shot—and continued down the hall, stopping at a door on his right. He hesitated briefly before turning the knob, then rapped lightly on the door as he pushed it open.

Dan Michaels looked up from his desk, pleased to be rescued from a mound of paperwork. He stood up from his chair as Alric entered, and reached out his hand. Alric could see that his warm smile held a trace of concern. They shook hands briskly.

"Sit down, please, John," said Michaels, his speech immediately revealing his American background. He was in his early thirties, slender, of medium height, and, even when relaxed, gave the impression of nervous flexibility characteristic of his former years of chain-smoking.

Alric took the seat in front of the desk, shifted once or twice to accommodate himself to its new leather contours, and looked over at the other man.

"I wasn't expecting you so early," said Michaels, also sitting.

"I was in town to drop something off at the museum. But if I've come at a bad time. . . ."

Michaels shook it off. "Not at all." He motioned to the stack of papers on his desk. "A pleasure to get away from this bureaucratic mess for a few minutes."

There was a short silence. Michaels smiled self-consciously, then, as if to fill the void, asked, "How's it going at the site?"

"Pretty well. We've been inside the pyramid."

Michaels looked up, interested. "Oh? I didn't know it would be so soon."

Alric smiled. "Neither did we."

"Learn anything interesting?"

"Too early to tell."

"They mention you every now and then in the local papers, did you know? You're quite a celebrity."

"I didn't know."

And then the silence was back. Michaels took a deep breath, let it go slowly. "But I guess you didn't come here to discuss archaeology."

Alric had been looking out the window beyond Michaels's shoulder. He could see that the sky had lowered a gray shroud above the tips of the New City; the earlier crystal blue was no longer visible. "Have you found anything?" he asked, without turning from the window.

Michaels shifted about in his seat, looked in need of a cigarette. "John," he began, "when you first came here I told you it would be difficult. And that chances were we wouldn't be able to come up with much."

The words had a familiar ring.

"Nothing?" asked Alric.

"John, it's just that—"

"Nothing?"

Michaels shook his head slowly.

Alric nodded to himself. "Yeah," he said softly.

Through the window he watched a single bird in slow flight, a spot of darkness against the low sky, drifting in and out of a flat gray cloud, drawing erratic circles, growing and shrinking in his field of vision, becoming a black point, a negative star, then disappearing, only to exist at a new and seemingly random point.

"You have to consider the situation in this country at the time," said Michaels. "It was in a state of turmoil, immigrants recovering from the shock of the war, reeling with the new freedom. At other times there would have been better records. And even then, perhaps not—a lone archaeologist in the desert. . . ." He shook his head slowly and put his hand on the desk, realizing that he was reaching for a pack of cigarettes that wasn't there. "Things were not as efficient—as thorough—as they are now."

Michaels's words seemed to pass through Alric. In truth, perhaps, he'd been expecting nothing else. He'd known it was a slender hope, the possibility of tracing his father, missing these thirty years, lost—or dead—somewhere in the Judean desert. He thought back to a childhood of not knowing, of ignorance of his past, his heritage; and the early years of his adulthood, the many blind alleys and false hopes. He had tracked down as many of his father's colleagues as were still living, gathered bits of information here and there, old memories of a man with a mission, a scientist, losing himself in the heady vision of new archaeological discoveries. For the thousandth time he pictured the lone man in the desert—how accurate Michaels's words must have been—the hardened, sun-browned hands searching carefully through the sand, the eyes mesmerized by the possibility of learning something new, something unexpected . . . What had his father been searching for?

"Dead," his mother had told him, simply. Then she had turned from him, squinting at the gray glare from the window. "He died before you were born."

"What was he like?" the boy had asked.

The woman's face had been weary, though she had not been old. She had looked back at him, then again turned away. "He died before you were born," she had repeated.

But his questions had multiplied as he had grown older, his mother's words shedding no light. And many times through the years he had thought back to that day in the attic, the worn black chest with the rusty latches, the aging manila envelope—and its strange contents. . . .

He looked up bleakly. "Where do we go from here?"

Michaels frowned. "I'm afraid there's nothing more we can do. Not without more information."

"I've already told you everything I know. Everything my mother was able to tell me."

Michaels picked up a pen and tapped automatically on a stack of papers. "John," he began slowly, "I know this is difficult, but could there have been any reason she'd have had to lie?"

Alric looked stiffly into Michaels's eyes. "No. Of course not."

"Can you be sure?"

"What do you mean?"

"I don't know, myself." A few seconds, a few more taps, then, "It's just that . . . it's understandable that your father could have disappeared once he had entered the country; he could have lost himself in any number of ways. But when he entered through Customs, there should have been *some* record. I've checked the British files, as well, for that period. And there's no record of him ever having entered the country."

"That's impossible," said Alric.

"Unless he'd had a reason to enter in secret."

"What are you driving at?"

"I told you. I don't know."

"I think you do," said Alric, with more anger than he'd intended.

Michaels leaned back in his seat. "I really don't, John. It just seemed odd that an American scientist could have come into the area without *any* record anywhere." He raised his hands in a conciliatory gesture. "But, as I've said, in those days anything was possible."

Alric sat back in the chair, resigned. There was really no place else to go, no other leads to follow.

"I see," he said quietly.

Michaels smiled sympathetically. "I'm sorry we haven't been of much help."

Alric nodded slightly to Michaels. "Well, it was a long shot in any event," he said, rising to leave. "Thanks anyway, Dan."

"Only wish I could have done more. You will keep me up to date on the research?"

Alric smiled weakly. "Sure." He turned and walked to the door.

. . . there, just below the pupil, an impurity. . . .

He stopped, turned back to Michaels, remembering another, a newer question, and wondering what other information the man might have access to.

"Dan?"

Michaels looked up.

"Have you ever come across the term 'Eluth'?"

Michaels looked quizzical.

"It might have something to do with some kind of . . . cult," prompted Alric.

Michaels thought for a moment, then shook his head slowly. "I don't believe so, why?"

Alric hesitated. "The name came up in some research I've been doing."

"Sorry I can't help you."

Alric smiled. "Be seeing you."

"Keep in touch."

Alric turned and left the room.

Michaels watched the door close behind Alric, studying the rich grain of the wood as though it were a manuscript. He turned back to his stack of papers, but soon let them rest, swiveling his chair around to look out the window at the lowering sky. He felt a cold shudder pass through his body, in spite of the closeness of the day, as if in response to the piercing cry of a lone circling bird as it faded easily into the clouds. In a few minutes he turned, pensive, back to his desk. He resumed his pencil-tapping; even, measured, as if keeping meter with his thoughts. Finally he reached for a blank sheet of paper, deliberately writing down a single word:

Eluth.

"What's doing?" asked Diana, smiling at Chandler from the entrance of his tent.

The archaeologist looked up, also smiled. "Looking for an excuse to take a break."

"Not going so well?"

"On the contrary. It's going *too* well."

She stepped into the tent, cocking her head in curiosity. "*Too* well?"

He nodded toward an open book lying at the edge of his desk. "I've been trying to make sense out of those signs we found on the model pyramid. But the problem is they're too ambiguous. They could mean any number of things. Or something entirely new."

She considered for a moment. "You think they might explain the little beads we found in the pyramid?"

He shrugged. "It seems logical, though at this point it would be dangerous to take anything for granted."

He closed the book and slid it across the table. "It's really like working in a vacuum. If I knew what type of civilization we were dealing with. . . ." His voice trailed off into a helpless sigh. "Our understanding has always been that the Sumerians were the first to use writing. But I don't know if we can really call this writing. Most of these symbols have been around for thousands of years, and used by many different civilizations." He paused. "And then there's the pyramid itself. My God, when I think of the theories that have been put forth to explain the Great Pyramid of Cheops: that it had served as a water pump, a granary, a tomb, a public works project, a temple where the pharaoh might undergo initiatory rites and his spirit might journey to the realm of the gods, so that he might be revitalized, to better fulfill his function of fructifying the land. . . . There's been endless speculation."

Diana was silent a moment, then asked, "Do you think the people who built the pyramid could have been trying to tell us something? I mean, like a kind of time capsule?"

Chandler smiled. "A bit whimsical, don't you think?"

She raised her eyebrows. "Oh? You never can tell. We certainly could use some advice."

He chuckled mildly. "I'm afraid there's not all that much that can be said with four symbols."

"I thought you said your problem was that there was *too* much."

He gave a short laugh. "You were captain of the debating team at Bryn Mawr, I presume?"

She smiled.

"But your point is well taken. And perhaps it's my own limitations that impose boundaries on understanding." His face clouded over briefly.

"Hey," she said, "I thought we were going to take that break."

"Right again. Time for a cup of coffee."

She grimaced. "You *will* rinse out that pot some time this month, I take it?"

He raised his arms in surrender, standing up from the worktable.

They both squinted coming out of the tent; the sun's light burned around them, sparkling in the billions of tiny stars of the desert sand.

"John's not back yet?" he asked.

She frowned. "No."

They strolled over to the campfire and crouched down. Chandler poked at it with a charred twig. "You're concerned about him, aren't you?" He flipped over a half-orange ember, so that the cold black side faced upward.

She looked up at him, her eyes answering.

He nodded, attempting a smile. "It's understandable, I mean, his interest. I think if I were in his place. . . ."

She shook her head mildly. "But it's so all-important. I don't want it to . . . become an obsession."

"Now, now," he soothed. "Look at what we're doing here, all of us, out here in the desert. What is it, really, but searching for our origins? You can't cure a man of wanting to know who he is, where he came from."

She nodded slowly. "I know."

They turned toward the fire, watching it catch slowly from a single ember. It crackled delicately, almost an icy tinkling.

Alric stood before a large wooden catalog, his fingers flipping through a section of cards. The library's main room was large, medicinally lit by long rows of fluorescent bulbs, with bookshelves reaching almost to the ceiling. The only other occupant was a middle-aged woman sitting at a long, counter-like table near the entrance; distractedly, she leafed through the pages of a magazine, having barely looked up when Alric had entered.

His finger now stopped midway into the drawer of cards, while with his free hand he reached for the pen in his shirt pocket. He quickly scrawled several index numbers on a scrap of paper and slid the drawer back into place.

He turned briefly to the woman, but, noticing her disinterest, decided to attack the shelves without help. He soon found his way to the proper section of books, mercifully situated near the bottom of the shelves. He smiled slightly, pleased at not having to ask the woman for the ladder, and pulled five or six books from the shelf, carried them to one of the several desolate reading tables, and sat down.

For a second he felt foolish, sitting there with his stack of books, like a schoolboy ready to cram for an exam. And at the same time he had to push back a remote nucleus of fear. He had a sudden impulse to leave. It would have been so easy.

Instead, he opened the first book to the index. Slowly, he ran a finger down the page, his eyes intent, searching for the listing. It wasn't there. Obscurely relieved, he closed the book and slid it across the empty expanse of table. He reached for the next book. Again the listing wasn't there.

Perhaps, after all, there was nothing. . . .

In the third book, a small old volume with fraying edges, his finger traveled slowly down the column of index listings—and stopped, the tingling in his fingertip spreading quickly through his body as he stared at the inconspicuous entry: *Eluth Initiates.* A cold barb stuck between his shoulder blades as he studied the cover of the book, realizing he had guessed right: *Arcane Practices of the Occult,* it read, in dull gold letters.

He wanted to lean back just then, wanted a moment's respite before plunging into this new pool of information; he wanted to tell himself it was just a coincidence, or perhaps he'd heard the name somewhere, remembered it unconsciously, only to have it regurgitated by whatever underground currents energized his psyche. And, suddenly, he wanted to close the book, stand quietly from the table, and smile politely at the middle-aged woman as he smoothly exited the room.

But his fingers acted of their own accord. They

flipped quickly through the pages, mechanically, it seemed to him—he could have been viewing from a distance—as anticipation grew warm in his blood.

Halfway down the indicated page, he found what he was looking for:

This latest eruption of the dark occult forces lying everpresent beneath the veneer of civilization took the form of a circle of initiates, a hidden order dedicated to the furtherance of the aims of the demonic powers from which they claimed to draw support. They called themselves the *Eluth Initiates*.

Alric sat back in his seat, his hands tightly gripping the pages of the worn little book. Slowly, he felt the warmth leave his body, replaced by an indefinable sensation.

It had actually existed—the words were on a band of continuous replay in his brain. *It had actually existed*. His earlier, halfhearted attempts at rational explanations were quickly and savagely pierced by the sharp edges of the cold, black letters on the page.

And in that instant he knew there was more.

With a growing dark knowledge bordering on fatalism, he again lowered his eyes to the yellowing pages:

Formed in Central Europe after the turn of the century, and disappearing shortly after the Second World War, this obscure group founded its beliefs in the Legend of Thule, for which the name is an anagram. Similar to the Atlantis myth, though in all probability far older, the Legend of Thule deals with a highly advanced civilization supposed to have existed at the northernmost limits of the world, somewhere in the area of present-day Iceland and Greenland.

The name of the continent was Hyperborea, and
its capital was Thule. It was said to have been
even more advanced than Atlantis, being in possession of motorized vehicles, rocket weaponry,
space vehicles, perhaps even nuclear power. But
eventually their control over the forces of nature, having become a "black force," turned
against them, unleashing a cataclysm of un-
equaled proportions.

Alric looked up from the book, scratching his
head.

Thule. The legendary civilization at the top of the
world, having disappeared somewhere in the dim
recesses of the past. He had come across the myth
several times in the course of his research.

But what of the mysterious group, the *Eluth
Initiates?*

Suddenly a shiver ran the length of his body—and
he had a fleeting vision of a dark circle of men in the
desert at night, the swollen orb of the moon, the
white shining of raised blades. . . .

He shook off the image, and continued reading:

The Initiates believed, however, that the destruction of Thule was merely the latest in a
cycle of birth–death–rebirth stretching back to
the beginning of the human race. Several such
civilizations had arisen in the primeval past,
great ages of man during which powerful na-
tions arose, and giant "Supermen" appeared, to
reign godlike over the mass of humanity. But,
inevitably, catastrophe would strike, as man's
control over the elements turned against him.
Life would be devastated, and the great civilizations, having reached the pinnacle of scientific
and artistic achievement, would perish. And during the long intervening ages of darkness, hide-

ous crawling mutants would inhabit a world of swampy wastelands.

Alric wanted to stop reading for a moment, relax and assess the strange information—and try to understand it in the light of last night's dream. But instead he found himself reading faster and faster, words becoming a blur on the page, as a bizarre new world opened up to him, frightening in his growing recollection of his night in the pyramid.

And the words, the letters, came still faster, now blinding in their speed—

He stopped. And his blood ran cold.

It couldn't be. . . .

He slowed his heart's racing by an effort of will, and began to reread the last paragraphs:

The Eluth Initiates developed, as their doctrine of beliefs, a fantastic cosmogony which not only attempted to explain, in mythico-scientific terms, the formation of the earth and solar system, the beginnings of life and its infusion with spirit, and the development of man and society, but presented a detailed picture of the universe, from its creation, to the ultimate catastrophe which would end the "cycles of time." At the core of their doctrine was the belief that the whole of cosmological creation, as well as the history of humanity, could be perceived in the perpetual struggle, transcendent throughout the infinite reaches of space, between the eternal combatants, fire and ice.

It should be noted, in this context, that the Initiates' belief system was, in fact, a corrupted form of the ancient mystical principles of the dualistic nature of the universe, a universe governed by the interplay between the forces of attraction and repulsion, light and darkness, life and death. The Eluth phenomenon was not an isolated instance in the history of mystical science, but rather the latest, albeit degenerated, cosmogony in a long line of Gnostic and Neo-Gnostic doctrines, including those of the Cathars, the Templars, and the Manicheans. The Initiates drew from the rich font of myths buried deep in the human psyche; their theory of cycles was but a reinvention of the Platonic world-view.

It was several minutes before Alric closed the book, his mind going over the last passages again and again, troubled and confused. It had been a brief reference, vague at best. But the connection was unmistakable.

Fire and ice. . . .

He leaned back, finally allowing the small book to rest on the table. He studied the cover, with its soft gold letters, the dark emanations from its pages almost palpable under the library's false daylight. He gave his head a small shake.

Mysticism. . . .

The word itself had come to be a curse to him—with good reason. Now it was an icy coal burning in his stomach. He'd fought it for so long, had succeeded in relegating it to a world far from him, distantly unreal and safe. But now it had returned to haunt him. And the idea of coincidence—that slippery phenomenon in which he'd never held much faith—seemed the only possible source of light in a strange new darkness.

Coincidence. How safe it sounded.

But he couldn't make himself believe it. And he couldn't quell the thought, faint but ever present, that his presence here had purpose, design. On some level, perhaps, he had believed that from the start.

And now . . . ?

With a slow, deliberate motion, he reached under his jacket to the inside pocket and pulled out a single wrinkled sheet of yellowing paper, unfolding it carefully, for it was brittle with age. He flattened it out before him on the table and leaned over it, reading for perhaps the thousandth time the precise handwriting.

His father's unmistakable hand.

*And how I am drawn down these last days.
. . . Yes, last days, I fear indeed, for it seems
that sanity escapes me—and what will take its
place . . . ? I am pulled down, drawn into a raging fire, deadly cold. But I must continue. To do
otherwise would be inexcusable. I only hope my
faith can sustain me.*

*I see dark worlds before me, and I read fear
in my own heart.*

*I see blackness; the ceremonies are unspeak-
able. . . .*

*Through mystic eyes I begin to see all: the
world is Fire and Ice, the demons live. Take our
bodies, our voices cry, we are your tools. Let the
river flow. Blood, all will be blood.*

*And here, in these sands it will be found, from
this place he will come forth. Buried in the sand,
millennia, he comes forth. I have seen his eyes.
From the raging pyre he will emerge:*

A new birth.

Son of Fire, Son of Ice.

It was a long while before Alric looked up from the tattered paper—the cryptic legacy left him by his father, which was to haunt him throughout his life. The page had been returned by the newly established government in Palestine, along with his father's few possessions: a dog-eared passport, rusty razor, taped-together photograph of wife and infant son—the last artifacts of his known existence. Alric had been thirteen when he had come upon them; his mother had always said there had been nothing. And then one rainy morning, looking for God knew what, he had found the manila envelope buried in an old chest, beneath a mass of papers, letters, yellowing photographs—and he had known that his mother had lied: his father had not died before Alric's birth, could, conceivably, still be alive. Alric had never told his mother of his discovery, but had secreted away the page, reading it over and over, trying to decipher its meaning, and wondering if these had been his father's last words—and if they had been meant for him.

Mysticism. . . .

He shook his head again, a confused gesture. What had his father seen—or thought he had seen—that could have turned him from the solidity of his science? What had pulled him away from the rational, the objective, the *real?* And could he, Alric, go under as well? It had always chilled him, how shallow beneath the surface the alien worlds seemed to be at times, how short a lapse was necessary for man to revert to the modes of the primeval. And now, his frighteningly real dream had impressed itself upon his waking life, had thrown him into a shadow world with a force that began to enfold him in dark, threatening arms.

But, simultaneously, a part of his mind rebelled against this newest bit of information, this newest link. Mysticism was (in spite of what Chandler might, at times, have thought) far from him. He was a *scientist*—how reassuring the word could sound— and this material was far from science.

He let himself be soothed by the word, as clear and clean as the light from the fluorescent bulbs overhead.

But was that all there was, the light without the dark? Had he not also felt the subtler reality of that other world, the world of the visionaries? Had he not, as a boy, lain awake at night, his head filled with the conjurings of the forbidden magicians (Hermes Trismegistus, Agrippa, Paracelsus—he could still recall the names), his eyes alert, as though expecting the gods to reveal themselves in the mysterious patterns of light and darkness which played across his ceiling?

He was not aware of how long he had been there, lost in his thoughts, when the middle-aged woman began clearing her throat, a bit louder each time, until he looked up and over at her. She smiled apologetically, catching his eye for the first time, and he understood that it had grown late; she was ready to close this section of the library and lock up.

He stood slowly from his seat, as if awakening from a thick sleep, and bundled the books together. In a moment he had returned them to their places on the shelf and walked over to her by the door. She stood poised with her hand on the light switch. He made a vague gesture of apology for having kept her, but her own gesture indicated that this was unnecessary.

He exited quietly through the library's heavy wooden doors.

The last ray of sunlight hung suspended over the city, painting the sky with the darkest colors of blood. It remained for a widening instant, an ethereal bead hung from an invisible strand, awaiting quiet and unnoticed dissolution. In the next instant it would have faded, as the sun sparked a new morning, left behind an old day.

The street bordering the museum grew quiet, as did most of the city at this point, the juncture of two worlds, light and dark. Those who had walked briskly along its clean, even surface during the daylight hours had now returned home from work, were sitting down to dinner, relaxing with the smooth flow of information concerning the day's events and the next day's plans.

But this dusk the museum street was different, though anyone walking along it would have had a hard time putting into words just why. He would have *felt* the difference, though, on the deepest level, in the densest fibers of his nervous system. He would have looked at the regular shape of the museum, noticed how a new coat of paint might be in order, thought back, perhaps, to an interesting exhibit he had seen in some forgotten year, and found little else to draw his attention to its boxlike structure.

But this evening he would have walked a little faster along this quiet street, telling himself that it was just the slight chill in the air, not unusual for this time of year. And to reassure himself he might have drawn his jacket a bit more tightly around his neck, though faintly conscious of the tiny beads of sweat along his nape.

Night had settled fully on the camp by the time Alric returned. He looked up at the black shroud of the sky, patterned with the six thousand pinprick spots of light and the faint glow along the horizon. For a few minutes he remained in the jeep, dwelling on the one link that seemed to unite the pieces.

The dream.

If only he could remember more than the smallest fraction. . . .

Visionary experiences within pyramids were nothing new; Alric had come across several of them in his research. They had, in fact, been the motivation for his spending the night in this newly discovered pyramid. He thought now of the researcher who, having spent the night in the Great Pyramid of Cheops, had emerged the following morning haunted by the images which had assailed his senses: the bizarre shadows and apparitions which had hovered around him, coalescing into terrifying faces; the sinister elementals, creatures of the underworld, which had surrounded him, threatening him; and, finally, the night's transformation from one of fear and horror to one of peace and clarity, with the appearance of the tall figures in flowing white robes, who had served to guide him toward a vision of knowledge.

And now Alric was faced with the dilemma of interpreting his own experience—in light of the information he had obtained at the library. And he had to decide how much to tell Chandler.

Setting his mind, he left the jeep and walked quickly toward the two tents, the thin canvas walls of each revealing a light from inside. He thought briefly about saying hello to Diana, but instead walked directly to Chandler's tent. Inside, he found the archaeologist at his table, leaning over a book.

"Carl, I have to talk to you," he said without introduction.

Chandler looked up, meticulously removed his glasses and set them on the table. "Where have you been till now?"

"In town," said Alric, quickly. "Listen, I've found out something very interesting."

"So have I."

Alric did not hear him. "I would have come to you sooner, but I had some things to check out."

Chandler was curious at the younger man's energy. "Well, am I going to have to guess?"

Alric did not smile. "Do you remember that pyramid investigator I was telling you about? The man who slept in the Great Pyramid?"

Chandler sighed. "Yes, of course. But you know what my opinion of the whole thing is."

"I know," said Alric, brushing aside Chandler's tone. "But do you remember the dreams? The ones he said he'd had that night?"

"More like hallucinations, I recall. Extremely vivid, he'd said."

"Yes." Alric paused for the first time since entering the tent. "Well, the same thing happened to me.

"What do you mean?" asked Chandler, cautiously.

"In the pyramid last night. A dream. Only it was real. It was as though I were there."

"I see," said Chandler, noncommittally. "And what can you remember about this dream?"

Alric slowed his pace, thinking back. "Well," he began, "there might have been more than one . . . or several fragments running together. It's hard to remember, pretty much is still unclear. But toward the end, right before I woke up . . ." He hesitated, seemed in need of a proper approach. Then he looked up. "Do you remember, this morning I asked you if you'd ever heard of Eluth?"

"Yes?"

"Well, it was in the dream, the last one." He stepped over to the cot before continuing. "There was a group of men, taking part in some kind of . . . rite." He stopped, allowing the image to clarify, then continued. "Then there was someone behind me, pointing to one of the men. He said the man had been seeking Eluth."

"It still doesn't ring a bell," said Chandler.

Alric looked up, catching Chandler's eye meaningfully. "I know," he said. "It wasn't that well known. But it *did* exist."

"*What* did exist?"

"Eluth. Or, at least, a cult that based its beliefs in the legend."

"I don't understand what you're saying."

"The name, Eluth . . . it's an anagram for Thule. This group was centered around the story of Thule."

"The legendary continent?"

"Yes," nodded Alric. "When I was in town today I did some research at the library." His voice grew emphatic. "It really did exist, Carl. The name in the dream . . . Eluth."

"I see," said Chandler quietly. "And you're sure you've never heard the name before?" he asked soberly. "You've done so much research."

Alric frowned. "That's just it. I should have come across the name, but I didn't."

"You can be that sure?"

"Carl, don't you think I know that that's the logical explanation? That I've heard the name somewhere and retained an unconscious memory of it? But it was so damned real."

Chandler let it go for now. "And what did you find out about this group?"

"That's also pretty interesting," said Alric. "You see, the Eluth Initiates—that's what they called themselves—were some kind of mystical cult. Not only did they believe in the literal truth of the legend of Thule, but they had as their central doctrine some kind of crazy cosmology which believed that the universe was formed by the conflict of fire and ice—a kind of cosmic interplay of opposing fundamental forces."

Chandler raised his eyebrows.

Alric shrugged. "I told you it was crazy."

"I don't see what possible relevance—"

"Please, Carl, let me finish."

The older man nodded reluctantly.

Before Chandler's cold stare, Alric recounted what he had learned at the library a few hours earlier about the peculiar beliefs of the group of occultists: the strange, mystical birth of the universe, at the beginning of the cycles of time; the great civilizations that arose and perished; and the mad cosmology which reduced all things in the universe to the relative balance of fire and ice. He thought briefly—and immediately rejected the idea—of telling Chandler about his father and his possible connection to the mysterious cult. But no, Chandler would not understand, and it would only make certain in his mind Alric's capacity for projection; all would surely seem a hallucination. So he stopped short, and the silence in the tent seemed to exude from the very pores of the canvas walls.

Then a curious transformation took place on Chandler's face. The cold, dispassionate gaze of the scientist standing tribunal before the flights of the mad prophet gave way smoothly and imperceptibly to a look that was a combination of recollection, interest, and association. When he finally spoke, there was a trace of concern in his voice. "I wonder if there might be a connection."

"What do you mean?"

"I've been doing some research as well," said the archaeologist, picking up a hardcover book lying open on his desk. "The signs on the little pyramid. The sun and the moon. . . ."

Alric thought for a moment, then connected. "Fire and ice?"

"Perhaps," said Chandler, leafing through the book. "Ah, here," he said, stopping at a page. He began to read. " 'The sun: symbol of the ruler, the driving force of matter, the procreative power, the power of intellect. When not balanced by its opposite pole, the moon, symbol of the transcendent spirit of the cosmos, the underlayer of consciousness in which reside intuition, spirituality, and compassion, the results are a civilization obsessed with violence, total control over the forces of nature, and the will to power.' "

Alric thought back to the story of the civilization of Thule, so advanced, but destroyed when its power had turned against it. He began to speak, but Chandler raised his hand slightly in order to continue.

"There's more," he said. " 'The original purpose of the pyramid'—and here the author means the Great Pyramid—'may have been to equilibrate the forces of nature, and by a union of the masculine principle, represented by the sun, and the feminine principle, represented by the moon, to make fertile the earth.' " He looked up from the book. "And the third sign— the five-pointed star—seems to be a symbol of that sacred union."

"And the last sign? The lens shape?"

"I'm not sure yet."

Alric smiled. "You *have* been doing some work."

Chandler put down the book. "It's all pretty interesting stuff, John, I'll admit. But at this point, I really don't know what it means. And this dream you say you had. . . ." He shrugged. "Could be just coincidence."

Alric took a deep breath and was silent, as thought creased his face. After a moment he looked up; an idea he had been pursuing for some time had taken form inside him. He looked at the archaeologist. "Carl, remember what Ahmad said? The pyramid alters time in some way? A man might be able to see different points in history . . . ?"

"John," said Chandler evenly, "we've been working here for months, now, and this pyramid research has been a concern of yours for years, along with your research into ancient civilizations. If you were going to have a hallucination, it's a natural motif. And being here, this business with your father, trying to find out about him . . . it's only brought things to a head."

Alric started at the last words. His *father*. Why had Chandler brought *that* up? Caught off guard, Alric managed not to let it show.

"Then how do you explain Eluth?" he asked simply.

"Like you said. You heard the name somewhere and remembered it unconsciously. Not the most dramatic of explanations, I'll grant, but certainly the most reasonable at this point."

Alric shook his head slowly. "It was so real."

"John, even Jung said that you have to exhaust all plausible theories before considering an extraordinary one."

Alric was silent for a few seconds, then said, "Carl, if a few years ago I'd asked you what caused mummification, what would you have said?"

"I fail to see—"

"What would you have said?"

Chandler grudgingly acquiesced. "Well, I suppose

104

what any other archaeologist would have said. The treatment of the bodies, combined with the dryness of the climate."

"Right," said Alric. "But then along comes an archaeologist who discovers the bodies of some animals accidentally sealed in the Great Pyramid. And even though they'd been untreated, they were preserved as well. That's when the physicists got involved. What is it, we asked, about the structure of a pyramid that affects the way things behave inside it? Years later we still don't know."

"What's your point?" asked Chandler, wearying of the old argument.

"Just that we don't know," said Alric. "We don't know about the pyramids. We don't even know all there is to know about electrons, or light, or gravity. The best we can do is describe the way they behave. And even that's only in terms of statistical probabilities. But as far as things *really* are, their *true* nature, we just don't know."

"But we have to act as though we did," said Chandler, "otherwise, what's the point?" He walked over to Alric, putting his hand on the younger man's shoulder. "John, I just don't want to see you get caught up in this."

"I already am," said Alric evenly, as he stood up from the cot.

The two men's eyes locked for a moment, then Alric nodded his good-night to Chandler, turned, and left the tent.

Chandler nodded slowly to himself. For a few seconds he stood still, listening intently to the desert silence. Then he turned and walked back to his desk, going over in his mind the discussion with Alric. The information that the younger man had turned up was interesting and could, conceivably, be relevant. The wild ideas held by the "cultists" were not unheard of; history had seen several such anomalies since the dawn of civilization. Flat earthists, hollow earthists, searchers for Atlantis, the list of mystic dogmas went on and on. But had Alric found a credible link? Could a dream be taken seriously? And how did it all tie in, especially in relation to his, Chandler's, research into the meaning of the signs?

Thoughtfully, he picked up the book from which he'd been reading, hefting it a few times as if gauging its weight. There was much work to be done tonight, he reminded himself, as he sat down heavily at the table and reached for his pen and pad, grateful for the cool wisp of night air entering through the gently swaying tent flaps.

A row of tiny scarabs lay across the shelf, marching with infinite slowness toward the end of time; across the room, a stone woman watched the progress impassively, remembering, in her crumbling eyes, the light of an earlier sun, the hands of a different race; along the wall a sage held counsel with a young pharaoh, warning of various intrigues, the many threats against the crown. In another room, a lion struggled defiantly in alabaster relief, its hind legs useless under the nerve-splitting force of the arrows which had torn through its flesh; a mummified head sat alone on a shelf, eerily reflective, the corners of the mouth turned slightly inward, giving a look of condescension; against a wall an Egyptian tablet displayed some of the symbols of the ancient culture: the ankh, eternal symbol of life, shaped like the heel and strap of a sandal; Nekjbet, the vulture goddess, who spread her protective wings over the pharaohs of Upper Egypt, grasping in her talons the royal ring; Wadjet, the crimson-garbed cobra goddess, patron of Lower Egypt; and the falcon, Horus, the cosmic sky god whose eyes were the sun and moon.

But another room of the museum was strangely cold, its two display cabinets etched in an etheric, crystal atmosphere. The gold pyramid glowed mildly in the darkness, housed within clear glass walls. And across the room the two small black statues stood silent watch, eyes at home in the night, listening, perhaps, for the faint whistling of the wind in the alleys outside.

Near the main entrance, the museum's night watchman sat down easily in the wooden chair by the large double doors. He reached across his small, school-style desk, and pulled a transistor radio a few inches closer to him, simultaneously turning it on and tuning to his station. He leaned back with the flow of music, opening the evening paper to an article he'd begun on the bus.

It was going well enough for him, he reflected on another level of consciousness: the kids were surviving school this year, and the meager pay increase next month promised to lighten the load somewhat. He let a satisfied belch escape, hearing its echo roll through the cavernous halls and chambers.

Above all, he was one of those rare, fortunate men who truly enjoyed their jobs. Sometimes, late at night, he would walk down the deserted corridors as if they were the halls of his own home, his own palace. He would admire the works of ancient art, drink them in until he was familiar with every chip in the stone, every crack in the wood. Then he would return to his chair as though from a full meal; he would adjust the volume on the radio and finish his newspaper, waiting for the first rays of dawn and the first sounds of life from the street outside.

(In another part of the museum, display windows were clouding over with a dark frost. A shadow moved slowly down a corridor.)

The watchman looked up from his newspaper, not sure exactly why. He had felt a brief, tingling sensation, little more than the vestige of a feeling he couldn't quite place. He shook it off, noticing the coolness in the air; he would have to check the thermostat. His eyes again lowered to the paper.

But the feeling wouldn't quite leave him. He let the paper fall to his lap, wondering about the strange sensation. But soon the music soothed him, allowing him to push back the unclear thoughts. He reached for his cigarettes, near the edge of the table. But his hand stopped at the first crinkle of the cool cellophane.

He had felt it again.

And still he couldn't place it. A vague recollection in the depths of his brain? Or an internal signal that might have meant nothing more than a poorly digested meal? He finally lit the cigarette.

Or was it . . . ?

He turned off the radio.

And his senses began to understand.

He stood slowly, uneasily, aware that something had to be investigated. He didn't know exactly what had told him: a faint odor, perhaps, or the shadow of a sound; or the trace of an animal warning in some rarely used part of his brain.

But he knew, with the basic knowledge of the body, that something was in the museum with him.

He dropped the cigarettes soundlessly into his shirt pocket, and walked slowly toward the first long corridor leading to the display rooms.

(And slowly it moved, the darkness, past the bits of culture.)

There was that time a few months back, he reminded himself, just like this. Turned out to be a cat. Couldn't figure out how the damned thing had gotten in. There had been a muffled scratching sound; no one else would have heard it. But this was *his* museum, and he understood its night silence with years of experience. Nothing escaped him. And, he admitted, he'd been somewhat frightened that night. Though he was certainly not like *some* of the men among his friends, the superstitious fools who warned him of the ancient spirits that must surely roam these corridors at night. They wouldn't have his job, they would say between sips of *chai*, for *any* money. But he was not superstitious; he knew that spirits only walked the pages of children's stories. And if he had been frightened that last time, it had been only natural. How could he have known that some alley cat, seeking to escape the heat of day, had entered through an open basement window or beneath the legs of an influx of visitors, to be trapped inside when the museum had closed.

He smiled to himself; it was certainly a cat.

And then he heard it clearly: a distinct sound, like the crystalline tinkling of a statue of ice come to life. He dropped the cigarette, cursing, and began to walk down the long corridor.

(And in that room it stopped.)

Although he was moving very slowly, the display rooms seemed to speed by him. The ancient friezes with their tales of royal intrigue; the many tableaus of varying size and texture, displaying men and women at work, in the hunt, or performing forgotten religious rites; the steles with foreign alphabets, some, perhaps, never to be deciphered: all passed by in a vague and muted collage. The works of art before which he had stood for long hours were reduced to coarse chunks of matter; his body was in a state of readiness.

He stopped.

There should have been a light on in the next display chamber; each room had a low wattage bulb burning at all times.

But the next chamber was dark.

He stopped at the entrance, reached into his shirt pocket for his cigarettes. He exhaled deeply, only just now noticing how his breath steamed in the frigid air. With a caution that surprised him, he took a step into the room and looked around, aided by the light from the hall.

Nothing seemed out of place.

He looked at the small gold pyramid, remembering

that he'd heard about it from the day guard. It was something that the American research team had found. Something very old.

He looked over at the other display cabinet, saw the Egyptian beadwork, the crouching bronze lion, the necklaces of golden leaves. And the two small statues. How their eyes seemed to grow in the darkness, he thought, how they became cavernous, how they invited you—

And the cigarettes flew from his hands with a force that stunned him awake. A smothered gasp escaped his lips as he careened headlong into the room, as if sucked into a vacuum chamber. There was a muffled, bursting noise from inside his chest, and he reached up a hand as though to prevent his heart from exploding. He tried to scream, needed to scream, but could not. A thick, dark fluid had begun to rise in his throat, drowning his voice, pushing outward until bursting into his inner ears. There was a vague, questioning look in his eyes, as he felt his mouth open, as he watched the blood spew forth as though from the eruption of an internal volcano.

Reflexively, his body tried to react. Slowly, as if fighting a wave, he reached down for his gun, but his arm was thrown sharply back, his hand crashing through the glass window of the larger display cabinet, knocking over the bronze lion. His wrist twitched cruelly over the crystal shards, again and again, until the radial artery was torn open, spraying the gold necklaces with a hot, red shower.

Detachedly, almost willingly, he heard his last sound: the dreamlike popping as his eardrums burst under the growing pressure. His hair quickly became matted as the blood erupted, slick and viscous, from his ears.

Suddenly his body was thrown against the cabinet with a powerful wrenching motion. His head flew back through the glass of the upper shelf with rubbery ease, as if the bones in his neck had turned to sponge. His body continued to struggle, but now in feeble, jerking spasms, as the edge of the broken pane cut deeply into the back of his neck.

And slowly, slowly, his head was turned, his throat being driven over the jagged edge of the glass.

It has been a long time in coming: there will be much pain.

The time of darkness approaches.

(The Earth will split, and again . . . for man's power has turned black.

She will open, vomiting her molten insides to rain death; fire will consume the land, cauterize it, engulf it in an igneous sea; the oceans will rise, collapsing the continents and thrusting up new summits; man will flee to the highest peaks, and struggle to bury his legacy before he is taken under.

And the sky will be black for a thousand years, veiled by the ashes of his civilization.)

The glare of blue attacks Alric's eyes, impresses itself upon him with a physical presence. He brings his hand up to shade himself from the sky's morning strength; he lowers his head.

When vision has returned, shapes again become distinct: there are people in the street, walking briskly, purposefully, wearing brightly colored tunics, similar in cut to the blue one he wears. Buildings sparkle, their angles painfully sharp in the warm clear atmosphere.

He continues walking, on toward the construction site, with an indistinct memory teasing him.

(And there are black, hollow eyes, watching, waiting. . . .)

Some of his people nod to him or smile as he passes.

To his right, a man stands in an arched doorway, observing his progress. Alric slows as he passes him, turning his head toward him, as a vague uneasiness crowds him.

111

Then he stops, looks closely at the man, but cannot remember what he sees: the body is indistinct, though he is not far away. And the eyes. . . .

The eyes are closed!

But he has been watching, Alric is certain—watching with closed eyes. . . .

There is a flicker of motion on the strange man's face. Alric takes a step closer, begins to see clearly: the white frame of hair, the wrinkled layers of skin, the toothless smile.

And with that smile the eyelids withdraw, giving Alric no time to retreat: he stares into the wet, black caverns of empty eye sockets.

The Blind Man gives a short laugh. His face twists into a demonic leer. And, slowly, a hand reaches out toward Alric.

Frightened, Alric shrinks from him.

The Blind Man laughs again, a harsh, tearing laugh, and continues to reach out to Alric.

And then he's running. (Footsteps echoing in his head.) His feet tear madly at the ground; his muscles strain for the salvation of dark peace. . . .

(And images unfold in frantic sequence, shocking clarity in the absence of reasoned observation: an old man, cruel, empty eyes; squirming, wet, black insects, a field of snakes; and they're with him now, no escape, inside him now, a part of him, a blood legacy; figure of a man with no face, only empty eye sockets; naked squirming on sacrificial stakes, a row of corpses, a glint of gold; and a large black cat with digging claws, glistening fangs, blood running from its mouth; blood, all will be blood, as the Earth is split; then blackness, cold, cold grave, damp earth and drained white skin; and the cat's face white with devil-smile, white as a corpse's; a splash of blood, and claws digging into the flesh above his belt, teeth tearing into his throat; and slowly a head is turned, driven over a jagged edge of glass; slowly, soundlessly, a cold steel hook passes up through a

nasal cavity; an eruption of thick, cold snake's blood, from the depths; and always that eyeless face, turning white, death-white, corpse-white and smiling, transmuting into formless black stone. . . .

And he's falling, struggling, gasping, all the time watched, coldly observed by those eyes, those dead, black eyes.)

With a gasp, Alric awoke, jerked up straight in his cot like a puppet whose strings had just been snapped taut. Around him, the tent was filled with a thick darkness, heavy with it; outside, the desert night was soundless and cold. For a few minutes he sat there unmoving, straight up, back rigid, breathing in great gulps of air. His eyes were wide and darting, though it was several minutes before he could make out a few ill-defined, yet nonetheless reassuring, shapes: the worktable, just a few feet beyond the foot of his cot; the amorphous mass of clothes piled on the chair in the corner; and, in the cot next to his, Diana's quietly sleeping shape. At length, his breathing slowed. He leaned back in his cot, pulling the sheet a bit higher on his body.

His eyes remained open.

A cool night breeze stirred gently around his tent as Chandler sat down at the overladen folding table that served as his desk. He pushed his glasses a half-inch higher on his nose as he leafed through the pages of a thick hardcover book. In a few seconds, having found the desired page, he set the book on the table and juxtaposed it with the scrap of paper on which he'd copied the signs inscribed on the miniature pyramid and its stand. His right forefinger remained stationary at each of the four symbols in turn as his left ran down columns of figures on the book's page. After he'd found the last symbol, he turned quickly to another page, reading it carefully, his brows furrowed in thought.

When he'd finished reading, he set the book down

open on the table and pushed his seat a few inches away, taking a deep breath. He folded his arms across his chest as an idea scurried lightly across the boundary of his consciousness; something that had skirted his awareness throughout the day, barely perceptible at the limits of his peripheral vision, then submerging within the folds of everyday distractions.

And there was something else; something Alric had mentioned earlier. . . .

In a moment he stood and walked to a small brown briefcase in the corner of the tent. He searched briefly among its contents, then pulled out a paperback copy of the book Alric had written on pyramidology. He returned to the desk and opened the book. He quickly found the page he wanted and began reading.

The secret of mummification may lie not in the treatment of the body but in the very structure of the pyramid. For completely untreated corpses of animals found in several of the pyramids were found to have undergone the same mummification process, the efficacy of which often equals that of the pharaohs.

That wasn't it, thought Chandler; not exactly. It was something else he'd read. Something about preservation. He turned the page, scanning it quickly.

And his eyes stopped.

Here it was. This was the section. Something in it set his mind on edge. If only it would come clear.

He found his red pen under a loose pile of papers, and drew a box around one of the paragraphs on the page. He tapped the desk top with the pen as he read and reread the words.

There appears to be something about the pyramidal shape which effects changes in any chemical, physical, and biological processes going on inside it. I have carried out numerous experiments in which a variety of items have been left in pyramids for periods of time ranging from a few minutes to several weeks. The results, though not always consistent, do seem to indicate that *something* different occurs inside pyramids. Food is preserved, water is purified, plants tend to grow better, the germination period for seeds changes, sometimes shortened, sometimes lengthened. Human subjects remaining in pyramids for a few hours have claimed easier relaxation, peacefulness, better meditation, faster healing, and even a feeling of rejuvenation.

He put the book down open on the table.

Yes, he was getting closer. But there was another part. Something that would just not clarify, that he would have to coax into the light. He tilted his head slightly, as if in response to a faint sound. Then he smiled.

Something in the signs.

He reached for the slip of paper and searched the four symbols for a clue. He knew there was something there.

Could it be . . . ?

He turned phrases over quickly in his mind: "the sun, symbol of the ruler," "the moon, the feminine principle," "the five-pointed star, symbol of sacred union." And there was the fourth sign, the lens shape. . . .

He looked up. Was it possible?

The events of the past few days collaged inside his brain: their entry into the pyramid, older than any of them had suspected; the finding of the chamber, empty except for the small gold pyramid; the mysterious inscriptions, reaching back to him across the eons; the flowerlike opening of the gold model. . . .

He quickly tore a scrap of paper from his note pad and reached for the hardcover book he had been reading. He copied down several phrases, then tossed his pen to the table and leaned back. He read the few words to himself, over and over, struggling to find the connection. Struggling to understand the significance of the sign that the Greeks had called the Holiest of Holy, the sign from which so many Christian symbols were derived. The small sign that resembled a thick lens, or a blank, iris-less eye: the *vesica piscis*.

And he had it.

He pushed his thick fingers deep into his shirt pocket, vaguely aware of the growing warmth in his blood. Finally he retrieved the tiny ovoid that Alric had found in the gold pyramid. He held it gingerly between thumb and forefinger.

"Could we have been so blind?" he asked in a half-whisper.

Quickly he stood and walked to the suitcase. This time he removed a small microscope and returned to the table. With a fingernail he scraped some particles from the surface of the ovoid. The two glass slides tinkled coldly as his trembling hands put the particles between the smooth clean surfaces. With some trouble, he managed to get the slides into the microscope. He hesitated briefly, then lowered his head and peered into the eyepiece.

And his eyes grew wide.

"Yes!" he said, after a few seconds, his body now shaking with mild tremors. He could no longer steady his hands to the focusing wheel.

At length he calmed himself. He leaned back in the chair and again studied the bead.

"Yes," he repeated, nodding slowly.

He had been sitting there for several minutes when a soft rustling sound from outside the tent disturbed his thoughts. He put the ovoid down in the crease of the open book and walked to the entrance of the tent. He bent through the canvas flaps and stepped outside.

He found the desert night mild but invigorating. Its darkness was broken only by the overhead haze of the Milky Way, which cast a muted glow on the desert floor, giving the appearance of a sparkling road leading to the horizon and beyond.

He looked briefly toward Alric's tent. He would, of course, have to wake him. Alric would not have wanted him to wait until morning. Not with something like this.

But just now he had to relax for a few moments. He had to sit down with his new discovery, close his eyes, and let it sink in. He went back inside the tent and returned to his chair. He leaned back, folding his hands in his lap.

He closed his eyes.

*

MORNING GREW UNOBTRUSIVELY in the small camp, more a fading of the darkness than a gathering of the light. The stars retreated imperceptibly, fusing slowly with the sky, until the two tents stood clearly in the sand, outlined in varying shades of brown and blue.

In his tent, Alric opened his eyes slowly, carefully, as if unsure of what they would find. The tent's interior was cast in dark green; the entrance flap swayed gently with the morning air. He found his head surprisingly clear of yesterday's strange discoveries; the cool morning served well to sharpen the world's lines, dissipating the miasma of indeterminacy.

He swung his legs noiselessly over the edge of the cot and reached for his pants, pulling them over his legs. He turned back toward Diana, but decided to let her sleep, at least until coffee was brewing on the campfire. He quietly left the tent.

Outside, the air was surprisingly chilly for this time of year, the skies a rich blue. He glanced briefly at the campfire, but walked instead directly into Chandler's tent.

"Carl, I—"

He stopped abruptly, just inside the entrance. Chandler lay motionless on his cot, his sheet pulled up to his eyes.

118

Something undefinable sounded inside Alric. Something very old.

"Carl . . . ?" He tentatively approached the cot. "Carl?"

Still no repsonse. Alric pulled back the sheet.

And froze, his limbs drained hollow, his stomach leaden with revulsion.

The archaeologist lay on his cot, hands folded over his belly. In the center of his chest was a splotch of blood, dark and caking. The two streams that had led from the source were dry, their pathways traced in deep red, from each nostril, down and around the lips, over the curve of the chin and onto the chest.

On the floor by the cot lay a gray and white mass, like a loosely coiled and dripping snake.

Alric stood paralyzed, unable to move or yell, unable even to retch, though his brain screamed for release.

The street bordering the front of the museum was beginning to grow crowded with morning commuters as the curator ambled briskly up the stone steps leading to the entrance doors. From the top he looked down and briefly surveyed the small section of town visible from his vantage point, watching a stopped bus add a new and varied group to the growing pedestrian population. He turned back to the large double doors, taking a last deep breath of fresh air as he rapped sharply on the dark wood. How clear the air was this morning, how clean.

After several seconds, there was no answer.

He knocked again, this time louder.

Still no answer.

He cursed mildly at having to search among his keys, again berated himself for not having labeled them, and reached into his pocket for the overladen key ring. After several attempts he found the right key, sighing as it slid smoothly into place and turned

with that familiar metallic click. He pushed open
the heavy door, then bent to secure it with the small
metal hook set in the floor. When the second door
had been likewise secured, he straightened and
looked around the cavernous entrance chamber.

"Musab?" he called, smoothing out his jacket.

He approached the watchman's small wooden
table. It was not like Musab to be away from his
post in the morning. And the radio was off; the only
sound was the rustling of a haphazardly dropped
newspaper, its pages opening and closing with the
currents of air entering through the open doors.

"Musab?" he called out.

Silence.

With his mind uncertain, vacillating between an-
noyance and concern, he approached the long hall
leading to the display rooms.

The time spent in the police station seemed unending. Alric sat in an uncomfortable wooden chair
in the inspector's office, staring fixedly at its drab
interior: the hanging pale green lamp, swinging in a
lazy arc with each gust of air from the open window;
the dusty, gray file cabinet, its drawers bursting
with folders; the assortment of yellowing photographs taped to the wall, displaying several children
of various ages. It had been his world for two hours
now, his universe. And still he had to remain. The
forms had been filled out, carried to the photostat
machine on another floor by an officious-looking
young woman; the American Consulate had been
notified and had sent over an overweight, red-faced
representative, who had pumped Alric's hand amid
profusions of sorrow and indignation, and had assured him that all arrangements would be taken care
of by the Consulate. And still there was more to be
done.

Images flashed through Alric's mind. At least he
had managed to keep Diana from seeing Chandler.

Her voice, calling him from outside, had forced him to action, had made him summon the strength to remove his eyes from the corpse. As though in a hypnotic state, he had turned and left the tent. She'd been about to enter, had been startled when he'd grabbed her by the arms, told her to take the jeep, go to the village, call the police. But she had obeyed, her eyes darting between his and the entrance to Chandler's tent, knowing that something was terribly wrong. And then she had run to the jeep, leaving him alone in the camp, alone with the two dark green tents. Alone with . . .

Inspector Yadin looked up from his desk, meticulously placing his pen on the pad on which he'd been writing. With a heavy gesture he smoothed his mustache, then ran a hand through his thick, dark hair, more from bewilderment than for preening. He was a large man, with a broad-shouldered, solid physique recalling an athletic youth which approaching middle age, had not yet dethroned. His quiet manner indicated a man who was sure of himself, needing to prove nothing. Alric had felt, at their brief handshake, that Yadin was the type of man whom, had the circumstances of their meeting been different, he would have liked. The officer glanced briefly at the pad again, then back at Alric.

"Is there anything else you can tell me, Dr. Alric?" he asked.

Alric shook his head wearily. "No."

"Are you sure? There are sometimes small details which we forget."

"I've already told you everything. I walked into his tent this morning and he was . . . like that."

Yadin picked up his pen, tapped it against the edge of his desk. "And you heard nothing?" he asked, for perhaps the fourth time.

Alric looked up, met Yadin's eyes. "I told you," he said evenly. "I didn't hear a sound. Don't you think I would have done something?"

"I'm sorry," said the inspector quietly. "But this is necessary. I'm just trying to understand how something like this could have happened without a struggle. Dr. Chandler was a large man."

Alric started at Yadin's words. The finality of Chandler's being referred to in the past tense cut sharply through his state of disbelief. For the first time since stepping into Chandler's tent that morning, he was awakened to the cold daylight. He exhaled long and deeply, as if squeezing from his system the last fog of unreality.

Yadin watched him closely, nodded understandingly, though Alric was not looking at him. He saw clearly that there was much work ahead of him.

By the time he had gotten to the first display room, the curator realized that his pace had slowed considerably. He shook his head and smiled thinly. It was foolish, of course, this unwarranted apprehension; surely Musab had simply fallen asleep on one of the long leather couches situated in some of the larger chambers. A reprimand would be in order.

But it had never happened before. And why had the guard turned off his radio, that damned instrument which each morning greeted the curator with a blast of meaningless noise? He tried to quicken his pace, but soon found himself moving forward with the same small cautious steps.

Yes, a reprimand would surely be in order. Sleeping on the job. He simply wouldn't have it.

There was a sharp cracking sound.

The curator halted stiffly, his heart beating furiously. He exhaled deeply and gave a nervous laugh as he found the source of the noise: he had trod on a fragment of broken glass. With careful fingers he removed the shard from the sole of his shoe, wondering where it had come from.

Then he became aware of the ringing.

He straightened, standing still for a moment, trying to place the sound. It was distant, so faint that it could have been coming from miles away. Yet at the same time it felt as though it were inside him. But unlike the familiar vibratory ring of the eardrum when all is quiet, this was a foreign sound, an invader, having entered his brain against its will.

He looked up, toward the next display room. He weakly called out the night watchman's name again, though this time he expected no answer. It had been a mere gesture, a failing bulwark against an obscure and growing fear.

And the ringing grew louder.

Alric watched the pale green lamp sway in the breeze from the open window, a rickety pendulum against the background of the faded walls; he nodded slowly his uncertain accompaniment. How quickly things could change; a blink of time was all that was needed. He narrowed his eyes in thought and realized that he couldn't place that blink, didn't know when it had come. He remembered the strange feeling that had been pursuing him since the start of the excavation, like an everpresent dark vapor, crystallizing slowly to black solidity. But no; it had begun before that. He couldn't place its birth.

He shook his head mildly, turned toward the window, heard fleeting disjointed sounds from the street below: a squeal of poorly adjusted brakes, a brief chord of horns, a shout cut off in midair. He wondered at how normality could so easily coexist with madness, how readily, understandingly, they accepted one another.

Yadin sat across from him, his old beaten desk between them. He looked up again from the pad, then, too, turned toward the window. He took a deep breath, letting the air escape slowly. "A bit noisy, no?"

Alric looked up vaguely, shrugged.

Yadin pushed himself away from the desk, leaning

back in his chair. He paused for a moment, studying Alric. "Tell me, Doctor," he said, with prepared casualness, "did Dr. Chandler have any political affiliations?"

"What?"

Yadin spoke carefully. "We live in a particularly volatile area, as you well know. If Dr. Chandler was involved with any political causes . . ."

Alric shook his head. "No. Nothing like that."

Yadin nodded. "And his financial status? Wealthy?"

"Middle class. A professor's salary."

"You said he had a daughter?"

"Yes. Single. In her twenties. Away at college, in upstate New York, I think. He didn't talk much about family."

Yadin raised his eyebrows. "Oh? Any problems with the girl?"

Alric looked up sharply at Yadin. "You mean, does she belong to some extremist group that blows up buses and hijacks planes?" he smirked. "No. No 'problems' with her."

Both men were silent, their eyes again finding the window. Outside, the sun beat down with growing strength; the street's babel rushed to a peak.

The phone on Yadin's desk rang.

He didn't know how long he had stood there, half curious of, half frightened by, that strange, ringing sensation, when at last he had understood that something was wrong, gravely wrong. He had given up calling the watchman's name, and had been trying to innervate his body to continue the search. He had noticed that the next room along this corridor was the one he'd been in yesterday with the American; it had been there that they'd placed the unusual gold pyramid, there that they'd—

And then he had seen it. Seen the dark, slick patch on the floor by the cabinet. Seen the strangely

124

sparkling and uneven floor, reflecting splinters of light like myriad tiny stars. . . .

And now it was harder than ever for him to move his legs, to give them the command to continue. Now it was harder than ever to keep the growing light-headedness from taking his body, relieving him of responsibility and allowing him escape into unconsciousness. But at length he prevailed. He walked the remaining few feet to the chamber's entrance, and stepped inside.

The floor was a ragged blanket of shards; his feet crackled piercingly with each shallow step. The glass was gone from the cabinets and windows—shattered, splintered, as if from a tremendous implosion. The case which had housed the pyramid was empty.

And everywhere was blood.

He turned his head quickly, involuntarily, from a dark mass propped in the corner by the window, sagging and covered with an inch-thick layer of fragmented glass, looking like a collapsed and crystallized snowman. He looked over at the larger display cabinet.

The fine beadwork had been crushed, turned into a coarse powder; the bronze lion lay on its side, twisted beyond recognition; the gold leaves of the two necklaces had been fused into a malformed broken cross.

Then he stopped. He felt the gorge rising in him, his bowels tightening like a steel coil. His hand came automatically to his mouth at the first sight of the dark tendrils hanging from the topmost shelf. But against his will, his eyes moved upward. . . .

And his screams echoed throughout the empty corridors.

The watchman's head stood in a crystal bed, dangling wormlike threads where a body should have been. The mouth was open, frozen in the throes of death agony, the eyes glazed and wide, as though attempting to better see the two cold black statues standing to either side.

The curator felt himself give way. He fled the room, trailing the coarse liquid which erupted from his mouth and spilled thickly through his fingers.

And he thought the ringing would burst his eardrums.

Yadin cupped the phone in his large hand, curtly speaking his name into the receiver, then awaited the flow of information. He listened for several seconds without speaking, his brow creasing darkly. "Yes ... What? ... I see," he said finally. He looked over at Alric. "He is, right now. Can you place the time of death? ... I see. ... And was anything else taken?"

At this, Alric looked up, curiosity apparent in his face.

Yadin finished. "I see. Thank you." He hung up the phone with greater force than he'd intended.

"Something was stolen from Carl's tent?" asked Alric.

Yadin hesitated for a second. "That wasn't about Dr. Chandler."

"What ... ? But I thought—"

"Dr. Alric," interrupted Yadin, "you delivered an artifact to the Museum of Antiquities yesterday morning?"

Uncomprehending, Alric nodded vaguely. "Yes. A small gold pyramid we'd found at the site the day before yesterday. Why?"

"Gold?"

Alric nodded.

"I see," said Yadin, again drawing his fingers over his thick mustache.

"I don't understand. What does all this have to do with Carl?"

"A guard was killed at the museum last night. And your pyramid was stolen."

126

"What . . . ?"

Yadin nodded.

"But how . . . ?"

"We don't have all the facts yet. Our team has just arrived at the scene." He paused for a few seconds, watching Alric closely. Then, "Can you think of any reason someone would have to steal it?"

Bewilderment seemed to form a veil between Alric and the world. "I don't know," he said, shaking his head. Then, grasping, "It's made of gold . . . very valuable."

"There are many other valuable objects in the museum," said Yadin. "Your pyramid appears to be the only thing taken."

Alric stared down at the floor and shook his head numbly. "Then I don't know." He looked at Yadin. "How was he killed? The guard?"

Yadin was silent, obviously debating.

Alric let a grim smile escape. "After today, I think I can take it."

Yadin gave a short nod. "The man's head was . . . torn off."

Alric winced in spite of himself.

Yadin again nodded. He studied Alric closely, his eyes cool with the same detached interest that the other might have applied to the investigation of a new subatomic particle. His gut reaction was that Alric was being honest with him. Twenty years of experience told him that the grief over Chandler had been genuine. He had noticed, perhaps half-consciously, the body's signs, difficult to counterfeit: the face, both flushed and pale at the same time, like fine red dust loosely settled on a layer of fresh snow; the lips, drained and cold, forming words mechanically, as if only from memory; above all, the eyes, those somnambulistic disks, with their enlarged pupils all but banishing the thin ring of iris. He wanted to again run his hand through his hair but became self-conscious of the gesture, and instead settled his arm heavily on the desk top. His eyes dropped to his notes, briefly scanning the precise handwriting.

He looked back up at Alric. "I guess there's no need to keep you any longer, Dr. Alric. You've given me all you can." As Alric stood, Yadin added, "Again, let me say how sorry I am. . . ." He stopped, realizing how mechanical it sounded, how hollow. Then, quietly, "This kind of thing does not happen often in our country."

Alric nodded, walking to the door. Before reaching for the knob he hesitated, almost turning back to the inspector. Was there any point in mentioning the cult of Eluth to Yadin, with their strange beliefs and practices? Could there be a connection?

"Yes . . . ?" asked Yadin, as Alric stood by the door.

No, thought Alric, quickly deciding to say nothing of the group. He really had nothing solid. At this point Eluth meant little to him—an obscure group that, for all he knew, had disappeared some thirty years ago.

He looked back at Yadin. "I'll . . . let you know if I think of anything that might be of help." He opened the door with a stiff motion and walked from the room.

Yadin looked after him, allowing himself a brief tug at the whiskers around his lips. And, as usual, his intellect felt that familiar surge, like a minute electric shock, at the inevitable process to follow: the maze of events and personalities which experience had taught him was like a chess game with real-life pieces; and the moves that had to be made with the utmost precision, until the quarry became known and was brought to a forced and losing endgame.

But at the same time there was a cold feeling in the pit of his stomach telling him that this was something new for him; something of a different kind. He found himself wondering, with surprising detachment, if the methods of police work were equipped to deal with it. And what he would do if they weren't.

He had heard of cases like this, of course, had read about them in American magazines. Cult murders. Certainly the two killings were related, committed by the same group of . . . And there he stopped. Group of what? Witches? Devil-worshipers? He recalled that case several decades back; he'd read about it as a boy. A girl had been found in the desert nearby, stabbed in what the newspapers had called "ritual fashion." Must have been thirty years ago. And there were always the unsolved disappearances, though statistically his district fell below the average in that regard.

But now this. Two murders within a few hours. Surely the papers would make the most of it, demanding action, as they always did, in the strident voices of those who were free to comment without participation.

He sighed heavily as he stood, feeling his age settle on him like the deadweight of a poor night's sleep. He reached for his jacket, hung over the back of his chair, and walked to the door. He did not look forward to going to the museum.

He closed the door thoughtfully behind him, listening for the small metallic click that would tell him the lock was in place.

The New City was alive with midday activity. It was as though an internal whistle had sounded, a signal that only city people could hear, and then the streets would fill, quickly forgetting the calmness of a few minutes earlier.

Alric left the jeep parked in front of the police station and started walking along the crowded downtown avenue. He had no destination in mind, it was only important that he walk, in a straight line, for as long as possible. His muscles would work out what his mind couldn't; his sweat would cleanse his body of all poisons.

He walked at a brisk pace, feeling obscurely relieved at each meeting of his feet with the hard pavement. And he noticed, with sudden disdain, the blankness on the faces of the passersby. Insect tribes going about their ordained business, coordinated on some preverbal level. How easily those faces could become indistinguishable, little more than splashes of color on a moving canvas. And how, as he quickened his pace, the shop windows sped by, their garish invitation unnoticed; even the English ones seemed in a foreign language. The street began to race by with dizzying speed, a disjointed composite of angles and shades. All motion was outside him.

With controlled desperation his mind fled the city, seeking sanctuary in the memory of the small protective hollow of their clasped hands as he and Diana would stroll through the park on a warm Sunday afternoon. He remembered how the touching of their flesh would tingle, as though coursing purified blood through their arteries to revitalize their organs and renew their spirit. And even the weight of his unknown origins would be lessened.

How long ago had it been?

He stopped abruptly, a part of him hearing the painful sound of tires sliding on asphalt. He looked up and noticed the red light; the car had missed him by a few feet, and its driver, a middle-aged man in a gray suit, was shaking his fist furiously at him.

Alric stepped back onto the curb and watched the car pass. In its rear window he caught a brief reflection of his face. The sight abducted him sharply from his reverie, chilling his brain awake with the merciless pull of materiality. For a moment he stood there, feeling incredibly small, incredibly alone. He felt like a pawn in the hands of greater powers, drawn, inexorably, to the desert, like those stone blocks at

Gizeh, inching toward their endpoint, self-crushing under their own weight. There seemed to be a heaviness in the air around him, pushing against him from all sides with the pressure of uncertainty: the uncertainty of his past, the uncertainty of his future.

And now Chandler was dead.

The light changed, but instead of continuing he turned around and started back toward the jeep.

It was early afternoon, and the camp was deserted; it had grown hot, the air still and oppressive. Alric remained in the jeep for several minutes, debating, his eyes fixed on the entrance to Chandler's tent. Perhaps it would be pointless, merely a gesture to relieve his conscience. But there *was* the possibility that the police had overlooked something, something that they wouldn't have seen as meaningful.

He gave a short, stiff nod, fortifying himself, then left the jeep and strode to the tent. He bent quickly through the entrance, knowing that he couldn't hesitate, couldn't let himself be intimidated by the memory of that morning, or it would be impossible. His eyes unaccustomed to the darkness, he walked carefully to the worktable and fumbled with the lamp.

He stood by the table, the light illuminating the interior with a pale glow. He looked around slowly, noticing how efficient the police had been. Nothing was left of the day's events, except for the white splashes of fingerprint powder on the table and chair, like ghost traces of the past.

And the dark stains on the floor by the cot.

He averted his eyes quickly, but knew that it would require constant vigilance to keep them from returning to the grisly reminders.

He pulled out the chair, seated himself, and scanned the items on the table's surface. He reached for the paperback copy of his book, lying open and face down. The section on preservation had been boxed in red. He read the paragraph, his brow creasing in thought, then put the book down. What had Chandler been looking for?

Near the center of the table was a low stack of hardcover books, most of which dealt with the symbols of the ancient world. Next to them was a microscope, its eyepiece reflecting a small glint of light from the lamp above it. Alric did not remember having seen it before. Perhaps the police had used it for something; he would ask Yadin about it.

A small slip of paper fluttered to the floor with a sudden air current. He leaned over and picked it up, began to put it back on the table when he noticed the writing. And the symbol drawn crudely above the words.

The lens shape from the model pyramid.

Chandler had found the fourth symbol, the one that had eluded him.

Alric quickly read the words written by the archaeologist only a few hours earlier. He shook his head in puzzlement. He reread them several times, narrowing his eyes as if to help him understand. Had the meaning of the symbol had some significance to Chandler, something that he, Alric, could not yet see? He shook his head again, then crumpled the slip of paper in his fist; his fingers tightened around the little mass until his knuckles grew white.

He stood stiffly, pushing the paper into his pocket. He walked quickly from the tent.

From where he sat on the low hill, the sun was a few degrees above the tip of the pyramid, casting a yellow haze over the distant flatlands. At this time of day the horizon seemed to merge with the sky in a nebulous union, signaling the approaching darkness.

A few dozen workmen were down below by the pyramid, continuing with the process of excavation; it would be several weeks before the structure was completely freed. Occasionally a random shout or command would reach him, but he paid little attention. He felt very tired, very old.

She had come up the hill from his blind side, sitting down quietly beside him. Her eyes, too, had soon settled on the pyramid's golden capstone, which seemed to draw in the sun's light like a magnet, reflecting it in broad, even waves. They sat together in silence, watching the pyramid, the sky, the desert.

At length, Diana spoke. "Looks like they haven't got much longer now."

He continued staring down the hill. "Another couple of weeks, I guess."

"I wonder how long it took to bury it."

He looked at her curiously, said nothing.

"Ahmad said they must have planned it this way," she continued. "That after a certain period of time, it would be uncovered."

"To what end?" wondered Alric.

She shrugged, flashing that smile that always made them both feel better. Down below, two workmen argued heatedly over the placement of a wood sand barrier. She turned back to him, her smile quickly fading. "Why did it happen, John? Why Carl? Why would anyone . . . ?"

He turned to her, put his arm around her shoulders as she slid down against his side. "He was a good man," he said, stroking her hair.

"Have the police got any ideas?"

"I don't know. He didn't have any enemies that I know of. Other than, of course, scientific rivals. But I can't imagine that line of investigation leading anywhere."

"It couldn't have been a terrorist thing, could it?"

"I don't see how. It wouldn't make sense. He was a scientist."

She looked up at him. "You think they could come back?"

"If they'd wanted us, too, they could have done it last night."

She shivered in his arms. "My God, when I think of what they . . ."

He held her tightly, as if trying to squeeze the shock and fear from her system. It gave him new strength. "This inspector Yadin seems to be a capable man. I trust him." He smiled grimly. "At least I don't think he suspects *me*."

She straightened, looking up at him. "*You?* How could he even . . . ?"

He shrugged. "It's only logical. I mean, we were the only ones in the camp last night. I'm the first one he'd have to cross off his list."

"Well, I hope he *has*," she said, settling back in his arms.

They again became silent, and again their eyes rested on the pyramid. It seemed to act as a psychic base of sorts, a home port. The sun was lower now, and, from their position, appeared to have settled gently on the tip of the capstone, balanced there for an instant, a small eternity, becoming a fiery crown atop the pyramid's own icy crown of gold.

After a few minutes, she sat up. "I forgot to tell you," she said. "You got a message from Dan Michaels. He said you should call him. I think he wants to see you."

"How long ago?"

"Not long. An hour, maybe."

Alric stood slowly, feeling his muscles unstiffen. "I guess I'd better see what he wants."

She nodded, then took his arm as they made their way down the shallow incline. At the bottom they walked to the jeep. She watched him slip behind the steering wheel.

He looked up at her. "I don't want to leave you here alone."

She shrugged it off. "It's all right. Ahmad said

he'd stay at camp, at least for a few days. I'll be fine."

"You sure?"

"I'll be okay." She smiled weakly.

He smiled back, then started the engine.

In a few minutes he swung the jeep into a tight U-turn, coming to rest a few feet from the telephone booth which stood outside the village's single canteen. The "business district" consisted of three stores and a small, dusty clearing where preschool children were usually at play amid high-pitched laughter and clouds of kicked-up dirt. But now Alric found himself alone on the street, the village's sole citizen on this quiet afternoon which seemed imbued with all the heaviness of late summer. He stepped into the phone booth without bothering to close the door, and quickly dialed Michaels's number, listening intently as the phone on the other end rang. Before it had completed its third ring, he heard the connecting click.

"Yes?"

"Dan? John Alric."

"John, hello. I see you got my message."

"Diana just told me. I was in town."

"Good, I just—"

"Listen, Dan, something's happened. Carl Chandler's dead."

"What . . . ? The man you were working with?"

"Yes."

"But how . . . ?"

"He was murdered, Dan."

"Murdered? But I don't understand. . . ."

"Yes," said Alric quietly. "It must have been late last night. In his tent."

The line was silent for a few seconds. Michaels's next words were almost whispered. "Oh, my God."

"I know," said Alric. "Things have been pretty bad here."

135

"I don't know what to say, John. I'm sorry. If there's anything I can do. . . ."

"No. Thanks. We'll be all right." A pause, then, "Diana said you had something to tell me."

"Yes. I was . . . doubtful about it. But now, under the circumstances, I don't think it can wait."

"What is it, Dan?"

Michaels was silent for a few seconds, then said, "Can you meet me in town?"

"I guess so," said Alric, curious. "But what's wrong with the phone?"

"I'd rather tell you in person."

"Where, then?"

"Damascus Gate in an hour?"

"Fine. I'll see you then."

Alric hung up the phone thoughtfully and left the booth. The street was still deserted as he walked the few paces to the jeep and slid behind the wheel. In fact, he was sure he'd seen no one since entering the town.

He let the thought drop as he turned the ignition key. The rough gurgling of the starting engine broke the sterile quiet of the afternoon, enticing a few small birds to sputter complaints in response.

Dan Michaels paced before the ancient stone walls of the Damascus Gate, alternately crossing his arms over his chest and burying his hands deep in the pockets of his jacket. His eyes moved randomly about the street, while he went over in his mind the disturbing conversation he'd had with Alric, trying to make sense from the disconnected facts he'd learned.

At first it had seemed an odd, though probably meaningless, coincidence, and had had little solidity for him. But with the death of Chandler clues were mounting in a dark and forbidding direction. Above all, it was imperative that possibilities such as this be checked out beyond reproach, no matter how tenuous the associations appeared.

And then there was the matter of the museum guard . . .

He was about to turn around again, to face north on his small elliptical path, when he spotted Alric approaching from up the street.

Alric nodded briefly to him as they met. "What have you got for me?" he asked. "Something about my father?"

Michaels motioned with his arm down Sultan Suleiman. "No," he said, as they began walking east on the broad street running along the wall enclosing the Old City.

"Then I don't understand," said Alric.

"John, yesterday you mentioned a name to me, just as you were leaving. Do you remember?"

Alric thought back, nodded. "Of course . . . Eluth."

"Why?"

"I told you. The name came up in some research I've been doing."

Michaels smiled. "What has your pyramid research to do with occultism?"

Alric turned to him. "What's your interest in all this?"

"A question with a question?" smiled Michaels.

Alric shrugged. "All right, there's no secret. Part of our interest—*my* interest—in this project, was to study the effects of pyramids on the human mind. Several years ago a scientist spent a night inside the Great Pyramid of Cheops. He claimed to have had revelatory experiences while in there. So Diana and I decided to spend a night inside our pyramid." They reached Herod's Gate and turned left, walking along Salah Ed-din.

Alric continued. "While in the pyramid, I had a dream—a kind of vision, you might say . . . anyway, it involved Eluth. I didn't remember having heard

137

the name before, so it would have proved interesting if the term Eluth had any meaning in reality."

Michaels's face had remained impassive during Alric's story. Now he said, "It did, you know."

Alric nodded. "I know. I read about it at the library after seeing you yesterday."

"Yes, well, it existed, all right."

Both men were silent for a moment as they walked. Alric could make nothing of Michaels's sudden interest in his research. Certainly the cult of Eluth had been little more than a historical curiosity—meaningful to no one other than Alric. So why Michaels's involvement?

At the corner, Michaels stopped and turned to Alric. "Listen, have you got some time? There's someone I think you should meet. It's why I asked to meet you here."

Alric's curiosity quickened. "Sure. Where?"

"We'd better take your jeep. It's a short drive."

In a few minutes they entered a small bookshop on Yafo Street. A little silver bell tinkled as the glass door swung open, and Alric guessed it was there more for its pleasant sound than for vigilance, the shop being too small for a new customer to go unnoticed. The smell of old books hit him immediately, and he surveyed the room, always fascinated by the mystique of crisp, yellowing pages.

The shop exuded an air of controlled chaos, with hardcovers and paperbacks everywhere, some in stacks of varying heights, others lying about open-faced, as if carelessly set down a moment ago. The entire store consisted of a single rectangular room, divided roughly into two sections. The front area was where business was apparently transacted over a waist-high counter a few feet from the wall (no cash register was in evidence, and Alric suspected that prices were highly negotiable). Several chairs and small, coffee-stained tables formed a little reading area, under the dusty oil paintings, antique maps, and astronomical charts which lined the walls. Toward the middle of the store began two long double-faced bookshelves, reaching almost to the low ceiling and stretching back to the rear wall.

It was from this back section that a small man appeared from behind a cardboard carton overflowing with books. He looked up and smiled at the two visitors, then walked quickly over. He took Michaels's hand warmly, then turned pleasantly to Alric.

Michaels spoke first. "This is the man I was telling you about, Sam, Dr. John Alric. John, this is Sam Stein."

The old man's eyes sparkled in his creased face, and he gave a small nod. "The pyramid man," he said, revealing a mild accent, perhaps German.

Alric smiled at the appellation. "Yes."

He took Alric's outstretched hand into his own small one, squeezing it with surprising strength.

Alric returned the firm handshake, immediately intrigued with the old man.

"So you're interested in Eluth," said Stein simply.

Michaels said, "John had a dream about the cult."

Stein raised his eyebrows.

"Yes," continued Michaels. "As I told you before, John is involved with pyramid power, and—"

"Pyramid *what?*" interrupted Stein. Then he nodded. "Ah, yes, the latest 'power.' Last year they were going to psychic surgeons to get rid of ulcers, now they're hanging pyramids over their beds to improve their sex lives." He turned to Alric. "Tell me, Doctor, does it work?"

Alric couldn't help smiling. "We try not to place judgments on anything quite so . . . subjective."

"It heartens me to hear that. The romantic spirit is not yet dead." He walked around the counter to a beaten-up straw chair. "You'll not mind if an old man sits down? Now, tell me, Doctor, what does this have to do with our mysterious 'seekers of Eluth'?"

Alric told him briefly about his original intention

—to spend a night in the pyramid, as had been done at Cheops. "It was during that night," he explained, "that I had the dream involving Eluth."

"I see," said Stein, nodding as if hearing familiar information. Then, "You have an interest in occultism, Doctor?"

"I'm a scientist," said Alric, a bit too sharply.

"Ah, yes, a *scientist*. And that tells me, since you're being defensive about it, that you have the heart of a mystic."

Alric smiled in spite of himself.

"A scientist," repeated Stein, his face growing serious. "So were they. Or at least they claimed to be." He shifted in his seat, then looked directly at Alric. "I met some of them, you know."

It was Alric's turn to raise his eyebrows. Michaels showed no reaction.

Stein nodded. "Yes. It was when they first formed their little group." He looked up at Alric briefly. "They even asked me to join at one point." He smiled, then sat in a reflective silence for a moment.

"It seemed harmless enough at first," he began finally. "No one knew where it would lead. Just some wild ideas about their 'magical heritage.' We of the so-called intelligentsia laughed them off."

"What do you mean by 'magical heritage'?"

"How much do you know about the Island of Thule, Doctor?"

Alric shrugged. "It seems to be a fairly common myth, similar to Atlantis. The idea of an ancient and highly advanced civilization. . . ."

"Destroyed by its own power," completed Stein.

Alric nodded.

Stein raised a forefinger in a professorial gesture. "Ah, but the Initiates believed that not all secrets perished with the island. That, in fact, powerful Beings remained, in a dormant state, and still capable of exerting influence over the destiny of man—hidden vortices of evil working within the historical process. And eventually, through communion with these Beings, great forces were to be placed at the disposal of the Eluth Initiates, who, with their newly acquired powers, would rise in victory and dominion over the earth."

"These . . . Beings were supposed to exert influence over historical events?" asked Alric.

"According to the Eluth Initiates," nodded Stein. "They believed there were certain centers of power, hidden from the mass of humanity, pushing, guiding from behind the scenes, one way or the other, in man's favor or against him—toward the Light or toward the Darkness. The Initiates sought out the creatures of Darkness, in the belief that they would soon rise up, destroying everything in their path. Only their human counterparts—the Initiates—would be spared, and set up to rule over the remnants of mankind."

Alric recalled the strange pages he'd read yesterday at the library. How unreal, how remote, the mad group of initiates had seemed—before Chandler's death. And before the death of the museum guard. Was there actually the possibility of a surviving remnant of this cult connected in some way to the murders? What Stein was talking about was not entirely new to Alric—the idea of "circles of humanity," the masses of the outer circle being guided, though unaware, by the inner, esoteric circle. It was a common mystical belief, though he had never taken it as anything other than metaphor. "Hidden vortices of evil," Stein had said, and, as obscure and allegorical as it sounded, after the two deaths, there were perhaps some things Alric would have to reexamine. He shook his head fractionally, feeling with dull wonder how quickly the implausible could become plausible, how fluid the world really was, how malleable. And, slowly, the question took root in him, whether there actually was substance in the long traditions of the mystics—and whether there was something more than the history books in school taught. Something infinitely darker. His throat was dry as he asked, "And did they ever make contact with these supposed beings from Thule?"

The old man shrugged. "Who can say? They *believed* they did. They even went to the point of vowing to commit suicide rather than to do anything to jeopardize their pact with the Powers." Stein's face grew dark. "And their pact was sealed with human blood."

At this Alric looked up. "Human sacrifice?"

Stein nodded gravely. "The Initiates believed that in order to awaken vision to the Evil Ones, the most brutally sadistic acts were necessary, and that only by these acts would the powers be bestowed upon them."

Alric said nothing, allowing Stein's last words to hang in the air before him. Slowly, he looked around, his eyes taking in the forms and shadings of the small shop: the stacks of aging books, standing like unsteady towers, awaiting one last gust of wind, or a final movement of the earth, before tumbling down to dusty oblivion; the two small lamps, under whose light customers would search the fragile volumes, perhaps for a first or signed edition; and the picture window comprising the storefront, through which he could see the slowly fading colors of the day. And there his eyes remained for a moment, perhaps seeking a link with a saner past, a bond with that safe life which had ended that morning with a sick splash of red.

Michaels, whose face had remained impassive throughout Stein's story, now spoke. "Yesterday you mentioned that they also believed in some kind of succession of lives?"

Alric looked up at Stein. "Reincarnation?"

"Oh, yes," said the old man. "You have to understand, their belief system was, in fact, a hodgepodge of many schools of mysticism, an unholy union of

Eastern religion and Western Gnosticism. But their kind of reincarnation only applied to the elite of Initiates. And there were no moral values, such as the law of karma. They believed that certain individuals come into being at the necessary times in history. Furthermore, they imagined they could perceive, in a prophetic vision, the fate of Europe during the entire twentieth century. In fact, some of their predictions were remarkably accurate."

"We have our psychics as well," said Alric.

"Ah, the voice of the scientist again," smiled Stein. "But, you see, they never claimed to be psychics—at least not in the normal sense. They believed they could perceive a grand vision, a kind of cosmic tapestry of time, an immense vista in which world destiny appeared on a continuous band, revealing both the history and fate of man. It was a vast panorama in which the same major personalities confronted one another on the world stage, in the past, present, and future."

"The Akashic Record?" asked Alric, recalling Ahmad's words.

"Yes," said Stein, mildly surprised. "That which is perceived by what the Eastern religions call the 'Third Eye.' The ability to perceive other incarnations in a kind of visual memory."

Alric scratched his head. There had been something else. Something obscurely familiar. Had it been the other night, in the pyramid? Or was it . . . ? But the feeling lasted too briefly, flashing only subliminally before his mind's eye and then disappearing, leaving too subtle a trace. And then—yes. The dream. But not exactly. The dream, yes, but also . . .

And it was gone.

He shook his head slowly and looked back at Stein. "It all seems insane."

"Yes," agreed Stein softly. "It was."

For a moment the room was so quiet it was as though all sound had crystallized, precipitating to the floor in tiny beads. Even the street outside did not dare invade their sanctuary. Only the books seemed to echo faintly in the stillness, vibrating in some distant, eidolic dimension.

Finally Stein repeated, almost in a whisper, "It *was* insane." He shrugged slightly. "But, as with most phenomena, there were degrees of involvement, degrees of guilt. We mustn't judge them all equally. Not all took part in the . . . practices indulged in by the inner circle. Some were merely misguided, alchemists born ten centuries too late."

Now Michaels again spoke. "You can see why we may have interest in this group. The government is, of course, anxious over the possibility of violent cults. The experiences back in America should make it all too evident why."

Alric looked at Michaels, his eyes narrowing. "Government?"

Michaels nodded slowly.

And now Michaels's interest became clear to Alric. He shook his head in amazement. How efficient they were. How damned efficient. An offhand question he had asked, and already the wheels were turning. He looked up sharply. "Yesterday you said you'd never heard of Eluth."

Michael's raised his hands apologetically. "I wasn't lying. I was curious, and brought up the name with Sam. Later I did my own research."

"But we're talking about thirty, forty years ago. What possible connection—?"

"At the end of World War II there seemed to be a small migration of . . . cultists to the Middle East, particularly Egypt and Syria. Some even to Palestine."

"Yes," agreed Stein. "You see, there had been a clandestine affiliation with certain esoteric sects in the Islamic world. And there may have been another reason for their migration here. . . ." He smiled. "But I'm afraid I'm getting ahead of the story."

144

"And you think some of them might still be around?" Alric asked Michaels.

"It's possible. Every lead must be checked out, no matter how apparently meaningless or improbable."

"Even dreams?" asked Alric ironically.

Michaels said nothing.

Then Stein said, "But you see, Doctor, the fascinating thing is that it all ties in."

"I don't understand."

Stein was silent for a moment, then said, "When Dan called me yesterday and asked me about Eluth, I didn't think much of it. But when he mentioned that you were with this archaeological team, something struck me. I remembered that the myth of the Island of Thule was rooted in a still more ancient legend, of which very little is known. It's a Tibetan legend about a great migration which took place long before Thule was founded." He stopped, standing up from the straw chair. "No, wait—let me show you."

He walked to the nearer of the two bookshelves and pulled out a large, old hardcover book. He brought it back to his chair and placed it on the counter. Quickly, he leafed through the pages. "Ah, here it is," he said, stopping at a page and swiveling the book around to face Alric.

Alric dropped his eyes to the open book. On the two connected pages was a plate of a painting done in medieval style.

"It represents a civilization which was said to predate Thule by thousands of years," said Stein. "Perhaps it was the birthplace of the human race, the primeval city. But it, too, apparently fell, the first in a cycle of great civilizations which rose to power and were destroyed by their own device."

In the open book Alric saw the representation of an ancient city, shimmering with cold power in the sharp light of the sun. Structured with such precision, it could have been the heart of some immense, unknown beast, its streets the veins and arteries, curving around or toward the central point. Everywhere buildings of white marble rose toward the sky, reflecting sunlight in broad, golden blades.

But it was an empty city. For in the surrounding land was a multitude of people, engaged in a vast migration. As wide as the city itself, this human river branched into two streams, each stretching endlessly toward opposite ends of the horizon.

Alric searched the painting for the cause of this exodus, but could find nothing. Again his eyes gravitated to the primeval city: its glistening walls, surrounding it like a protective womb; the peculiar machinery left in its streets, as if set down only a moment ago; the gleaming white buildings, empty now of their human lifeblood. . . .

And, in the very center—the small pyramid with the capstone of gold.

It was a full minute before Alric was able to look up from the book.

"You see?" asked Stein.

Alric nodded, though his eyes were remote.

Stein continued. "Your dream was more than some kind of strange coincidence. The Eluth Initiates may well have been rooted in a myth whose birthplace is this area."

Alric said nothing.

He turns a corner, starts down a broad avenue. At the end of this street he sees the construction clearly for the first time.

A gold-topped pyramid.

"Is something wrong, John?" Michaels asked Alric, who had suddenly gone pale.

Alric turned to him. "There wasn't just the one dream," he said numbly.

Michaels and Stein were silent, watching Alric.

He continued haltingly, as if just emerging from sleep. "The one in which Eluth was mentioned was

146

the last one. It was the only one I could remember. But there was more. I can remember . . . being in some strange city. I seemed to sense it was at the dawn of civilization." He looked up at them, pointing at the picture.

"It was *this* city."

They all looked down at the representation and studied it in silence for a moment. The city seemed to exude a kind of power, a magnetic pull along unseen lines reaching out to them, without words, and in mystery.

"But I still don't understand *why*," said Alric finally. "Why Eluth? Why the pyramid? What possible connection . . . ?"

"Earlier you mentioned the Akashic Record, Doctor," said Stein. "There are those who believe it was the function of the pyramids to allow vision of what the mystics call the 'turning points in time.' "

"What do you mean, Sam?" asked Michaels.

"You see," Stein went on, "the Initiates, among other occult societies, believed there were certain points in time, coming every thousand years or so, when history could go either one direction or the other. And those points were when the Powers reached out and attempted to tip the balance." He picked up the open book and quickly found another page. His lips moved silently as his finger ran down the paragraphs.

"Here," he said, stopping midway down the page. "Listen to what it says: 'According to legend, God gathered up the unholy spirits and cast them down into a deep cell. There they remained, sealed within the walls of darkness, until, once in a thousand years, a man would have it within the power of his free will to release the fiends to walk the earth again.' " He closed the book thoughtfully. "Once in a thousand years," he repeated softly.

"And the Initiates believed we were at such a turning point?"

"Or approaching one," speculated Stein. "You see, their belief was that whenever man's knowledge becomes corrupt, a divine manifestation—what in Sanskrit is called an 'avatar'—incarnates to give mankind a new revelation. The Oriental tradition teaches that the earth has already seen ten such incarnations. And at the end of the present cycle, the cycle of fire, the primordial avatar will come to reduce the world to ashes."

"The cycle of fire?" asked Alric, startled by the connection.

Stein nodded. "The Initiates returned here, to the desert, to summon the powers of evil—and to await the birth of their dark messiah."

Alric's mind locked onto the obscure passage in his father's letter, while he struggled with its meaning: *A new birth. . . . Son of Fire, Son of Ice.*

"Yes, Doctor," continued Stein. "The Initiates thought that the time was imminent. Again the world would be split by the battle between the powers of light and darkness. The neo-pagan occultists would be locked in a death struggle with Judaeo-Christian civilization—the latest and most violent eruption in a war that would go on until the end of time.

"They believed that the time would soon come to light the fire. In the words of the Revelation 'Satan would be loosed from his prison.'" He paused for a few seconds, then finished. "The time of chaos was fast approaching."

Alric was silent. *Son of Fire, Son of Ice. . . .*

The heat of day wants to press the life from him, fuse him to the moment.

And suddenly he's running, pushing away from his people.

He stumbles, falls to his knees . . . and a face, shrouded, yet darkly familiar, smiles through the crowd. . . .

"Can you remember any more?" asked Stein.

148

Alric looked up quizzically.

"Of the dreams," explained Stein.

Alric looked at the old man for a few seconds as if he had spoken a foreign language. Then he nodded hesitantly, thinking back, trying to regain the elusive memory. But it wouldn't come; with his effort it only sank deeper. Finally he became passive, allowing his mind to go blank, and gradually the images began to form before him.

"It all became unclear," he said slowly, "a series of fragments flashing into my mind. . . ." *And a face can be seen, even at this distance* . . . He hesitated. "I . . . I'm not sure I can put it into words." *The chiseled features, the sensitive mouth* . . . He shook his head. "All I can remember is a voice, whispering . . . the reference to Eluth. . . ." He felt a dark tremor pass through his body.

. . . and the star-shaped fleck of gold just beneath the left pupil.

"I see," said Stein, nodding to himself. Then, after a few seconds, "Well, Dr. Alric, I guess that brings us back to where we began. The serpent is biting its own tail, as the mystics would say."

Alric looked out the front window and noticed that it had grown late; outside, the streets were returning to activity as the business day ended. He turned back to Stein, studying the old man in the gray light of dusk.

"One more thing, please, Mr. Stein?" he asked. He hesitated, then continued, "What do *you* believe of all this? How much of it was real?"

Stein was silent for a long moment, looking steadily into Alric's eyes. When he spoke, it was slowly, with a tired voice. "After all these years, Doctor, I honestly don't know. I don't know if any contact was made with the Powers—or even if these Powers existed, except in the minds of a handful of madmen. But I do know that the evil that has been brought about in this century has been overwhelm-

149

ing. Is it totally unimaginable that there are forces that manipulate from behind the stage of human affairs, their mortal counterparts acting as mere puppets?"

His eyes held Alric's with a cold spark of curiosity. "Did the Dark Powers really exist? Or were the Initiates madmen?" He shrugged mildly. "Who can say? But belief is the fine line between reality and fantasy—and, in a way, perhaps it made no difference."

The room was silent again for a moment; the street sounds entering seemed remote, unreal.

Alric nodded slowly, extended his hand to Stein. "Thank you for your time." He smiled weakly. "It's certainly been interesting."

Stein rose from his chair and took Alric's hand. "Think nothing of it, Doctor. You've merely given an old man an excuse to hear himself lecture once more." He smiled warmly at Alric.

Alric looked over at Michaels, who gave a brief nod and smiled his good-bye to Stein.

The cool air greeted them mildly as Michaels opened the front door, stimulating the small silver bell to life once more. They passed through the doorway as if exiting an alien world, and were surprised to find out how little the old one had changed. They stood silent for a moment, each feeling palpably Stein's earlier metaphor: the serpent biting its own tail; the myth of eternal return, the wave flowing into itself. For a moment Alric wondered what the old man's eyes must have seen in his life, those sad brown eyes which still held the vital spark of humor.

"Quite an interesting man," he said, at length.

Michaels nodded. "He used to teach at the University of Munich."

The two men looked at each other, each feeling that something had changed, but neither knowing exactly what. Michaels gripped Alric's hand firmly.

"Listen, John," he said, quietly, yet intently. "I

don't know about Sam and his 'Powers of Darkness' —I'm not in a position to be a believer. But I do know that people have been killed, and if any of these . . . *cultists* are still around . . ." He looked meaningfully into Alric's eyes.

"Just be careful, John," he finished. Then, with a brief nod, he took his leave.

Alric watched Michaels's retreating figure for a few seconds, then turned back toward the jeep, parked at the end of the block. The streets were again filling with people as the day quickly gave way. The sun had dropped below the city's false horizon, and the sky retained only its last traces of color. The night chill was rapidly entering.

He wanted to go quickly to the jeep and drive back to camp; the coming night aroused fears for Diana's safety, though he knew Ahmad would not leave her unguarded. Alric *wanted* to walk quickly, but didn't. Instead he slowed his pace, trying to assimilate all that he had learned, all that had happened in the last few hours.

It was a growing web of madness, coming up from behind him and surrounding him with a cold wet touch. And there was nothing he could do. He tried desperately, but could find no patterns in which to think, no words that would dispel what was happening; he could find no everyday labels of experience or comforting channels of familiar knowledge. He could only dwell on the dark underbelly of knowledge, the mutable distillation of intuition: mysticism. He had fought its pull throughout his life, though without verbalizing why, without ever acknowledging the fear, but burying it under the edifice of rationalism, the bulwark of the "scientific method."

And now it was all coming apart. . . .

The madness seemed to have become a part of him. And he knew on some preverbal level that it hadn't begun only that morning, in Chandler's tent.

Nor had it been yesterday at the library, or the night before in the pyramid. Something was all wrong, had been all along. And yet he knew he *had* to be there, right where he was, it *had* to be him. Perhaps he had always known.

But he didn't know why.

Now he *did* quicken his pace, as if to ward off the eerie feeling that grew inside him, to try to work it off with his body. How much longer would it go on, how much longer would the pendulum swing in the same direction, before making that merciful turn back toward normality, sanity, toward everything he'd told himself his former life had held? How much longer before the cycle began to wind back along familiar paths? How much longer would the world splay out before him, curving away from him in a direction that made sense mathematically, but meant nothing to the body?

He stopped.

For an instant it had flashed before him on some internal screen. It had been dazzling in its brevity, but he had seen it clearly enough to remember every detail for the rest of his life: the dark circle of figures in the desert night, chanting the unholy words of the ancient ritual. The prone girl, her wrists and ankles tied to wooden stakes in the ground, her body glistening pale white in the glow of the full moon. The sacrificial blades in the hands of the believers, raised high, as though questioning the gods—and then driven downward into her helpless body again and again, her blood spurting, hot and steaming, onto the cold desert floor. . . .

And Alric understood the reality of Stein's words: *the unholy covenant—sealed in human blood.* . . .

He no longer knew if his eyes were open or closed, and, for a second, no longer cared. He was caught. *The serpent biting its own tail.* And yet, something inside him struggled—for there was a part missing from the picture, some transcendent purpose, a meaning within the madness.

If only he could . . .

Without knowing why, he buried his hand deep in his pocket and pulled out the small, crumpled scrap of paper he'd found that afternoon in Chandler's tent. He opened it carefully and reread the words scribbled in haste by the archaeologist—the words which spoke cryptically from beneath the sign that so resembled a white, iris-less eye:

> *Vesica Piscis—*
> *Union of opposing masculine and femine cosmic principles.*
> *Symbol of the sacred marriage of the spiritual and material worlds, of the sun and moon, of heaven and earth.*

He stopped reading for a second, looking around him as if to extract an answer from the air itself. He again looked down at the small sheet, and read the final short line—the last words Chandler had ever written:

> *The primal unit of creation.*

He shook his head to clear it, confused and disturbed by his failure to understand. And the feeling of displacement grew inside him, along with the frustration of not knowing. How easily, how swiftly, it could return.

The serpent. . . .

And it was growing dark so quickly, as if the light were being sucked from the world by the pull of interstellar vacuum. His eyes quivered in response to a vibrating world. *A face, shrouded, yet darkly familiar . . . his eyes . . . and a coldly observing figure, death-white face, eyeless . . . a fleck of gold. . . .*

No!

The world became a jumble of dark, wrestling colors; the faces of the people grew blank. Insect tribes . . . *the dark man nudges him, the eyes, look at the eyes . . . surfaces are breached and forms flow into one another. All lines are curved, meeting at infinity. . . .*

And time is the shortest distance between two points.

He looked up, his eyes glazed and large.

Through the crowd, a face—Death's head grinning.

And then he *did* care, then he *could* move again. With a sharp motion of his head, he shook himself awake and free. He looked farther up the block, saw the jeep at the corner. He took a deep breath and walked the remaining few yards.

Alric pulled the jeep up onto the small patch of packed sand a hundred feet from the tents. Darkness had completely overtaken the desert, and the silence seemed stronger this night, almost painful.

He reached a hand to the ignition key—it was almost a tentative gesture—then sat back, trying to gain control over the indefinable sensation that threatened to take possession of his body, and trying to untangle the web of other feelings surrounding and invading him. Without moving his head, he let his eyes survey the small campsite. He unconsciously nodded at a reassuring sign: a light could be seen through the canvas wall of his tent. His body relaxed slightly in the knowledge that his anxiety over Diana's safety had been unfounded.

Then he noticed the light in Chandler's tent.

His mind quickly searched for a reason Diana would have had to put the light on in the other tent. But no, she wouldn't have gone in there. Perhaps he had forgotten to turn it off that afternoon. Or perhaps—

Then he saw it. A brief flicker, a fragment of a shadow, against the near wall.

There was someone inside.

Cursing himself for not having a gun, he noiselessly opened the jeep door. He pushed back the memory that kept rising involuntarily into his consciousness: the image of Chandler, as he had lain in his cot that morning. He swung his legs out in a smooth motion and stepped out, feeling a cold sensation as his feet touched the sand, as if expecting a snake to curl around his ankle and glide silently up his leg.

He stopped abruptly at the side of the jeep. Something had occurred inside him; a connection had been made on some instinctual level.

And, for the briefest instant, he knew.

He slammed shut the jeep door and walked determinedly to Chandler's tent. Without hesitation he ducked and stepped through the entrance flaps.

Just inside and to the right of the entrance, Ahmad crouched in the corner, going through Chandler's suitcase.

"Forget something?" asked Alric.

The guide looked up, began to speak, but Alric's foot came up fast and caught him under the chin, sending him sprawling backward onto the floor of the tent. Before the guide could recoup, Alric was above him. He reached down and grabbed the front of Ahmad's shirt, lifting the smaller man to a standing position.

"All right," he said in a low, steady voice. "Now, tell me what you know about Chandler's death."

The guide breathed with difficulty, not yet able to speak.

"John!" yelled Diana, from the entrance of the tent. "What are you doing?"

Alric did not turn from Ahmad. "He knows something about what happened to Carl."

"What . . . ?" She shook her head in confusion,

"Listen, John, he asked my permission to look in Carl's tent."

Alric started to answer, but Ahmad stopped him with a gesture of his hand.

"He's right," said the guide, still breathing heavily. "I have not been honest with you."

Gradually, Alric relaxed his grip.

Ahmad wiped a drop of blood from his lower lip, and began, quietly. "At first we believed we could accomplish our task without your knowledge. I see now that this was wrong. And now, the death of your friend entitles you to know."

Alric released the guide entirely, allowing him to take a step back.

Diana came farther into the tent. She looked questioningly at Alric, but his eyes were fixed on the guide. "What's this all about?" she asked quietly.

"I'm not sure. But I know he's involved. "Is that true, Ahmad?"

She turned to the guide. "I had nothing to do with the death of Dr. Chandler," he said softly. "But I cannot escape responsibility. We should have known their power was growing, and that they would stop at nothing. We should have been prepared."

"What are you talking about?" asked Alric sharply. "Who do you mean by *we*? Who are *they*?"

Ahmad took a deep breath, then turned to Alric. "Doctor," he said, "how much do you know about the history of this desert?"

"I'm beginning to learn quite a bit."

Ahmad nodded slightly to himself. He was hesitant, as if still debating whether or not to talk. Alric found himself wondering if the guide had actually taken some oath of secrecy.

Finally Ahmad spoke again. "There is a tradition here," he said, his voice dry, "that stretches back to the beginning of the human race. Back to when humanity was less removed from its origins, and men still remembered that they were descended

from gods. There existed a highly developed civilization. . . ."

"There's nothing new in that," interrupted Alric.
"Every culture has a similar myth. Atlantis, Lemuria,
Thule. . . ."

"Thule?" asked Ahmad, raising his eyebrows in
curiosity. "I see you have been busy."

The remark disturbed Alric, but he said nothing.

Ahmad said, "The legend of Thule is itself derived
from the civilization of which I am speaking. In the
mythologies of all races are the stories of these
people, revealing fragments of information concerning their extraordinary mental abilities, and their
powers of magic."

Alric recalled Stein's words of a few hours earlier.
*The Thule myth was rooted in a still more ancient
legend, of which very little is known . . . a Tibetan
legend of a great migration. . . .* Was this what
Ahmad was talking about? The very roots of civilization? He nodded briefly to the guide, allowing him
to go on.

Ahmad continued, "Many thousands of years before the birth of Christ, these people thrived. And
their scientific accomplishments were legion: they
could extract the life power from seeds, and use the
forces of nature to realize continent-wide endeavors;
they possessed huge powered ships and sophisticated
flying machines; art and science reached their
highest degrees. . . ." His face almost glowed, as if
he were presently witnessing the deeds as he de-
scribed them.

"And their speech," he continued, "was unlike
ours. It went far beneath the thin layer of the con-
ceptual. Their words were keys that unlocked the
forces of the universe. With them they could control wild animals, improve the growth of plants, heal
sickness, and rein the destructive forces of nature.

"But perhaps their most fascinating aspect was
their mental faculties. Unlike us, they did not per-

ceive the world through the sensory organs alone. They lived in a sea of consciousness, in which the universe was perceived directly, mirrored in transcendent images that revealed objects in their entirety and essence. Theirs was not the shadow world which we perceive.

"But most important," said Ahmad, and here his tone changed subtly, meaningfully, "was their gift of genetic memory."

"Inherited memory?" asked Alric, looking up.

The guide nodded. "Yes. Their memory was passed down through the bloodline, a genetic inheritance which allowed them to recall the experiences of their ancestors as clearly as they remembered events in their own lives. In this way knowledge was passed down from father to son, and the wisdom attained by each generation was not lost. They were ruled by a line of priest-kings, in whom this faculty was the most perfectly developed."

Alric was silent, remembering the painting in the book, the primeval city supposed to have existed before Thule; the city whose inhabitants had used strange machinery, then left everything behind in haste as they fled for some unknown reason.

The city of the gold-topped pyramid.

"What brought about the end of this civilization?" he asked.

Ahmad gave a small shrug, barely perceptible. "In the beginning, man communed with the celestial hierarchies in a direct vision. He and the universe were one, radiations of the same primal force. But, through untold centuries, he evolved away from this union with the macrocosm, and toward the three-dimensional world. He began to worship his godlike powers, and not their divine origin, giving up the reality for the shadow. Some believe it was the aim of Lucifer to cut man off from this Vision, thus confining him to the world of matter. Split from his ground of being, man began to use his powers only for the fulfillment of his vain pleasures, until his control over the forces of nature turned against him, and a cataclysm was unleashed which destroyed his civilization and transformed his land into desert."

"This desert?" asked Alric.

Ahmad nodded.

The three of them were silent for a moment. Outside, the wind, which had pushed at the tent in occasional gusts, dropped to a low whistle, then died.

Alric spoke again. "And the survivors?"

"When it became known that destruction was imminent and unavoidable, a new race was founded, which was to watch over the future development of humanity in the millennia to come, and to serve as unseen guide of the spiritual evolution of man.

"With this aim before them, these last remnants of the civilization migrated eastward, where they set up a vast cave community at the foot of the Himalayas. But dissension was to come to the underground encampment, disputes over what would be the rightful course for mankind to follow. And, eventually, they divided into two groups, each following a very different path.

"The first of these groups believed in enlightenment through meditation and self-knowledge. They practiced the ideas of compassion and humility later associated with Christianity. But, as they had known would happen following the destruction of their civilization, their greatest gift, the function of inherited memory, began to weaken. Successive generations retained less and less, becoming increasingly isolated from their godlike origins. Because of this, in fear that one day all would be lost, a small sect left the sanctuary, in search of its heritage in the desert." Now he paused for a long moment, his eyes growing firm with decision.

At last he said, "I, and all the members of my village, are the descendants of that sect. We are a brotherhood that seeks to preserve what remains of the tradition of the Wisemen of the Golden Age, and to rediscover what was lost."

Alric thought back to his early impressions of the villagers, those dark, quiet people, with their intelligent eyes. He had always felt strange around them. How they seemed to look inside him, to know more about him than he did himself.

But there was something more, he felt, with a vague unease. Something inside him that he wanted to free, but could not. His face betrayed no emotion as he grasped for what seemed a fragment of memory, buried just shallow enough to signal, but too deep to reach. Something in Ahmad's words had struck a sleeping nerve. He let the feeling pass, looking back at the guide. "You said there were two groups?"

Ahmad nodded. "The other group turned to the practice of forbidden magic, mastering charms that could call up the winds and seas, and incantations that could create hallucinations in men's minds, or cause the healthy to sicken and die. They developed the power of shape-shifting, capable of changing at will into the forms of serpents, cats, and wild animals, even into stone. And, in their worship of evil, they founded a violent and powerful city consecrated in the name of the Dark One."

"Thule?" asked Alric.

"Yes," said the guide. "And from there they sought to command the elements and rule over humanity. But their civilization was destroyed, consumed by its own evil, and the unholy spirits were driven underground, where they remained, awaiting what they perceived as the final turning point in time. At the inauguration of that epoch, the leaders of the world would enter into a pact with the dark powers, which would be sealed with blood sacrifices."

"And the Eluth Initiates?"

"They believed that as the time drew near, the

Beings from Thule could be summoned . . . and they saw human sacrifice as the most powerful way to attract their attention. They came here to prepare the way, to call forth the dark powers . . . the creatures called *Eluthi*."

"What does all this have to do with Carl?"

The guide's face showed true sorrow as he spoke. "After carrying out their . . . rites, the Initiates disappeared. What happened to them, no one can say. Death? Madness? No trace of them remains. But the summoning had been performed, the Eluthi invoked to await their time, to look for the sign in the desert, gathering strength. . . ."

"And do you want me to believe that these . . . spirits are responsible for Carl's death?"

"It appears that the Initiates accomplished their task," the guide said solemnly.

Alric inadvertently dropped his gaze to the dried stain on the floor by Chandler's cot. He quickly looked away. "But why?" he asked.

Ahmad was silent for a moment, and Alric again had the feeling that an internal debate was going on.

Finally the guide said, "I told you that my people returned to the desert in search of their heritage . . . but their purpose was also to protect their legacy— and to await its fruition." He paused again, then seemed to commit himself. "The Wisemen of the Golden Age knew that their civilization was on the verge of destruction—but they were determined that from the ashes of their world there would be one survivor. So, under the rule of the last of the priest-kings, the pyramid was built."

"*Our* pyramid," said Alric. It was not a question.

Ahmad nodded. "Yes. The great pyramids of the Egyptians were mere reflections, the dimmest memory of the original of the Golden Age. Egyptian civilization was the last to retain a glimmer of remembrance of the teaching."

"And the purpose?" asked Alric.

"The pyramid was built to endow their descendants"—and here he smiled with mild irony—"to endow their descendants, at their eventual coming of age, with the secret, the birthright. . . ."

Alric started at Ahmad's words—they had been a direct quote from his own book.

But the guide just nodded. "Yes, Dr. Alric, you don't know how literally right you were." Then he stopped again; his smile faded.

"Go on," said Alric, trying to disregard the chill that ran between his shoulder blades like a trickle of ice water.

Ahmad frowned. "But I'm afraid we've lost, in any event."

"What do you mean?"

He looked up at Alric, trying to assess the impact his words would have. "I found out earlier that the gold pyramid was stolen from the museum last night."

But Alric just nodded. "I know."

"Then you also know a man was killed."

"Yes," said Alric. "Your . . . *Eluthi?*"

"Yes. But the real theft was not of the pyramid, but of that which was contained within it."

At this Alric looked up. "And what was that?"

Ahmad was silent for a full moment. His eyes were almost black in the light of the tent's single lamp. Then, with no change in his voice, he said, "The purpose of the pyramid was to preserve and keep viable the seed of the priest-king."

Alric felt the ice spread from his back around his shoulders and down his legs, enveloping his entire body in a crystalline hold. He could not speak.

Ahmad went on. "The Wisemen were, above all, scientists. They discovered a means of forming genetic material into a stable substance which, inside the protective womb of the pyramid within a pyramid, could remain in a state of viability indefinitely."

He exhaled deeply. "And that is what I was searching Dr. Chandler's tent for. I thought that perhaps you or he had discovered a way to open the pyramid."

Alric said nothing, but reached into his shirt pocket and pulled out the small envelope. He opened it and dropped the four ovoids into his hand.

Ahmad's eyes widened; a shudder of relief spread the length of his body and he grinned broadly.

Alric studied the guide's reaction. "You don't seem very surprised," he said.

Ahmad continued smiling. "Let us say I am more relieved than surprised."

Alric replaced ovoids in envelope, envelope in pocket. "And Carl?" he asked.

"I can surmise that the Eluthi soon discovered the pyramid to be empty, and came here in search of its contents." His face creased with concern. "They vie for the soul of the unborn descendant."

"Why didn't they kill us, as well?"

Ahmad shook his head. "I don't know."

Alric turned from the guide, took a few steps toward the worktable, then looked back at him. "And you expect me to believe that the pyramid was supposed to serve as some kind of . . . eternal gene bank?"

"I don't expect you to believe anything," said Ahmad evenly.

Diana stepped over to Alric and touched his arm. "Could it be, John?"

He looked at her without expression, then turned and walked the remaining few feet to the worktable, still dappled by the eerie patches of fingerprint powder. He sat down, pulled the small microscope over to him, and removed the slides. He began to reach for the envelope in his shirt pocket, but stopped the motion abruptly: he had noticed the smudges between the faces of the glass slides. He reinserted them, then bent his head to the eyepiece.

In a moment he looked up, nodding to himself. He stood up from the seat.

"It can't work," he said simply.

"Isn't it possible, John?" asked Diana.

He turned to her with a sharp motion. "*No*, it isn't possible." His voice was loud and edgy, breaking the quiet atmosphere of the tent. "Even now we're nowhere near having the ability to do something like this. Not without refrigeration. And even then, genetic material can only remain viable for a few years."

"What about the research?" she asked. "In preservation? You said yourself—"

"Our research was with plants. Or pieces of meat. What he's talking about is impossible." He realized he was almost yelling. He softened his tone, shaking his head to add emphasis to his words. "It couldn't remain viable for that long. We're talking about thousands of years."

Ahmad said, "The pyramid alters the structure of time. Within its field, molecular activity is slowed down, just as with freezing."

Alric turned back to the worktable, shaking his head in wonder; he rapped his knuckles on the tabletop. "So *that* was the purpose," he mused. "The ultimate purpose."

Ahmad was silent.

Alric turned back to him. "*Why*? What was on their minds?"

The guide spoke slowly. "At the necessary time in history the pyramid would be discovered . . . the descendant would be born."

"And the Eluthi want to prevent that?"

Ahmad shook his head. "The descendant can be a force for good *or* evil. The Eluthi want possession of him, of his soul. They want him as their messiah."

Alric was silent, waves of meaning flowing through him. Uncomprehending, he understood. Unbelieving, he knew.

A new birth. Son of Fire, Son of Ice. . . .

It was a moment before he spoke again. He tapped his shirt pocket with two fingers. "And what's to be done with these?"

"In accordance with the teaching handed down, a girl will be chosen from among the unmarried of my village. She will bear the descendant."

"How will she be chosen?"

Ahmad seemed to consider for a moment, then said, "You may be present. It is to be done tonight." Then, anticipating Alric's next question, he said, "Within the pyramid, and within the bride, the seed will again become solvent."

"How long can it remain viable?"

The guide frowned. "Outside the pyramid, not long, I'm afraid. A day or two at most." He looked at Alric. "Which is why it must be done tomorrow night at the latest."

Alric was silent for a moment. Then he asked, "And you believe this?"

Ahmad returned Alric's gaze unwaveringly, his nod almost imperceptible.

It was a huge cavern, just above the foot of the rocky hills rising sharply from the desert floor. Alric guessed that it had served as a meeting hall, or hidden sanctuary, for whichever band of heretics existed in a given period. He looked up toward the ceiling, lost from view in the darkness; he could imagine great bats hanging there, upside down, watching through the centuries with their near-blind, incurious eyes as humans performed the ceremonies of antiquity.

He and Diana held hands, as they had since leaving the jeep and following Ahmad along the invisible path winding around boulders and between the few stark trees growing in the coarse soil. They stood there silently, a few yards inside the hidden entrance, and watched as six young women formed a circle at a point near the center of the grotto.

Beyond the women, in an area slightly raised from the floor of the cave, were three men in flowing white robes, each standing before a torch, the only sources of light in the cavern. These would be the village elders Ahmad had mentioned before they'd entered the chamber. In front of these three men, in the middle of the low platform, was a small stone altar, upon which sat a single object. Even at this distance, and in the weak light, Alric knew what the object was: a small gold pyramid, less than half the height of the model they had found at the site.

The three robed men moved for the first time since Alric, Diana, and Ahmad had entered. As though at a predetermined instant they raised their arms as one body, stopping when their hands were chest high. Before them, the six girls linked hands and began a slow clockwise revolution.

Alric found their serene motion hypnotic, as again and again they orbited soundlessly, like six celestial bodies, their long hair trailing like dark comets' tails.

It was several minutes before he became aware of a faint sound coming from the front part of the chamber. At first it was a low whistling, and, from the wavering of the torches' flames, he realized that air currents were entering, perhaps through ducts built into the mountain itself. The sound grew steadily, and he could now feel a wind on his face, coming from deeper in the cavern. The torchlight threw violently dancing shadows on the rough walls, and he wondered if former times had seen the shadows of wildly dancing humans, engaged in ancient orgiastic rites.

The flames finally went out, left and right simultaneously, the middle one after a fierce struggle with the wind. With the dying light, the girls' motion also died. And then the wind was gone. The chamber fell silent and pitch dark.

And they waited, the three robed figures, the six

village girls, the two Americans, and the dark, enigmatic guide.

The complete blackness stretched before Alric, seeming to reach back for him in a cold embrace. It enfolded him, downing him in that half-pleasant, half-vertiginous feeling experienced at the verge of sleep. And also, perhaps, at the verge of death, Alric told himself, in an effort to keep his balance. But it was getting harder all the time. And it was so quiet, so black . . . if only he could let it take him, let the darkness take him—perhaps it wouldn't be so bad.

And then he saw it, though at first he was not sure if it was in the chamber or merely a ghost spark on the inside of his eyelids. But yes, it was there, outside him: a fine sliver of white in the darkness of the cavern's interior. It was no more than a shard of light, all but lost in the depths of blackness. But it grew; imperceptibly, but steadily, it grew. And then there was another light, this one diffuse and barely discernible, a pale finger reaching down from the lost heights of the cavern and uniting with the glowing splinter.

He narrowed his eyes, at last understanding the origin of these apparitions: there was a narrow channel cut into the roof of the cave, leading through to the outside. And when the moon reached the right point in its orbit, it was exactly above the hole, its light falling on the gold pyramid, sending a thin white stream into the belly of the cavern.

He turned to Diana as her face was briefly lit by the spectral beam, then eclipsed by a slight adjustment of the girl standing in the direct line of the reflection from the pyramid. He could only see the girl from behind, and watched how the ghostly light entered her dark hair, shrouding her in its diffuse glow.

And he understood: she was the chosen girl.

She would bear the descendant of the Golden Age.

The moon's cold silver grew steadily on the pyramid's gold surface, and Alric envisioned the glacial white orb becoming full in the cavern's starless false sky.

*

ALRIC FELT DEPLETED, as barren and wasted as the desert around him, as he and Ahmad drove in silence along the dirt road leading to Ahmad's village. Last night was still with him, even in the bright sunlight which now surrounded them like a silver chalice. That strange vision in the cavern would, perhaps, always be with him, the blue-white light entering through a slender channel, reflecting off the pyramid into the depths of the chamber, falling on the girl's unseen face. And silence. Deep, pervasive silence, as dark and cold as the interstellar reaches. He felt he now knew what it was to be a planet, or sun, circling within the pressure of another dimension, existing in vacuum, guided only by the perfect curves of gravity, matter's original thought.

And he remembered last night in Chandler's tent, the ghostlike traces of fingerprint powder, the dark patch on the floor by the cot. And Ahmad's strange tale, dropping all the pieces into place.

All except . . .

He strained mentally, though he didn't know what he was reaching for. But something was still missing; its absence grew inside him with a cold hollowness.

And there was something new: a coarse thread of fear that scratched roughly at his throat and reached down into his belly, coiling there like an unholy fetus.

They passed quickly through the village, heading east. The few structures were desolate; in the dusty clearing a child's toy lay abandoned like a relic of a forgotten age. Now Alric understood the village's strange silence.

They continued until the road became little more than a mule trail. The jeep strained along the sudden rises and drops, occasionally a jagged rock scraping piercingly at its underside. After a few minutes Ahmad motioned Alric to pull over in front of a small mud-brick house. They left the jeep and walked up the narrow stone path leading through a small vegetable garden. Alric inhaled deeply, drinking in the pleasant fragrances of the plants and flowers. The bright clear greens and reds were a visual respite from the unending browns and tans of the desert.

Ahmad knocked on the door, and in a moment a small woman came and let them in. She spoke no English, but from her manner Alric could tell that she and Ahmad knew each other. She had a pre-occupied look about her, like a woman in the midst of preparations for an important guest or an up-coming holiday. But no, decided Alric, it more resembled the distracted look of concern one has for an ill relative.

In the small, spare dining area to the left of the entrance, a stocky middle-aged man stood from his seat at a large wooden table. He nodded to Alric, who remained by the door, and shook hands warmly with Ahmad when the guide came to him by the table.

The two men spoke quietly while Alric stood by the doorway, waiting. He looked around curiously, studying the simply furnished home and the sun-browned faces of the two villagers, who somehow seemed unawed by the events. At one point the woman approached him, asking with her eyes if there were something she could get for him. He shook his head and smiled at her. She returned the smile with a face that creased heavily around the eyes, then left him, perhaps sensing that he needed to be alone. He breathed deeply the heady aromas from the garden, allowing himself to sink into his thoughts, trying to somehow find the point at which it had all begun, as if by this knowledge he could still alter the events. And he tried to find names for the various sensations that now flitted in and out of his field of awareness, but failed in the effort; all was too unclear, too hazy. And the truth was, he was *feeling* very little; all was now observation. He had been removed as a motive agent, reduced to the role of spectator, the I in the dream, stuck helplessly to a spot on the ground and forced to watch events go on around him. And this dreamer could not open his eyes to the rescue of daylight—because he realized that the nightmare was outside of him as well as inside. It was real. And his eyes were already open.

As he stood there, immersed in his thoughts, a girl silently appeared from another part of the house and walked toward the front door. He was immediately struck by the fluid grace of her motion, and thought back to last night in the cavern, the slender shape of the young girl—the chosen one—outlined faintly in the blackness, her dark bolt of hair invaded by the light reflected off the pyramid. Now he saw her face for the first time, her large, brown eyes and dark skin, he saw that she was beautiful.

She smiled shyly at him as she passed and went through the open door to the garden. He watched as she knelt by a flower and bent low to smell its petals, then inspected a nearby small vegetable patch, here and there removing a dead leaf with delicate but nimble fingers.

Alric felt Ahmad's hand on his arm, and turned to face the guide.

Ahmad nodded. "Let's go now. We'll come back tonight."

The girl looked up at them as they passed, and Alric smiled at her, again feeling the garden's gentle vibrations enfolding him.

A few minutes later they had reached the other side of the small village, and were again in the realm of the Judean desert. Alric removed a hand from the steering wheel to wipe some sweat from his forehead and turned to Ahmad. "How do they feel about this?" he asked.

The guide looked at him curiously. "Honored," he said. Then he added, "And somewhat fearful."

Alric said nothing, but turned back to the road that stretched before them like an uncoiled desert snake.

From the protective shade of a low plant, it had watched, cold, lidless eyes impassive, ivory fangs glinting softly in the shadows, sleek and curved inward. At the ready. . . .

It had watched the humans, waiting.

Now it moved, slowly, slithering out from the darkness. It came alive, for time was growing late. Somewhere it knew: another step had to be taken.

Legless, it glided. . . .

Inspector Yadin looked thoughtfully at the small book that had been sent over earlier, the white edge of a business-sized envelope protruding from under its cover. Finally he slid out the envelope and tapped it a few times against his open palm, as if debating whether or not to open it. He turned it over and studied his name, written on its face in neat blue script. Then, with a quick motion, he turned back the unsealed flap and extracted the single white sheet.

His eyes were expressionless as they scanned the page; it was a short note from the government man,

as he had known it would be. He meticulously re-
folded the letter and slipped it back inside the
envelope.

He glanced up from his desk, as he had been
doing all morning, realizing with a grim smile that
he was looking around the room as if for a life preserver; somehow it was immensely important that
he keep his mind within the confines of his small
office. But the sight kept coming back: the face
of the old curator, white and drawn, his eyes vacant
circles, his head nodding involuntarily every few
seconds, as though in the affirmative to some question heard only by him; the small display room,
its floor a rough blanket of glass fragments, crackling sharply with each step—except at the slick,
clumped areas; the dark mass by the windows,
propped up in the corner like a sandbag against the
splintered glass sea; and the two display cabinets;
the small, empty one, its windows gone, standing
like a cube of air—and the other, larger one against
the wall. . . .

He shook his head slowly, without meaning to do
so, and was surprised to realize that his years on
the force had not prepared him for this.

He reached for the small book.

Alric found Diana sitting by the campfire, elbows
resting on knees, chin in palms. Her eyes were wide
and unfocused, as if looking into an uncertain distance. He sat down beside her and studied the
flames as they fed on the last fragments of wood,
then slowly ebbed to an occasional flicker.

At length she turned to him, summoning a weak
smile.

"Eaten yet?" he asked.

She shook her head.

"Hey, I've got an idea. Why don't we head into
town, get away from here for a while?" He hesi-

173

tated awkwardly. "You know, try and sort things out."

"No, it's all right here. There's really no need. . . ." She looked up at him. "How'd it go?"

He looked back at the burnt twigs. "I guess there won't be any . . . problems." He stopped, remembering the girl, her dark, beautiful face, and the small garden, growing well under her gentle touch. "We're going back there tonight," he said, then paused. "And then to the pyramid."

A slender flame shot up near the center of the fire; there was a small pop from within the ashes.

"What do you think of . . . what Ahmad told us?" she asked. "I mean, is it possible?"

He shrugged. "I don't know. Maybe it *is* possible. But I don't believe it." He paused for a moment. "I'm going along with this until I find Carl's murderer."

She turned to him. "You don't think Ahmad was involved?"

Again he hesitated. "No."

He felt a tiny bead of sweat trickle down his temple, distilled by the pressure of the afternoon sun.

She said, "But just think about it, if it were true . . . what it would mean."

He shook his head. "I don't *know* what it would mean."

"A descendant of that race, born after thousands of years." Her face seemed to grow brighter with the idea. "He'd *have* to be different, something special. The only survivor of the Golden Age."

Alric said nothing, her words reminding him of the picture he had seen yesterday in Stein's book: the primeval city, sparkling in varying shades of gold, the creation of an extraordinary people. Was their descendant to be heir to their secrets, a benevolent emissary of the first, the archetypal civilization of man? Or would he be the evil messiah of Eluth,

come to end the present cycle and reduce the world
to ashes?

And he thought of the silent watchful eye, the
vesica piscis, etched in the gold model pyramid; he
could visualize it hovering over the golden city like
a lens cut into the sky. Chandler's last words kept
coming back to him: *"the union of opposing masculine and feminine cosmic principles . . . the sacred
marriage of the spiritual and the material worlds,
of the sun and moon, of heaven and earth . . . the
primal unit of creation."*

So *that* had been their purpose, of which the later
pyramid builders, with their great monument to
Cheops, had been only dimly aware. Ahmad's tale of
the original civilization would have been easier to
dismiss—were it not for the many references in
Egyptian lore to the mysterious land of the *Great
Ancestors*, the remants of which had been reputed,
in legend, to have instructed the pharaohs of the
early dynasties in the ways of the forgotten wisdom.
Could Ahmad's civilization be identified with this
ancient race? And was the pyramid—and its contents
—their ultimate legacy to the human race? The heir
to the throne of the Golden Age, come to . . . ?

And there he stopped. There his mind went dark,
and the world went gray, out of phase . . . and he
knew it was within his power to end it, as it would
never again be. Within his power to regain control
over events, and let the world clarify itself once
more.

With a somnambulistic motion he reached into
his shirt pocket and pulled out the small envelope.
He studied the dying flames, wondering how quickly,
how coldly, they would consume the paper, then
melt and vaporize its unholy contents. And he wondered if it would end his uncertainty, if the world
would again become defined, and if sanity would
return.

Without emotion he watched the last flame die

with a soft crackle. He understood that it was too late.

He replaced the envelope in his pocket.

Yadin closed the small book and reread the note left by the government man. When he had finished, he dropped the page to his desk, leaned back, and ran a hand through his thick, dark hair, wondering what to make of the new information. Certainly there was nothing that could be called hard evidence. He went over in his mind the facts gathered from the sections of the book indicated by the government man, trying to determine if there could be a meaningful link, or if the slim leads would prove false ones. The possible connection was obvious: a clandestine society of adepts dedicated to the furtherance of the cause of black magic, considering themselves servants of the Dark Powers and taking strong measures to protect their secrets—death being the punishment for revealing their rites. His own first thoughts had been along similar lines, considering the bizarre manners of the two deaths. And there had been evidence linking the cult mentioned in the book to several ritual murders. But the group had disappeared over thirty years ago, and there was nothing solid connecting them with this part of the world—though, according to the book, many of the inner circle of initiates had turned to the Middle East following the end of World War II, feeling stronger ties with certain Eastern occult sects than with the Christian world.

Yadin considered: occult esotericists in the Middle East? Perhaps seeking union with other hidden sects, more likely to be found here than elsewhere?

To what end?

Yadin could find little in the book that might offer enlightenment on this question, except for a few obscure passages referring to the cult's belief in the coming age of darkness—and their vow to keep eternal vigil until the time of "Supreme Revelation," when the Powers would come forth from the depths to wreak havoc on the world.

A shiver ran down the inspector's back, and he leaned away from the book on his table. Suddenly the scene at the museum sprang into his head again, and he fought to eject it. But it kept coming back: the image of the night watchman's severed head— the wide, questioning eyes, the thickly matted hair, the twisted red tendrils hanging loosely from the shelf. . . . He shook his head briskly to free himself of the grisly picture.

And he wondered if there was a connection.

But the most interesting of the sections noted by the government man was the one concerning the strange beliefs of the mysterious group: the mystic concept of the power of the blood, and the occult rites whose aim was to bring about a metamorphosis in human evolution—the birth of the "New Man." Rites which inevitably involved torture and human sacrifice. The group members had believed the blood ceremonies necessary for their communication with the non-human Intelligences guiding them, and pre-paratory to their awakening in themselves a higher consciousness of the flow of history and the overall destiny of man. In this way, they initiated them-selves into knowledge of the hierarchies of evil and the true aims of the Luciferic Principality working within the framework of history—thus becoming the willing vehicles for the powers of evil in the twentieth century.

Yadin had reread the passages several times, trying to figure out exactly what had been on the govern-ment man's mind. Had he suspected that survivors of the cult were alive today? And returning to the practice of blood sacrifice to unite with the dark powers? Or that some new band of deluded occult-ists had emerged, engaging in similar rites of black magic and ritual murder? Yadin shook his head in a gesture of uncertainty. These were lines along which he was not accustomed to thinking. Nor was his government friend given to mystical flights. Yadin wondered what other information the man might have.

He reached for the book and opened it again. Perhaps there was something he was missing. Certainly any connection between the cult and the archaeological team was unapparent. Why had Chandler and the watchman been singled out by the killers? And what was the significance of the small gold pyramid? And its theft from the museum?

He looked up briefly, noticing how dark it had grown; only the last few rays of day entered through the grimy windows, throwing the room into a muddle of muted hues and long shadows. He thought momentarily of standing and walking to the light switch, but was too settled in his seat. Instead, he leafed through the book until he found a particular page.

In the poor light, he squinted down at a few short lines derived from an ancient legend—one that gnawed at him with its cryptic meaning:

> *To them it will be left,*
> *the choice, whether to secure*
> *the demons in their cell—*
> *or break the seal*
> *and set them free to roam the world.*

A shrinking band of gold lay along the horizon, blending imperceptibly with the blue-black shades of the upper sky, forming the indistinct boundary between day and night. Below, the desert released its heat quickly to be carried away by the rising wind.

A single headlit vehicle drove east along the dirt road that ran through the desert like a dry riverbed. Its two occupants were silent, each immersed in his own thoughts. Ahmad, in the passenger seat, looked straight ahead, his dark eyes narrow and sharp, as if trying to discern unfamiliar shapes in the growing darkness. Behind the wheel, Alric thought about his strange companion, trying to understand the several things which seemed to remain hidden—for something continued to tug at the perimeter of his awareness. "I see you have been busy, Dr. Alric," the guide had said in the tent last night, seeming to have anticipated Alric's involvement in the mysteries of the ancient civilization. And why had he taken such an interest in Alric's earlier research, quoting a passage from his book on pyramidology?

And why, knowing the small pyramid's contents, had Ahmad made no attempt to take possession of it?

The jeep slowed to a stop a few feet from the small vegetable garden in front of the mud-brick house. Again Alric's mind filled with the image of the girl, so darkly beautiful, surrounded by her flowers and plants; again he remembered her soft touch as she had tended to the new buds. He wondered what she must be thinking of what was to be done tonight.

Along the short stone path Ahmad slowed, reaching for Alric's arm. He was looking up at the front door, which stood open, allowing a spill of light onto the walk. His eyes indicated that something was wrong. The two men quickened their pace and stepped through the door.

In the dining area the girl's mother sat crumpled in a chair by the table, face buried in her hands, sobbing fitfully. Her husband, on one knee by her side, murmured softly to her. He looked over briefly at Alric and Ahmad. His face was grief-stricken, his eyes red and puffed.

Ahmad rushed through the open door to the girl's bedroom, leaving Alric by the front door, uncomprehending. Suddenly, an undulating wail arose from deep in the woman's throat, growing from a quiet sob to fill the house, then dying down to a whimper. Alric felt light-headedness wash over him like a cold, white light. A pounding grew in his chest.

When Ahmad returned, Alric saw shock in his face for the first time.

"She's dead," said the guide in a dry, quiet voice, as if reluctantly giving up a protected secret.

Alric stood still, leaning against the doorframe and allowing himself a few seconds of not believing. Then he felt strength return to his body with a sense of finality. He walked through the door to the girl's room.

He stopped just beyond the entrance and looked across the room to where the girl lay on her bed, hands resting by her sides. He watched her for a long moment. Nothing about her reminded him of death. Her skin retained its brown richness, her expression its quiet life. But she wasn't breathing.

He walked over to the bed and took her wrist. There was no pulse. He began to lower the hand, but stopped: his finger had found an irregularity, a small break in the smoothness of the skin. Feeling a return of weakness, he turned the hand over. Just above the base of the palm were two clean puncture marks, space about an inch and a half apart.

He replaced the hand by her side and left the room, gently closing the door behind him.

"Eluthi?" he asked quietly, when Ahmad had turned to him.

The guide said nothing, but returned Alric's gaze.

They left the mud-brick house, the darkness surrounding them like a sheath.

The scent of flowers from the girl's garden was still with Alric as he and Ahmad arrived back at the camp. In the mild yellow glow from the dashboard he detected a curious look on the guide's face, a creasing between the eyes that seemed to indicate not only concern but a growing realization of what the true situation was—a situation which, for Alric, was becoming ever more unclear and diffuse. He turned the ignition key and listened to the engine's rough growl dissipate quickly into the rapidly cooling night air. They sat silently for another moment, then simultaneously opened the jeep's doors and stepped out onto the sand, returning to Alric's tent. Alric bent through the entrance flaps, Ahmad pressing behind him. Inside, Diana lay still on her cot, her eyes closed.

Ahmad stopped abruptly, grabbing Alric's arm.

"Wha—?" began Alric, twisting back toward the guide.

Ahmad silenced him with a short wave of his hand. His eyes were clear, intent, sharply focused. For the present, all traces of uncertainty were gone. With a concise movement of his head he motioned to the sheet loosely draped over Diana's feet.

Alric saw nothing, turned back to Ahmad.

But the guide's eyes remained on the sheet, his face taut. He resembled an animal ready to strike. Alric looked back at the cot.

And then saw it.

The slightest flicker of movement, a faint rippling in the smooth whiteness of the sheet.

A short sound escaped his throat, but Ahmad's grip on his arm tightened to the point of pain. He forced his jaws shut; his eyes narrowed in intensity. The two men stood motionless, watching the small rippling of the sheet. Then Alric felt an indistinct murmuring in the center of his stomach. His eyes widened. Now it was his own restraint that held in check his need to cry out.

Two pale, slender threads had begun to emerge from beneath the sheet—two hairlike antennae, swaying with a slow, mesmeric rhythm.

He watched in horror as the head appeared, colorless and round, followed by a pair of venomous jaw-

181

like claws. And then the body, in slow, sinuous movements, until the first dark segment was revealed, then a light one. Black and white, the alternating segments squeezed from beneath the sheet. Black and white again, and again. Until the entire foot-long body was visible, its myriad pointed legs moving slowly like slithering living thorns.

Alric felt the building pressure of revulsion in his stomach, felt his facial muscles constrict with painful tension, as he watched the centipede crawl steadily upward along Diana's bare leg. He looked farther up to where the coarse blue material of her cut-off jeans began. The centipede was now a few inches from the frayed edges. Alric bit his lip as the creature stopped at the hanging white threads, moving its head around as if scouting new territory. The antennae slipped easily under the material, and then the head disappeared. Alric felt a drop of blood roll from his lower lip. His mind shrieked in soundless prayer.

And again the head was visible, coiling back upon its body as if afraid of the dark. It moved along the edge of the cut-offs. Slowly, toward Diana's hand, by her side on the cot.

Alric parted his lips, letting a breath finally escape. He watched the insect reach her hand and coil its body along her knuckles and wrist, then begin its ascent up her arm. But her hand twitched briefly at the strange touch, and the creature stopped. It lifted its head, twisting it from side to side, the antennae moving apart and together, swaying to some unknown measure. Then the creature returned to its path, writhing rhythmically upward along her arm.

Alric looked at Diana, her face turned away from him on the pillow. He prayed fervently that she wouldn't awaken. Her breathing was slow and regular. He saw her neck, smooth and white, imagined he could sense the blood flowing easily through the jugular, thought for a moment he could see the gentle rise and fall of the carotid. It was hypnotic, the regular motion. Rising, falling. . . .

And with a blinding knowledge he knew what was going to happen. He watched the centipede's slow progress and *knew*—while at the same time realizing the absurdity of attributing conscious intent to the creature—that the jugular was its destination. He could see those small claws digging quickly, silently, into the flesh under her jaw, and yet deeper to penetrate the vein, discharging their venom with a mechanical pumping motion, sending it coursing into her bloodstream with dizzying speed, into her heart, into her brain. . . .

Ahmad's hand tugged at his arm, shaking him with quiet urgency. The guide pointed to the jacket draped across Diana's chest and shoulders, then stepped lightly over to the worktable and reached for a heavy hardcover book near the edge. He returned to the center of the tent, handing the book to Alric.

Alric gave a small nod of understanding. Each man took a step toward the cot. Ahmad reached down slowly to the sleeve of the jacket, hanging over the side to the floor. The centipede was a few inches from the edge of the jacket.

Diana's eyes opened: slowly and with clarity, as if she had only been pretending to be asleep, like a person suspecting a prowler in the house.

Alric knew that she felt the thing on her arm.

"Don't move," he whispered in controlled tones, pushing back the desperation from his voice. "Don't turn your head."

Her eyes were wide and clear, her breath shallow and quick. Alric could sense her terror, could feel the creature on his own arm, the light pressure of its moist, squirming body, the maddening tickling of its countless legs as it moved upward, always upward toward the throat. . . .

"Just don't move!" he repeated.

His breath tightened as the centipede reached the jacket—and hesitated, its head moving in a slow circle, its antennae twitching briefly. Then, slowly, it climbed atop.

With a sharp flicking motion Ahmad ripped the jacket from Diana's shoulders, throwing it to the floor.

Alric brought the book down hard, and felt a cold, thick splash hit his knuckles. Overturned and split, the centipede writhed madly, its legs wriggling in the air like two rows of unearthed worms struggling desperately for the dark safety of the ground. Wanting to retch, Alric brought the book down again, bursting the creature with sickening ease. The frenzied motion stopped. He saw a brief glimpse of pale mangled insides before covering the mass with the jacket.

He found his way to the cot and collapsed upon it.

Diana, having lurched forward at Ahmad's action, now stood on the other side of the cot, her body stiff with shock, her face drained white. She looked down at the crumpled jacket on the floor, bringing her hand up to her face. "Oh, my *God* . . . !"

Alric turned to her, shaking his head numbly. "A few seconds later, and . . ."

Trembling, she sat down beside him, arms limp at her sides. She was breathing heavily, but color was returning to her face. Alric put his arms around her and squeezed her to him until his own heartbeat slowed.

She looked up at him. "But what are you doing back? I thought . . . ?"

Alric looked over at Ahmad, who stood by the table, leaning back against it, palms on the surface. His brow was again creased, his eyes at the same time distracted and intense.

"The girl's dead," said Alric, turning back to Diana.

"What . . . ?" She shook her head uncomprehendingly. "But how . . . ?"

Alric said nothing. He looked at Diana, feeling with a tightness across his chest how close they had come. And, at the same time, he saw how well, almost naturally, she was taking all that had happened. He wanted to reach out to her and assure her that there was nothing more to worry about, but he could not; he didn't believe it was true. But at the same time he saw her strength, and it assured him that she could bear whatever was to come.

He turned to Ahmad. "What are we supposed to do now?"

The guide shook his head.

"No *contingency* plans?" asked Alric, with more than a little sarcasm in his voice.

Ahmad's eyes had gone dark, could have been black in the weak light of the tent. It was impossible to tell whether they were turned inward, or to some imagined scene. His expression resembled that of a man with a dreadful decision to make, as though the future hung on his next words.

Alric felt uncomfortable at Ahmad's silence. He shifted uneasily, then said, "There are other girls in the village."

Now Ahmad looked at him, catching his eye. "We haven't the time," he said. "It must be done tonight."

The silence returned. Alric thought he could hear the sound of the wind from deep in the desert, a low wailing.

Diana sat up straight in the cot, uncertainty seemingly lifted from her face. She had made a decision. "Well, then, its simple," she said, matter-of-factly. "It'll have to be me."

Alric sprang from the cot and whirled around to face her. "No!" The word exploded from his mouth as if he had been anticipating her statement. He glared at her.

She stood also, and went to him. She reached a hand up to his face. "Don't you see?" she asked, touching his cheek. "It's the only way."

He backed away, shaking his head in disbelief. It seemed a bad dream from which he could not wake up.

"Think of what it would mean," she continued.

"I don't give a damn about what it would mean! You're my wife, not a goddamned guinea pig!"

Again she reached to him. Her voice was soft. "We can't give up the chance. It's the only way."

"Then it won't be done," he said, pulling away.

"But it *has* to."

"Who says it has to be done? *Him?*" he snarled, turning to Ahmad, his eyes blazing.

The guide straightened, pushing himself away from the table. His eyes met Alric's. "She is right," he said, in a dark, cold voice. "It will be done."

Alric started at Ahmad's words. He began to respond, but caught himself. Instead he took a few breaths, conscious of the oppressive sensation which now invaded his very pores. It was a feeling he could not name. He calmed himself by an act of will. When he spoke again, it was in softer tones, the voice of reason. "This is insane," he said, shaking his head. "You can't actually believe . . ."

Ahmad's eyes stayed with Alric's, his silence answering.

The moment lengthened in the tent; Alric could feel himself drowning it it. Again his voice rose. "*You* can believe!" he shouted. "But I need proof! I'm a scientist, goddammit, not a mystic!"

Ahmad was silent for a full minute, the lamp directly behind him surrounding his head with a diffuse light. Then, slowly, his pupils dilated, making his eyes dark circles under his brow. His breath became shallow and fast; his face seemed lit with a numinous inner light, becoming deep red, almost glowing.

"Look," he said hoarsely, and gestured broadly with his arm to an imaginary scene, smiling with manic intensity. *"The seeker of Eluth."*

Alric took a step back; it had been an involuntary motion. Recognition came over him in a cold splash. He stared at the guide in utter astonishment. *He feels a hand on his arm, restraining him. He turns to the dark figure, the face obscured within its pale hood. "Look," says the man, pointing toward the ritual site. "The seeker of Eluth."*

Ahmad nodded slowly to Alric, his rapt expression unchanging.

Alric's voice was a harsh whisper. "How could you have known?"

And now a stifling heat oppressed him, squeezing the breath from his lungs.

A face, shrouded, yet darkly familiar, smiles through the crowd. . . .

"It was *you!*" cried Alric. "It was *you* in the dreams!"

Ahmad said nothing, his face a fervid mask.

Uncomprehending, Diana's eyes shifted rapidly between the two men. She made a tentative move toward Alric, but he was already out of reach, bending through the tent flaps. She turned to Ahmad in bewilderment, but neither made any move to stop Alric.

From outside they heard a roar as the jeep came to life and began driving through the sand toward the road.

Alric sat silent in the jeep, hands resting on the wheel, eyes peering through the dusty windshield at the gate to the Old City. He listened intently to the utter silence of the night, almost surprised by it, as though he had expected the walls of the ancient city to hum with the interwoven recollections of its thousands of years; as though a faint echo should always be heard, a fabric of voices, vehicular creakings, and the muted vibrations of old stone. But this night was soundless, cool and clear; he could have been on a dead planet, a planet of ice. He gave a small nod, as if fortifying himself, and stepped from the jeep. With dull urgency he strode through the stone gate, his destination unclear.

As he walked, his footsteps echoing briefly down the deserted streets, he urged his brain to action, recalling how clear problems had seemed to come while he was walking through the park on warm afternoons. His body's motion would stimulate his mind's, and all puzzles had seemed to have solutions, all doors, keys. For a moment he imagined he could see the greens of Central Park, the blues of the lake, the sharp outline of New York above the branches of the trees.

But he saw that his world had changed, irrevocably, and would never return to the clarity of the past; the small envelope in his pocket assured that. Unconsciously he reached up and tapped the pocket, like someone momentarily concerned that he'd forgotten his keys. The soft crackling of the paper brought home to him where he was. A shudder ran through his body.

And what now to make of Ahmad, the willing guide? How could he possibly have known the details of Alric's dream?

Alric found himself thinking of drugs, minute doses of hallucinogens, perhaps slipped into his food. But no, he shook his head; he knew that wasn't it. And he knew that the reality was here, somewhere in the Old City, the ancient city.

And here, in his shirt pocket.

The descendant of the Golden Age, bearing the genetic inheritance of millennia.

To what end? For what purpose?

He stopped abruptly. The alley to his right looked vaguely familiar. In the faint moonlight filtering down between the deserted buildings to either side, he could make out dark outlines along the ground:

the shapes of cardboard cartons, old crates, a broken wheelbarrow. He turned into the alley, walking slower, his arms outstretched to guide himself along the walls of the buildings.

Yes, *Ahmad*. . . .

And his strange tale about the beginning of history. Of the Golden Age of Man. Had he known all along of Alric's dream that night in the pyramid? *If* Alric could now still call it a dream. Or had the guide implanted it in some unknown way?

The City of Gold, the city of the ancients. Had this, in fact, been its site?

Alric stumbled over a broken crate and heard a frantic squeaking as a small lumpish body scurried along the ground, fleeing what had been its home. He walked carefully the last few yards until the alley ended, opening onto a broad square. He stepped out and continued in moonlight.

City of Gold. . . .

And its bizarre legacy, dropped into his hand like a cosmic joke. For he, more than any other man, would have to see it through to the end. He couldn't keep a grim smile from escaping. And he couldn't help recalling Stein's mention of the belief of the Initiates: that certain individuals incarnate at the necessary times in history. . . .

He hadn't noticed when the change had come, or if there had merely been a gradual decline in the state of his surroundings, but now he slowed his pace and looked around to discover that he had taken the right path: he was in the ruins—that part of the Old City not yet fully excavated, whose origins were lost in the furthest recesses of the past. The structures of antiquity lay broken on the ground like stone skeletons. The angled light and shadow painted grotesque images around him: concrete skulls seemed to leer at him from half-made graves of broken glass and rubble. He nodded, as if in acknowledgment of some unstated fact. He tightened his jacket around his neck and buried his hands in his pockets.

He had no idea what he would do when he found them, but he was drawn here nonetheless, as if by a sympathetic transfer of knowledge between the shattered frames around him and his own bones, leading him toward awareness of the fact: *the Eluthi dwell here.*

Creatures of the night, of the ruins, their presence was palpable; it exuded from the misshapen stone vertebrae like the rancid smell from a corpse. How much human suffering had been brought about in their unspoken name? How many had died? Through the centuries the screams of their victims could be heard, a low wailing against the pulse of history. Alric wondered how many times their cold, bilious breath had been felt by men, how many times their purulent spirit had invaded the pores of civilization, like some virulent disease for which the body had inadequate protection.

And it was an ancient disease, he knew, as old as knowledge, born with man's expulsion from the Garden: the disease of imbalance, the struggle between flesh and spirit, between heart and mind, the splitting of human modalities into left and right. The disease of power without compassion, of knowledge without wisdom.

His mind reeled in circles of ice and fire, fire and ice.

And he felt totally unprepared to meet them.

And the thought kept coming back, again and again, pounding in his brain with primitive pounding rhythm: *he, more than any other man. . . .*

Suddenly fear washed over him in a cold wave, making his stomach weightless, his limbs unbearably heavy. His senses were numbed by a dreamlike feeling of dread.

He knew he was being watched.

He quickened his pace, and it was as though he

were a passenger in his own body, watching—almost indifferently—as his legs moved faster and faster. And then he was running across the broad square, and his running frightened him, as if it acknowledged the true danger. But he couldn't stop, no longer knew how to stop. The ruins became a maze around him, broken lines and curves that came back upon themselves, crouching structures and shadowed angles that seemed to point at him with gnarled, bent fingers.

And everywhere watched by those eyes.

Those dead, black eyes.

He heard his breathing, furious and painful in his chest; he felt the strain in his arms and legs, the pumping of his heart. And, with dull force, the vanity of his effort impressed itself upon him. He allowed himself to slow, and finally stopped.

He looked up, and noticed for the first time that through the hoary frame of the gutted ruins surrounding him, the angular shape of the New City could be seen. He stood still for a moment, looking at its frantic spires pointing toward the sky, gleaming polished stone coldly reflecting starlight, standing as if in defiance to the will of time: the mark of man, scratched tenuously in the sand. He remembered the picture of the City of Gold, the *first* city, and suddenly understood with a potent new knowledge: it was to have been the superstructure of Man, standing midway between him and the universe, its living body pulsing life-current between the two, maintaining balance and equilibrating the forces of the cosmos.

He walked forward, caught in a feeling both familiar and remote . . . and a part of his mind became the city, seeing through its coarser eyes. While at the same time a part of him resisted, wanting to end the darkness—and the light. If only he could somehow propel his body through the hidden vortex, get caught up in the clockworks, and by his sacrifice bring an end to the momentum of time . . .

. . . and he continued along the sunlit surface.

The street glistens in the bright morning sun. The air, as always, is warm and dry. He stops by a fountain and looks at its clear, cool surface. He sees himself, his crystal blue eyes. . . .

Around him people walk along briskly, purposeful yet unhurried. And he, too, must walk. He is expected at the construction site. So well, so easily, the work progresses. And many years away . . .

An idea stirs vaguely in his mind, but is scattered by the sun's glare and wafts quickly away, the only proof of its having been, a faint tingling at the base of his spine.

The circle is complete, he understands.

There is a man who looks like him, standing in an arched doorway to his right. He slows his pace, quickens his breathing. The world threatens to darken as he walks past the man, trying desperately not to catch his eye—

The ruins returned in a violent flood of blackness, pinning Alric to the stone beneath him. He stood as he was, unmoving, allowing the forms and shadows around him to gradually regain their solidity. He counted his breaths, his pulsebeats, let his mind adjust to the darkness after his eyes had. Finally he turned his head a few degrees to the left and to the right. He was standing in the center of a broad street; to either side were the carcasses of ancient buildings, some still rising up dark and solid against the glow of the night sky. He remembered: yes, he was in the ruins in the Old City, surrounded by the remnants of a forgotten civilization. His eyes widened. And behind and to his right . . .

He shook his head, took a deep breath; a shiver rolled down the length of his body, expending the surplus energy threatening to spark from his skin. He took a tentative step forward. The ground held firm. He allowed himself a moment's reassurance; perhaps he would not have to turn. Another step, and then another, oh, God, and then—

He froze.

He had heard it. As clear as it was soft. And the tiny hairs on his back quivered in response to the unearthly rustle from behind.

Behind and to his right.

He stood rigid, glacial, his eyes wide and immobile, fixed yet unseeing. The skin along his shoulders tingled with tiny ripples, sending icy beads of sweat rolling slowly down his back. His jaw was closed tight, his teeth a solid wall, the pressure sending sharp pains through the muscles under his ears.

He knew he would have to turn.

Again the soft rustling, like a leafless tree swaying in the wind. But there was no tree. And there was no wind.

He turned slowly to face the dark figure, shrouded in the broken shadow of an ancient arched doorway. Then, with somnambulistic strength, he approached it. Black hollow eyes watched him from beneath overhanging brows as he took the last few steps. . . .

And stopped a few feet from the Blind Man.

In the dim, mottled light, Alric looked into the old man's face. Framed in a tangled mass of hair and beard was a chronicle in flesh, deep lines etched between thick folds of skin, sagging downward under the insistent pull of gravity. But it was not the face that he had imagined. Absent were the loose, fleshy lips, dripping spittle from a toothless, infected mouth, the bluish nose, broken and bulbous, the excrescent skin, red and craterous, puffed beneath the eye sockets. Instead it was a face that retained the ghost of a former dignity. The mouth was firm, indicating remaining teeth, the lips sensitive and wide; the nose was large and straight, had once been aristocratic; the high forehead was wrinkled but clear. Alric involuntarily averted his eyes from the deep brows, remembering Ahmad's story of this strange man's self-mutilation.

The Blind Man moved his head, a slight nod, acknowledging his awareness of Alric's presence. Alric felt intensely watched, and found himself irresistibly drawn to the sagging eyelids.

A charged stillness prevailed, a meeting of two worlds.

And then, slowly, incrementally, the eyelids withdrew, pulling themselves back amidst the folds and revealing the secret they had so long and assiduously guarded.

Alric stepped back in shock.

Two spheres, like polished stone, gazed back at him from icy depths of blue—and the sight exploded in his brain.

But it wasn't the color that nailed him to the ground, and mercilessly ripped through the fabric of his being: for in the left eye, just below the pupil, was a tiny, star-shaped fleck of gold.

The surge of knowledge drowned Alric, overloading his senses and draining him at the same time. He stared at the old man, unable to move or speak.

Again the aged flesh flickered with movement. This time the lines around the mouth raised slightly. He was smiling.

"I see they will work," he said, in a voice that was surprisingly mellifluous.

Finally, Alric found his own voice, strained and harsh in his throat. "They said that you . . . plucked them out."

"A latter-day Oedipus?" mused the old man. "No, I'm afraid, nothing quite so dramatic. Though, perhaps, in a way it might have been easier."

"But you kept them *closed*?" asked Alric, incredulous. "For thirty years?"

"Blue eyes stand out in this land."

Alric shook his head quizzically. "The authorities?"

"It wasn't the authorities I was fleeing," said the

old man. "And after all," he smiled, "self-imposed blindness does have a long tradition." He paused for a few seconds, considering. "Perhaps the truest punishments are the self-imposed ones."

Then his smile faded. His eyes were on Alric, but looked through him, watery and distant. It was a few moments before he spoke again, and when he did it was with immense weariness.

"There was a woman, there," he began quietly, "at some of our . . . gatherings. Poor, miserable wretch of a soul, she would go into a trance, and we would all sit around her, ourselves entranced with a vision of the New Man that was to emerge, and with the promise of a mystical heritage. And before our eyes, shades of long-dead initiates would appear in ectoplasmic shrouds around her, exhorting us with prophecies of the elementals who would come to our aid, and the long-awaited Dark Messiah who would come to abolish history and release us from the chains of time. And we would watch the terrible dream unfold, until the air around her became stifling and we fled the room, gagging."

He paused for a long moment, then, slowly, continued. "We all sensed the time was at hand. The demons would be released to attend the birth of the awaited one." He focused on Alric, looking deeply into the younger man's eyes. "It was not difficult for us to believe."

Alric searched the old man's face, as if attempting to trace the lines of history in the deep furrows. He looked into the eyes, those cold blue orbs that held so much power over him, and in them he could see the credulous young men, meeting by candlelight in curtain-shrouded rooms, their faces fervent, haunted, as they raised their voices with the power of belief, as their ears reverberated with the incantations— and as their minds followed, at first only half-driven by the words of the black magicians placed in their midst. At first. . . . But then the darkness would grow, hypnotic with its heady promise of power, thickly sweet with the threat of pain. And the black masses would come, the demons invoked with ancient pagan rituals—and with blood. The deep pull of violence would enfold them in hot, cold arms.

And he understood. It *hadn't* been difficult for them to believe. And it hadn't been difficult for them to wait in charged anticipation for their messiah, the Dark Prophet who would come, seeking to encompass the world in his icy grip.

"It was not difficult for us to believe," repeated the man of the ruins softly.

A strange calm seemed to have descended around them, as though an impalpable barrier surrounded them, encapsulating them from the rest of the world. Alric was silent for a few seconds, allowing himself to experience a moment's freedom from thought. He looked around at the sagging hulks and crumbling foundations, and for a moment felt as if he had become one with the stone, sharing its peace.

Finally he looked back at the old man. "And now, what's to happen?" he asked.

"The battle for the soul goes on, as it always will," said the old man. "The creatures dwell in shadow . . . awaiting their time." He paused for a moment, then said, "They prepare for the birth."

Alric looked up at the last words, uneasiness taking possession of him. The terms had been different, but the meaning was the same. Ahmad's words echoed in his brain. *"They vie for the soul of the unborn descendant."*

"The warring goes on," finished the old man.

An awareness took form inside Alric, as if fashioning itself from the empty colors and broken light around him. *The demons gather at the periphery of civilization, like the smell of corruption lingering in the ashes. Deathsmoke hovers in the air, obscuring the stars and enshrouding the day.*

The warring goes on.

Alric gave a slow nod of recognition. He knew what had to be done.

He looked up at the old man's face, eerily illuminated by a single shaft of moonlight. "Why here?" he asked. "Why have you come here?"

"It began here," said the old man. "And it must end here."

"And the Eluthi?"

"They can do nothing to me."

Alric took a long look at the old man, framed by the crumbling archway. He reached out and lightly touched his hand.

"Do you know who I am?" he asked.

The old man looked closely into Alric's eyes. Slowly, he nodded.

Both men were silent for a moment.

Then, Alric asked, "How do you live here?"

Again, the flicker of a sad smile. "The question is: how can I die here?"

"Is that what you want?"

The reply was barely more audible than the drawing shut of his eyelids. "It is what I want."

Alric nodded slowly, to himself.

The Blind Man heard Alric's footsteps fade gradually into the night, as if swallowed by the stone.

The full moon was a spherical jewel balanced neatly on the pyramid's gold tip. Surrounding it was the dark field of sky, silent, waiting.

The man and woman walked in the moonlight to the wooden ramp and descended slowly to the entrance of the pyramid. They passed easily through the series of tunnels and came to the central chamber. The only chamber. The womb of the pyramid.

The woman spread the sleeping bag on the floor in front of the vacant stone pedestal, which stood now like an ancient cosmic altar.

The man stood by the pedestal, his blue eyes almost black in the pale light of the pyramid's interior. He ran his hand along the edge of the cool stone, and felt the deep, clear inscriptions transfer their information through his fingertips. His face was haunted.

(*He pulls her up by the shoulders so she can look directly into his face.*

"Tell me what you see," he says, his voice cool and foreign.

"What?"

"Tell me what you see." Slowly.

"I don't understand.")

Still standing, he removed his shirt with deliberate movements. He turned, took a step toward the woman, knelt by her.

(*"In the left one. Tell me what you see there."*

"I've seen it a thousand times."

"Do you see it now?"

"Yes, of course."

"Do you know what it means?"

"I don't understand. It's just—")

He stood again and returned to the pedestal. He let go a deep breath, feeling the muscles in his chest tighten. He gave a small nod to himself, then rested a palm on each side of the pedestal, looking down into its highly polished surface. The face within its false depths looked unfamiliar, as if being seen for the first time.

He bent low, as though to confirm the knowledge that already held fast to his soul.

(*"Just what?"*

"It's just an impurity." Frightened at his behavior.

"It's hereditary, did you know? Passed on from father to son. Like a kingdom."

"I don't understand what you're saying."

"It means I understand why it had to be me all along. Why I had to be the one to come here. Why I have to be here now.")

He looked into his own eyes.

And there, immersed in crystal blue, was the tiny gold fleck he had seen ten thousand times: a curiosity become proof, a hereditary link.

A star which had glowed softly in the sun's light.

(*"It means I found my father today."* A grim *laugh.*)

He turned slowly to his wife.

Part Two

*

THE PIERCING CRY of sliding tires, immediate, painful; a man's hoarse shout, a head straining through an open cab window, a fist clenched hard and shaking; the oddly coordinated sequence of flashing lights, green, yellow, red; a conversation at a store window, animated speech, a few brief laughs; masses of bodies, descending into or emerging from the underground passageways running beneath the city like an arterial web, supplying people in groups resembling quickly assembled militia, coming together, separating. And behind and through it all, like an aural tapestry, the hum, the city's sullen breathing. Continuous, ever present, driving.

He walked south along Fifth Avenue, proceeding apace with the light-hindered afternoon traffic. To his right, beyond the low stone wall, Central Park was a multi-colored enclave in a realm of concrete grays. Occasionally he would look through the arching branches into the depths of the park, his eyes escaping the city streets, which seemed to have grown alien, grotesque, with his separation. The briskness of midday Manhattan was no longer invigorating to him; even the familiar smell of wet sidewalk on rainy afternoons was no comfort: the memory seemed old, brittle.

A few weeks after their return, the time spent in the desert already seemed little more than a dream, an old photograph losing its colors to the air. When he thought back, it was with a thick, sleepy quality, like vision through old and yellowing glass. But he did not often think back. He tried to let the memory slip easily from him, mercifully, into the depths of an unreal past. It was only in the twilight hours that it would return, and he would find himself disoriented, looking frantically for a familiar sign or an old feeling, until the fear passed, and once again the spectres became no more than receding memory.

But New York seemed no more real. The complexities and frenetic life, which had in earlier times sent small shocks through his system and assailed his senses to the point of exhilarating pain, now left him untouched. Alric felt himself trapped between two worlds; unable to rejoin one, unwilling to accept the other.

So he walked.

(A knob being turned, a door opening quietly. He does not react as she enters the room.

"John?" Softly, touching his shoulder.

He looks up.

"Were you asleep?"

He shakes his head and turns away from her, looking out the window across the room.)

He had notified no one of his return. A pile of un-opened letters grew daily on the coffee table in the living room: from the university, from his colleagues, from his friends. There had been no return to pyramid-related work; and after a few brief attempts at a framework for a new project, all work of any sort had come to a halt. For hours at a time he would sit in silence at his desk in his study, hands folded in his lap, eyes closed.

Diana didn't disturb him when he was like that, just as in former times she wouldn't interrupt him while he worked on his doctorate, or prepared an article for publication. She had begun reading a lot, a habit she'd lost after leaving school, and she would busy herself around the apartment, mending things, straightening, trying to keep occupied. But she couldn't keep from remembering how it used to be between them. She often thought back to their first years together, recalling the cool intensity in his eyes, the firm cast of his features, the quiet deliberateness that others had often mistaken for aloofness.

Now he would just sit, his face dark, unsettled, as if indecisive in choosing which expression to assume. And he would think.

Today, though, she had entered his sanctuary. For there was no longer any doubt.

Through the closed door he had heard her speak softly on the phone in the living room, then hang up the receiver. He had heard her steps as she had approached the door to the study. His head had moved slightly at the turning of the doorknob.

(She bites her lip with the effort of committing herself. Finally, the words:

"I just spoke to Dr. Murray."

He stands, walks to the window, looks outside. The sidewalk is dark with a light morning rain.

"And what does Dr. Murray have to say?" Matter-of-factly, without turning.)

He had not opened his eyes as she had entered. With a chill feeling he had sensed her behind him, near his shoulder. If only for a few seconds longer, he had not wanted to know. His eyes had tightened, involuntarily, as if to keep out the one remaining fact, inexorable as the secret deep inside them. But instead of darkness, he had seen a pyramid bathed in moonlight, a small chamber with blue-glowing walls, an empty altar—and himself observing himself observing himself mirrors against mirrors until all had become one, and he had been reduced to an object in the hands of the powers, driven by his past to completion of the act. . . .

If only for an instant longer, he had not wanted to know.

("I'm pregnant, John."

A pause.

"I see." Still without turning from the window.

Her tongue comes out briefly to moisten her lips.
"Is that all you can say?"

Now he turns to her, his face suddenly dark.
"What the hell do you expect me to say? What do
you want me to do? Run around handing out cigars
and say that I hope it's a boy?"

"John, it's your baby too."

"Is it?"

"You know it is!" She takes a step toward him.

"I don't know a damned thing."

"Well, I do. I know. It's inside me. I know it's
your baby."

He looks away from her, walks back to his desk.)

A thick cloud covering had begun to settle over
the city, lowering steadily toward the tops of the
highest buildings. At 72nd Street Alric turned west,
heading into the park. The air was brisk, an occasional gust of wind skimming off the surface of
the lake to stimulate the branches and leaves to
hushed chatter. He gave his head a brief shake and
buried his hands in his pockets.

He had not believed—had not allowed himself to
believe. It had been an act of madness. He had
struggled to purge it from his mind; but every time
he had looked at her he had wondered if their madness had taken root. In the present, in New York, it
had seemed unthinkable. But he had attempted to
prepare himself nonetheless.

And slowly, by degrees, the terror had seemed to
grow distant; six thousand miles distant, countless
centuries distant. The images had stopped running
through his mind, as they had those first few days—
and nights—in colors of overwhelming strength. He
had fought the memories, had separated himself
from them with the wrenching violence of birth.

And, again, perhaps he could not really believe. . . .

Then the words had come; he had heard them approach, enter his domain. And he had not, after all, been prepared, had had no defenses. There had been nothing for him to say, nothing for him to do but walk from the room, from the apartment, into the streets of the city.

He looked around, noticing the stark colorlessness of the day. The park seemed at home in the center of the city, at home in the grays. It was a seasonless day, as drained as he was, dominated by the cold mist that hung in the air like a dead hand. He unpocketed his hand to push a stray lock of hair from his eyes, then gathered his jacket more tightly around him. Though it was late spring, the wind from the lake was chilling.

In walking, he tried to bury himself in his surroundings, numb himself in the cold. But he could not keep his mind from her words—and the way she had looked at him when he had left. But the words had been more intolerable than he had imagined—giving expression to the impossible. He could no longer tell himself that the madness was over. And he could see no way out of it. He felt strangled by the circumstances, by his history—and by the revelation she had made to him that morning. One which the most hidden fibers of his being had intuited from the beginning. *She was pregnant.* The impossible had come to pass. The past had driven the present to its knees. And when he looked ahead he could see no future.

"How do you know it's not your baby?" she'd asked, and he'd seen the tears well up in her eyes.

"What?"

"How can you say for certain it's not possible?"

"Come on, Diana," he'd said, turning from her.

She'd grabbed his arm, trying desperately to turn him around to face her. "You said yourself you didn't believe the whole thing."

And then he'd turned back to her, his eyes blazing.

"And *you* said you did. You were the one who suggested it. You were all for it."

Her hand had dropped from his arm and fallen limp at her side. She'd begun to sob, and the words had sounded strangled in her throat. "I was wrong. Everything was so crazy there. I didn't know what to do."

He'd taken a deep breath, a hesitant step toward her. "I'm sorry. It's not your fault." But the words had been cold, empty.

She'd brought a hand up to her face.

He'd looked at her for a moment as she'd stood there, her body trembling—and suddenly he'd wanted to reach out to her, put his arms around her and whisper a few comforting words. His hand had moved tentatively toward her, and then stopped— and he'd realized that the dark knowledge churning inside him had made contact impossible. He'd shaken his head in his inability to act.

He'd turned and left the room.

And now he was away from it all, again in his refuge, though he expected only transitory comfort. He looked to his right and down at the lake, which spread out before him, curving away and out of sight beyond the small stone bridge. He stopped for a moment, leaning against the low wall bordering the steps leading down to Bethesda Fountain. He turned his attention inward for a moment. There had been a brief sensation that there was something he was overlooking. He shook off the feeling and turned from the lake, heading down the broad, benched avenue leading toward the park's exit at Fifth Avenue and 59th Street.

The park was sparsely populated on this workday. Here and there a pair of secretaries sat and hastily finished sandwiches amidst mutual complaints of life's rigors. To his right sat a thin young man with a torn sweater and violent twitch, deeply immersed in conversation with himself.

Alric felt hopelessly separated from everything around him, and the weight of who he was bore down on him with unyielding pressure. He looked straight ahead, his body braced as if heading into a stiff wind. Gradually, he quickened his pace; until it goes, he told himself, must keep walking until the feeling leaves. And then, without his knowing why, an image flashed into his mind, briefly, but with great clarity: an old doctor, a large metal desk, gray rain. And words. Words falling like ax blows. Words he had banished from his consciousness—and which now held a new, perhaps ultimate, significance.

What had they been?

It had been in some long-forgotten past. Last year? What had that white-haired doctor told him as he had stood before that neatly arranged metal desk, thinking back over the months of not knowing, and about the final tests which had brought him there?

What had he said?

The concrete was suddenly painful under his feet; the city discord swelled threateningly in his ears. He looked up and found he'd exited the park. He stood on the corner of Fifth Avenue and 59th Street, as New York surrounded him with its rush of sound and motion. Across the street a cabby was yelling, the veins on his neck purple and bulging; an odd confluence of car horns sounded a brief atonal strain; the acrid odor of burned rubber assailed his nostrils. And everywhere the lights, blinking mindlessly to unknown rhythms.

Like the blinding glare of a light turned on in the dark to drown a nightmare, the city bore down on him and wrenched him from his world, and, for the first time since his return from the desert, impressed upon him its solidity, its reality.

And he remembered.

Remembered the words and phrases that had disturbed him so at the time. Remembered them as if they had been spoken only an instant ago.

The old doctor had said that it was possible.

Unlikely, but *possible*.

Again Alric could see the small man in his immaculate office. Again he stood before that gray metal desk.

"Could we ever . . . ?"

"It is possible. But very unlikely, I'm afraid."

Alric had nodded.

The doctor had continued. "Of course, one can never be absolutely certain in the case of a low sperm count. However unlikely, the possibility of impregnation always exists."

And he'd gone on to give examples: a couple he'd seen not long ago . . . childless for seven years . . . fine baby girl . . . and another case in. . . .

Nothing mattered now.

Except that it was possible that he was the father.

Unlikely, the doctor had said, yes, and at the time the word had hit Alric with the force of absolute fact; there had seemed no hope. But now the slim chance *had* to be considered. For how much more unlikely the idea of . . . ?

He shook his head sharply, recoiling at the thought, and at the painful memory. It had been madness. And in the bright light of New York he could see that. It was an insane coincidence. It *had* to be. That was so clear now that he thought he must have been blind not to have seen it. It *had* to be his child. The alternative was unthinkable. Yes, of course.

Unthinkable.

He was a scientist, and he had to consider the most probable.

He walked briskly along the heavily peopled avenue, suddenly propelled by the words of the once-cursed doctor. *"It is possible,"* he had said. Nothing else was needed. Nothing. Just the one word.

Possible.

He clung to it as if it were a life preserver. The

old doctor's words—their significance—echoed through his brain like a clear chorus of churchbells. And it made sense. It *had* to make sense. He could see that now.

At every turn of his head the city seemed to lend support. He drew strength from its solidity, from its sheer mass. He looked up, watched the buildings reach toward the sky like grasping stone arms until they buried themselves in the growing layers of mist that had begun to envelop the city. He could feel the power, cold, pulsating, immediate. The city was a part of him, inside him, and at the same time it surrounded him like a protective shell. *The superstructure of Man.* . . . In a thousand voices it reached back, evidence of its reality. And in the internal voice of his reason he demanded to know that the nightmare had ended, and could no longer threaten him.

He walked along Fifth Avenue, breathing deeply the exhaust-tinged air, feeling armored by the city, by the present.

And in his mind the words formed themselves, slowly, tentatively, at first just a whisper, barely audible over the animal pulsings of his body. Again and again he could hear them, growing in strength, in substance, with each repetition. Faster and faster, again and again, a dizzying motion of words. Until the internal pressure built to the point of cauterizing pain:

I am the father.

Rather than dissipating under the sun's peaking strength, the mist settled thickly over the city, muting the light until all became dark gray. Under the shroud the usual small dramas would be repeated with the consistency afforded only by randomness: at the intersections, uneven lines of cars would lurch forward as traffic lights turned green; pedestrians would leap to the safety of the curb, turning to offer muffled curses to unseen drivers; the intermittent roar of subways would resonate through the ground in small man-made tremors; and everywhere, the flow of people, like blood cells circulating through the veins of the city.

At one corner a man stopped at a red light, watching a slow stream of cars pass before him. In the darkened rear of a taxicab he caught a fleeting glimpse of his reflection; he saw his face, his blue eyes dark, distracted, remote. He looked up and around at the stems of the great buildings whose tops were lost from view. The city's steel and concrete eyes seemed to return his gaze, dispassionately, coldly untroubled by the thickening fog. He stifled a shiver that began to run between his shoulder blades.

He became aware of a sound, at once immediate and distant: a million discrete bursts which together rose and fell with a hypnotic sway. He tilted his head, training his ears on the sound which was as unnoticed to the city as the roar of the blood was to the eardrums: the ever present collage of voices, pressing in from all directions, each with its own intensity, its own message. A million conversations, a million soliloquies. In his own silence, he stood listening. Occasionally a fragment could be drawn from the mosaic, and vague meanings could be distinguished, unevenly punctuated by the urgent cries of car horns.

And somwhere in the distance, he could hear faint laughter.

*

SHE STOOD BY the kitchen counter, her hand poised at the switch of the food processor, studying various remains on the countertop—a few fruit peels, an occasional splash of powdered substance—while mentally running down the list of ingredients for the health drink she'd found in last week's Sunday supplement. She gave a small nod, certain she'd left nothing out, then flicked the switch. The blender hesitated into motion, at first gurgling roughly, then settling into the smooth hum that told her the drink was ready. She flipped off the switch, removed the mixing container, and set it on the counter.

She glanced up at the calendar, taped askew to the wall above the sink. In a few days she would lift the present month, with its prosaic orange sunset, and attach it above with the small metal tack that held past months in place. For the third time that day she figured out how much longer it would be, smiling at the unconscious twitching of her fingers as she counted off the months. Three more to go.

She poured the drink into a tall glass, watching intently the viscous liquid's swirling progress to the top.

Things were better between them now, she reflected, recalling the first few weeks with an internal shudder. Tensions and fears had eased with time. Six months and many thousands of years separated them from the desert, and their experience there grew faint and unreal in the sharp daylight of New York. He seemed to be free of the madness that had strangled their relationship during those two months; perhaps he had even come to believe what she felt in her body to be true. But he never spoke of it. Without the conscious intent of either, an understanding seemed to have arisen between them which held things in place—without words. And perhaps it was better that way, even necessary; the semblance of normality would have to suffice for now. After the baby was born they would know for certain. Somehow, they would know. And then it would be over. But for now all understandings had to be unspoken: their verbalization could only lend body to the thinning skeleton of dark memory.

Still, it was not as it had been; it could, perhaps, never be. She understood that, and accepted it. Just as she accepted his uncharacteristic indecision, his periods of depression, the long hours he would spend in dark, impenetrable silence, seemingly blind to the world. This, too, would change. With time. He would see, she felt confident. When the baby was born, he would see.

How neatly it could all be encapsulated in that one short phrase. How much was locked within the simple words: *when the baby was born*. Yes, he would see. He would look into its face, its eyes . . . and he would know. As she now knew, with her own secret knowledge, the dark knowledge which traveled in her bloodstream, *their* bloodstream, that transcendent fluid which fed the fetus, and in turn fed her.

He would see.

She gave the drink an unnecessary stir with a long spoon, watching the spinning liquid funnel in the glass. For a moment she studied the skin on the back of her hand. How pale she had grown lately; she would have to get out more. She smiled grimly, remembering all she had heard about the "glow of motherhood" that was supposed to have infused her with something approaching divine spirit. Yes, she would have to get out more.

She tilted her head slightly toward the living room; the front door had just swung shut. She picked up the glass and drank the contents quickly, grimacing as she replaced it on the counter. She hesitated momentarily, then turned and walked briskly into the living room.

Alric closed the hall-closet door and turned to her with a nod as she entered.

She smiled. "How is it outside?"

"It's nice."

"Not too cool?"

"No." He walked to the living room sofa and sat down wearily. He looked up at her. "How're you feeling? Pain any better?"

She shrugged. "It's not bad. Dr. Murray says it's just nerves. Everything's fine on the inside."

He nodded, then leaned forward and reached for the newspaper lying on the coffee table.

Diana turned toward the kitchen, then stopped, drawing a breath. With a quick motion she turned back to him.

"John, I spoke to Tom," she said.

He looked up from the paper.

She continued quickly, "I invited him and Marie for dinner tonight." She expelled the air from her lungs, watching Alric uncertainly.

He rose from the sofa, tossing the paper aside. He walked to the window and gazed outside. On the street, dead leaves had formed dark puddles against the curb; at an angled distance he could see the bare tops of trees in Central Park. He spoke softly, the syllables even and distinct. "I told you I didn't want to see anyone just yet. At least, not anyone connected with the work."

"No!" She surprised herself with the anger in her

voice. "You don't want to see *anyone*." She stopped, taking a step toward him. "Look at me!"

He turned from the window, though his eyes did not meet hers.

"John, I'm tired of this. I don't know what I'm supposed to do. You won't have people over. We don't go anywhere." She stopped abruptly, looking pleadingly at him. She spoke more softly. "We've been back for six months. Aren't things ever going to be normal again?" The quiver in her voice was unmistakable.

He took a deep breath, and looked at her for a minute. For the first time, he noticed how pale she was, how weak she looked. He stepped over to her, lifting a hand to her face and pressing his palm against her cheek.

"I'm sorry," he said softly, putting his arms around her shoulders. "You're right. I don't know what's been wrong with me. It *would* be good to see Tom again. Maybe even get back to some work."

She looked up at him uncertainly, her eyes darting back and forth hesitantly between his. "You mean that?"

He pulled her to him and held her body tightly against his. "Yes," he said quietly, his eyes fixed on a random spot on the far wall.

"We're thinking maybe in a year or two. . . ." said Marie Scott, flashing a warm smile at Diana. "I just don't think I'd want to leave my job yet."

Diana nodded hesitantly, looking over at Alric, who sat expressionless on the couch. He had said little throughout dinner, had seemed uneasy and socially awkward.

"How much longer do you have?" asked Marie.

"About three months."

"I've heard great things about Dr. Murray."

"He's a fine man," agreed Diana.

Across the room, Tom Scott shifted restlessly in

his seat, looking occasionally at Alric, who seemed unwilling to meet his eye. The change in his former professor was marked. He spoke little and with hesitation, and there was a constant distracted look about him. Tom thought back to the years he'd spent as Alric's assistant at the university, and how Alric would tackle each new problem with a reserve of intellectual energy that had astounded the younger man. And how firm Alric's resolve had been at the beginning of the pyramid research, in the face of opposition from the more traditional-minded among the faculty. Now he sat mute, seemingly immersed in a private world. Following his abrupt return from the excavation in the Judean desert, he had given up his position at the university and broken off all correspondence without explanation. Concerning the research—or the bizarre death of Chandler—not a word had been forthcoming. The project itself had seemed to have been dropped cold without ever seeing the light of publication. Tom looked closely at Alric, now thinking twice about his decision to approach him with his new ideas. He glanced over at an oblong box that lay on the coffee table.

The glance was not lost on Diana; Tom had said nothing about the strange package he'd brought with him, propped under his arm like an unwrapped Christmas present.

She smiled at him. "Well, Tom, are you going to keep us in suspense forever?" She gestured toward the box. "Or do we get to see what's inside?"

"Yes, Tom," urged Marie. "I'm curious, myself."

Diana turned to Marie in surprise. "You mean you don't know what's in there, either?"

Marie shook her head. "He never lets anyone near anything he's working on." She smiled ironically. "I think he's still not convinced I'm not a spy from Brooklyn College."

Tom seemed to hesitate for a moment; then he smiled. "All right," he announced with mock dra-

217

matic emphasis, "The time has come." He turned to Alric. "John, I've been meaning to discuss this with you for some time."

Diana tensed with a pressure that shot a pain through her abdomen. She watched her husband intently.

Alric looked up at the young man.

Tom continued, "Do you remember where we were when you left? I mean, with the experiments?"

Alric shook his head sharply. "I'd really rather not—" He stopped himself, catching the look in Diana's eye. He knew she was right. He had to bring himself back, stop living in fear of the past. For a moment he was silent, struggling quietly to shake the vague feeling of discomfort tingling in his stomach; he understood it and was not going to let it control him. It was *now* that he had to free himself, or he never would. He smiled uncertainly at Tom. "Yes," he said finally. "Optimistic findings, but nothing conclusive." He exhaled deeply. It had been easier than he'd expected. He smiled to himself.

"Exactly," agreed Tom, nodding. "Inconclusive. But why?"

Alric shrugged. "I guess it was only natural at that stage of investigation."

Tom shook his head. "But, John, I believe we were approaching it from the wrong angle. I mean, look at the kind of experiments we were conducting; so many of the results could be attributed to subjective phenomena: suggestion, expectation, even auto-hypnosis." He paused for a moment, allowing Alric to consider his point. Then he said, "But if there were a test, something that *had* to be objective, as well as convincingly precise. . . ."

"What do you mean?"

"Just this: we suggested the possibility that pyramids in some way alter the structure of time. So, in order to test that theory, what we need is a clock." He searched Alric's face for reaction.

"Go on," urged Alric, anticipating Tom's line of thought. At the same time, he noticed, on another level, that the strange feeling had left him. It had been as easy as that. He now only felt the old intellectual surge that had always accompanied the challenge of scientific problems.

"And fortunately," continued Tom, with growing enthusiasm, "nature provides us with one. The perfect clock."

"Of course," agreed Alric, nodding quickly. "It's so simple we should have thought of it long ago. Use a substance with an easily measurable half-life."

Diana smiled at Alric's obvious interest. She had gambled, but apparently had guessed right. She traded glances with Marie, then turned to Alric. "You mean like radioactive dating?" she asked.

"Exactly. Except carbon-14 has a half-life of almost six thousand years. We'd have to use something considerably shorter, like a sample with a half-life of a few hours or a few days. You see, if we know the size of a sample and its rate of decay, we can predict how many atoms will remain at any given time. The only variable would be time itself."

Marie turned to her husband, pointing to the box. "Don't tell me you've got something radioactive in there?"

"Ah-ha!" said Tom. "The box." He leaned over and reached for the cardboard carton, quickly folding back the flap at one end. He removed a series of polished metallic tubes.

"What—?" began Marie.

He raised a finger to silence her, then turned the box on its edge, allowing several smaller pieces of tubing, bent at sixty-degree angles, to fall to the carpeted floor. Then he, too, sat on the floor. In a moment, using the smaller pieces as connections, he had constructed a model pyramid, about a foot and a half on a side.

Alric looked down at it, feeling a slight pain as it reflected the room's light sharply into his eyes.

And again the feeling, vaguely disturbing. . . .

"Our newest experimental model," said Tom. "Stainless steel impregnated with minute particles of gold. Seems to enhance some of the effects." He pointed to a small platform built into the base and rising a third of the way to the apex. "It's at the same relative height as the King's Chamber in the Great Pyramid."

The small pyramid sparkled, and the pain in Alric's eyes grew. Along with the feeling. He began to speak, but the words did not come out. Suddenly he found he could no longer keep his eyes focused in the strange, reflected light, and it was hard to keep a thought clear in his mind. And growing harder. But must try, must try. . . . Again he opened his mouth, feeling his facial muscles constrict with the familiar pressure, his vocal cords tense in preparing to modulate. But still the words would not emerge. Across the room he could see Diana; her lips were moving, but so slowly, it seemed. She was talking miles away, centuries away, forming words in soundless slow motion. And it was even harder to hold on to his thoughts. With dull recognition he began to understand what was happening: the darkness was returning. And the cold. It crawled along his spine like a wet slithering centipede. And then he could see them, indistinct shapes, like unformed dreams, nightmares, approaching; could see dark threatening arms reaching out to . . . *No!* Can't let it happen! *Must* not let it happen! Must not let the darkness return. Must hold on, find something familiar, something . . . in the fading light, Diana's lips, moving in the patterns of words. Yes, something familiar, some *now*. But this was familiar too, this feeling that crawled, inside him and around him, on his flesh and under it. And the cold, shadowy arms. . . . He tried to focus on Diana's lips; if only he could hear the words. . . . And then he realized with pure, cold terror that he *could* hear them—but they were unrecognizable. They made no sense to him. Nothing made sense. Nothing except—

Blackness.

The blackness of a deep cavern. Endless. Cold. Dead. Stretching before him, curving away in non-direction. The space between the stars. The surface on the inside of the eyelids. The line between past and future. The point. . . .

And he blinked: a glimmer of light, a ghost-spark touching down, reaching out, directly before him. A shard of golden light, clear and cold. Growing steadily, achieving definition. Compelling.

Triangular.

Brilliant shadow of a pyramid's capstone.

Enter.

And the light grew, touched off by the golden spark. Grew like wildfire.

Day.

He takes a step, then another. The ground feels solid, vaguely reassuring, warm beneath his feet. He is on a broad avenue near the center of the city. A hundred yards in front of him stands the gold-topped pyramid. Its construction has been completed.

He continues on in the bright sunlight.

There is a white-robed man, a Wiseman, standing before the entrance to the pyramid. He smiles as Alric approaches. . . .

". . . as close as possible to the real thing," Tom was saying. "As close as possible to the conditions that must have existed. . . ."

Diana had been watching Alric, and had noticed his silence. His eyes were blank; he almost seemed to be in a trance. She frowned deeply. Perhaps she had been wrong to invite their friends. She closed her eyes, lifting a hand to her forehead.

Marie turned to her. "Are you all right?"

221

"Oh, I just feel a bit weak. I'd better be getting to bed." Her eyes were on Alric.

"Can I get you something?" asked Marie.

Diana shook her head. "I'll be fine. Thank you."

"Sorry," said Tom, glancing at his watch. "I didn't mean to keep you up this late."

"Yes, he did," smiled Marie. "He's been dying to talk to John about his ideas."

Diana said, "It's all right. Really. I guess I haven't been getting as much sleep as I should lately." She watched Alric, as his eyes seemed to clear. She momentarily wondered if she had imagined his distraction. Then she frowned again, knowing she hadn't.

Alric stood, looking hesitantly at Tom and Marie. "Thank you for coming," he said hoarsely.

"Will you be coming in?" asked Tom, also rising.

Alric looked up quizzically.

"To the lab?"

Diana cringed, watching for her husband's reaction.

But Alric just nodded, saying, "Yes." He looked back at Diana. "Very soon."

Tom motioned toward the model pyramid. "I'll just leave it here, then."

"What . . . ?"

"The pyramid. Why don't you just hold on to it for now?"

Alric nodded vaguely as Diana walked Tom and Marie to the hall closet. The couple put on their overcoats, and Tom turned back to Alric. "I'll see you soon, then, John?"

"Yes," answered Alric, remaining by the couch.

Diana smiled at the young couple. "It's been nice seeing you again."

"It's been too long," said Marie, touching Diana's hand. "Next time at our place?"

Diana nodded as they opened the door and exited.

She looked down the hall after them, then slowly closed the door, leaning her head gently against it. After a few seconds she turned, now leaning her back against the door. She looked at Alric.

"Where were you?" she asked softly.

Alric still stood by the couch, studying the small pyramid curiously. At her words, he looked over at her. "What . . . ?"

"Where were you before? Before they left?"

Alric studied her face for a moment. Finally he shook his head. "I don't know."

"The dream?" she asked.

He shrugged. Then he nodded.

She sighed heavily, walking through the living room to the dining area. She hastily began setting things in order, plates clacking sharply in her hands. "Were you serious?" she asked, without turning from her task. "About going back to work?"

"Yes," he answered, without hesitation. He turned to her. "And thank you."

She looked over at him. "What for?"

"For getting tired."

She smiled. "What's a wife for?" She replaced a low stack of dessert plates on the dining table and walked over to him. Her smile faded as she looked up at him.

"Is it over, John?" she asked quietly.

He looked down at the miniature pyramid on the coffee table.

"Yes," he said, toying with the shiny steel model. He repositioned it closer to the center of the table, then straightened and moved over to her, putting his arms around her.

She slipped hers around his waist and pressed her face against his chest. "Oh, I hope so," she said, her voice muffled by his body. "God, I hope so."

They embraced for several minutes, until Diana winced, uttering a short cry. Alric stood back from

223

her, momentarily alarmed. Then he smiled. "Baby kick?" he asked.

She smiled, again pressing her body to his.

A low growl, base, feral, from the depths; he can see the black band across the horizon, growing, a dark pestilence.

Closer.

A searing pain tears his insides; a hand reaches out to him, deformed, bloody, leprous. And the pounding, the pulsing: the heartbeat of the earth—or is it his own, bursting in his chest? And then the ground is gone, so quickly that he cannot remember its firm touch—and he falls, sucked down with a force that tears the breath from his lungs, that empties his blood of all warmth; drawn down and smothered, faster and faster, with dizzying, sickening motion. Still faster, can no longer hold on to sense, can no longer see. No longer see! Pain across his eyes, burning, stinging; claws attacking, ripping, slick with his blood. And always the growling, the rumbling from the bowels of the earth, always louder, always closer . . . and the pain . . . and the pounding, steady, even, furious, about to burst his eardrums, relieving him of yet another sense; an unholy thunder, a chorus of pain. And always closer.

Closer. . . .

Alric opened his eyes to the primitive fear of the dark, a fear that soaked his skin and the sheet around him. He could see nothing, and did not dare the movement of his arm to the lamp that reason told him was right beside him on the night table. So he remained motionless, feeling the soft pressure of his eye muscles as his eyes darted uncertainly in the dark. He lay rigid and sweating until finally he saw something that allowed him to release the breath trapped in his lungs since he had opened his eyes: the fragile band of light entering beneath the curtains from the street and falling on the carpet near the window. He let the breath escape slowly, and with it felt the tension withdraw, leaving him spent on the bed. And, as though to fill the vacuum left by the escaping air, a blinding rage began to well up inside him, soon devouring the room's darkness in pulsating shades of red. A rage at himself, at his inability to let go of the past and escape the horror in the desert. Rage at his powerlessness in the face of madness. Rage at the dream that would not let him go, that held him in an unbreakable grasp. And rage at the fear. But the rage, too, eventually passed, as if subdued by the cool air entering with the light from the window, and by the sound of Diana's easy breathing beside him on the bed. His own breathing became regular, and he soon found himself drifting, sinking deeply into darkness, only remotely aware of the ambivalence of his need for sleep and his fear of dreaming. Yes, cool air, soothing around his temples, around his hands and feet. And darkness. . . .

His eyes opened wide.

In an instant he was awake with the immediacy of midday sunlight: he had not imagined it this time, he was sure, had not dreamed it, as he had countless times before, usually in the cold hours just before dawn.

This time he had heard it clearly.

Closely.

He did not blink, as if fearing that the instant of darkness was all *they* needed to invade his soul and take him prisoner. For he knew that they were there: he had heard the eerie rustling sound coming from the living room. A gentle rustling, like the whispering sound of a shroud being pulled back, slowly, to reveal—

He caught his breath, stopped his thoughts before they could overpower him. He shook his head, even allowed himself a brief smile. He remembered where he was: no longer in the desert, no longer in *their* world, but in New York. Where they could no longer reach him.

Yet, still, the sound. . . .

He slid his legs over the side of the bed and stood, walking quietly to the door. Without hesitation he turned the knob and went into the living room. He stepped carefully in the darkness, reaching for the lamp by the sofa and turning it on. Squinting in the sudden rush of light, he looked around, quickly taking note of the secured chain-lock on the front door. Nothing appeared out of place. He shook his head briefly, annoyed with himself, then again reached for the lamp.

But he stopped the motion abruptly, suddenly aware of a faint sound. His arm fell to his side and he stood perfectly still near the center of the room, listening. It was something he had heard before: distant, yet at the same time with him in the room. Or inside him. He searched the room with his eyes, finding nothing that could account for the sound.

And it grew louder.

What was it? And where?

And yet louder. Painfully loud. He remembered that first night in the pyramid, that strange ringing; Diana had heard it as well.

The voice of the pyramid.

And it grew still louder, with such a sudden surge that he almost cried out. Why didn't Diana hear it as well and wake up?

Before he could move, the sound jumped another quantum level, burning its way through his ears and into his brain, a vibration that shook his body and threatened to shatter his skull, breaking him down to a fine entropic powder; in his agony he hallucinated waves of himself, spreading ever outward, his soul dissipating, shrinking away from the pain, away from the body, and toward the cool void.

Where was Diana?

He could see himself disintegrated by the powerful vibrations that pounded through his ears and quaked his brain. And all the while, he felt his arms at his sides, useless under the paralyzing pain. He concentrated his remaining consciousness on them, his nerves shrieking the command to move. And finally, with immense effort, he brought his hands up slowly, the arthritic movements of an old man, and cupped his palms over his ears to keep out the ringing, the pain. And through the tears that boiled from inside his head he at last noticed it.

The model pyramid.

The smooth steel tubes shone brilliantly in the mild glow of the single lamp, seemingly with a preternatural radiance, sending light streaming into his eyes as if through a prism. He was mesmerized by it, and somehow his mind struggled for a vague bit of knowledge, a saving insight. Without conscious intent, he brought a hand down in an agonizing motion toward the pyramid's glowing tip until his forefinger made contact with the cool steel.

And it all stopped.

The ringing. The glowing. The pain.

Gone.

Gone so suddenly and completely that he was left stunned by its absence, swaying vertiginously with the strange feeling that comes with the shock of waking abruptly from a tortured sleep. So clean was the split between this new reality and the memory of pain that he wondered if he had imagined it. And again he wondered if he were going mad.

Before he could complete the thought, the curtains were thrown violently back from the windows by a gust of freezing air. He started at the force of the eruption, then silently cursed himself for having left the window open. From outside he could hear the shrill cry of a wind signaling the approach of winter. The curtains rose higher, almost to the ceiling, and hung there, perpendicular to the wall, fluttering in broad ripples, like two flags on a stormy day. He walked over to them, shuddering against the cold air. He leaned awkwardly over the coffee table and reached for the window to close it—and caught a glimpse of the street outside.

He stepped back in shock, knocking the lamp to the floor with a shattering crash, throwing the room into darkness.

His eyes were nailed to the street below.

But it was not the street that he knew, where he had been walking only hours ago. It was a street in ruins, its two uneven rows of split and crumbling sidewalk separated by a long black scar of crater-marred asphalt. The buildings across from his were gutted hulks, sagging precariously, as if the slightest movement of the earth would knock them down to a fine dust. Broken glass and rubble were visible everywhere like a thousand festering sores: it was a city empty for centuries. He moved his head sharply. There had been movement at the foot of the building down the street. His eyes widened in horror as a living mass spread slowly, a dark lapping wave. And then the vile squeaking reached him, as the horde moved unchecked from glassless windows and empty doorways, uniting in a dark sea: a thousand furry bodies, with teeth glistening in hideous blank-eyed smiles. And bits of flesh dangling from their viselike jaws. . . .

He recoiled from the sight, taking a step backwards into the room and reaching out a hand for the support of the soft arm.

He froze, suspended in an instant of terror.

He had heard the soft rustling sound from behind him.

In dreamlike slow motion he felt the blood stop in his veins and arteries, clinging in tiny beads to the inner walls of the vessels, crystallizing to narrow tunnels of ice beneath his skin. His stomach quaked in response to the sensation that ran along the length of his spine like the cold touch of a serpent's tongue. A long, low hiss sounded through the room, like a prolonged death rattle. The stench of putrescent flesh invaded his nostrils, forcing its way into his pores, his brain, dizzying him. He felt his throat contract in small gagging spasms, sending ripples of pain across his chest. And yet he knew that he would move, that he *had* to move. That he would turn, would pivot on his center of gravity like a planet of ice. Would turn to face what was standing behind him.

And then he *did* turn, though he had no awareness of the electric whisperings of his nervous system that had given the command.

She had not been sleeping well lately. And there had been more pain than she'd admitted to her husband. She'd been doing the exercises in the book, when it didn't hurt too much, and Dr. Murray had reassured her that the pregnancy was normal, and that natural childbirth was possibly a good idea. But her sleeping was erratic at best, and the long hours spent lying awake drained her for the next day. When she did finally fall asleep, it was shallow, like that of an animal easily aroused to possible dangers in the night. Just nerves, the doctor had said.

When she opened her eyes, this night, she didn't know if it had been in response to one of the burning twinges that knifed through her body at irregular intervals or to a noise from outside. She sighed heavily, rising up on her elbows, and studied the darkness of the room. It was a full minute before she realized that Alric was not beside her in bed. Shaking her head mildly, she reached for her housecoat draped over a chair. She stood stiffly and walked to the door. As she pushed it open she was greeted harshly by a blast of frigid air. Shivering, she wrapped the housecoat tightly around her, wondering why Alric had opened the window.

Then she stopped.

There were no lights on in the apartment. Could he have gone off somewhere in the middle of the night?

"John?" she called.

Silence.

"John, are you in the kitchen?" she called into the darkness, though she knew that she would have seen the light from where she stood. She stretched a hand across the wall, searching for the overhead light switch. The light went on with a white pressure that hurt her eyes.

She gave a short scream, taking an involuntary step backwards.

Alric was sitting in the corner of the room, cross-legged, head bowed. Beside him was the broken lamp. Behind him the open window blew in freezing air with a low howl.

Her hand came up to her mouth. "John! What are you doing?"

He did not react.

She shook her head numbly, then moved to the window and closed it. She turned back to Alric, standing directly over him.

"What are you *doing?*" she demanded, anger now replacing fear. "What happened to the lamp?"

He said nothing, merely gazed expressionlessly down into his lap.

"*John!*" she cried, frustration welling up inside her.

Then he moved. He tilted his head slowly toward her, his eyes blank and intense at the same time, an odd thin smile on his lips. She realized that he wasn't seeing her.

She stared down at him, the urge to cry about to overwhelm her. Stifling the impulse with an effort

230

of will, she turned sharply on her heel and walked back to the bedroom.

A part of him had heard the bedroom door slam shut, though he had not reacted.

He remained in silence. Numb.

He sat in the corner for a time he could not measure, eyes fixed on a random spot on the opposite wall. Outside, the first pale band of sunrise appeared on the horizon; in a short while the city would come to life.

Finally he moved. His head turned toward the coffee table, a few feet away.

Upon it sat the pyramid.

In silence, he watched.

Waited.

The pyramid sent crystal flecks of light into his eyes, and beyond.

*

DIANA SLAMMED SHUT the kitchen window with a convincing thud, keeping out the wind that grew noticeably colder each day. For a moment she looked out at the street, where the few remaining clusters of leaves swirled in intricate mutating shapes. She remembered, as a young girl, fantasizing living, magical creatures in just such formations, the way children often did with clouds or flames. But the wind soon died down, and the leaves, deprived of their spirit, fell to the ground with soft crackles.

She turned from the window, returning to the sink and placing a can of tomato juice on the kitchen counter. She leaned over, resting both elbows on the formica top, and peered into the shiny surface of the toaster just inches away. She frowned deeply at the reflection in the polished surface: the pallid skin stretched tautly across her broad, high cheekbones, offset only by the dark half-circles under her eyes that seemed to grow fuller and darker each day, like waxing black moons; the lips, drained and cracked, no longer used to smiling; the hair, hanging in loose, matted clumps like a wasted frame around her face; and the eyes, which seemed to recede a little more each day, as if to escape the sunlight. She lifted her chin and ran a hand along her neck, rubbing it gently. How sensitive her skin had become, like the tenderness accompanying high fever. And how the burning pain would unexpectedly attack her from inside, how it would rack her body and make her want to cry out. When had it been that she had last slept through the entire night? That she hadn't been awakened in the indistinct hours, her body still quivering in the wake of a sudden flare of pain? Or merely to black dissociation and cold sweat?

Just nerves.

She let the reflection recede from her as she straightened, taking a step back from the counter. There was no use in brooding. She would simply have to eat better, get more vitamins; perhaps she could will herself to sleep at night. It disturbed her that her general weakness had not allowed her to keep up her natural childbirth exercises with the frequency she would have liked.

She reached for the tomato juice, poured herself a tall glass, and raised it to her mouth, feeling the cold tingling as the liquid touched her lips.

In the living room, Alric sat on the sofa, head buried in the first section of the *Sunday Times*. He read for the third time the opening sentence of an article which held little interest for him; a moment later he would have forgotten its content. He had begun to read voluminously, compulsively, especially the newspapers, desperate to retain his link with the world, with the present. Only the science pages were left untouched. And when he'd finished the paper he would toss it aside and turn on the television, watching the various newscasters repeat the same stories on into the night. Other times he would go on long walks, no matter how cold it was, attempting to keep his senses filled with impressions of the present, trying to strengthen his sense of time, his connection with reality. For whenever he eased up, whenever he allowed his attention to slip, it would come back to him. . . . Again he began the article.

The splintering crash reached him with a sharpness that wrenched the paper from him and onto the floor. He stood quickly, secondarily realizing that the sound of breaking glass had been accompanied by a short, stifled cry that had been his name.

In an instant he stood by the entrance to the kitchen, his eyes wide at the broken glass and red juice that spread in puddles along the counter top and onto the floor. Diana leaned on the counter with one arm, the other across her belly, as if holding a bursting shopping bag that threatened to spill its contents. Her eyes were agonized and pleading.

"John! Something's wrong . . . !"

He broke from his paralysis and ran over to her. She grasped at him with the clutching fingers of an old woman, her body shaking in his arms. Slowly he led her from the maze of broken glass and spilled tomato juice.

"I'll get you to bed," he said softly, trying to calm her with his tone.

"Something's wrong!" she cried again, her eyes wide, like those of a frightened animal. "Inside!"

They walked carefully, like a couple brittle with age, guiding themselves along the walls. They reached the bedroom and he eased her into bed, pulling a sheet up over her.

"I'll call Dr. Murray," he said, straightening.

As he turned to leave she grasped his arm with manic strength. "John, I don't want to lose it!" Her cry became a hoarse gurgling in her throat.

"It'll be all right," he soothed, touching her cold

fingers. "It'll be okay. You're not going to lose the baby." He gently pulled away from her and walked quickly from the room.

He ran to the phone.

Dr. Murray closed the bedroom door quietly behind him, meeting Alric's questioning look with his soft, brown eyes. "I've given her a sedative," he said, in the hushed tones of practiced confidentiality. "She should be out for a few hours."

He stepped farther into the living room, stopping opposite Alric, whose face had grown pale in the intervening hour. He struck Dr. Murray as a man who had been getting very little sleep.

"What's wrong with her, Doctor?" he asked. "She's not going to lose the baby?"

The doctor made a perfunctory gesture of dismissal. "Oh, no, John. They'll both be fine." His well-lined face creased into a reassuring smile, and Alric relaxed noticeably. "The baby has a nice, strong heartbeat, and there's no sign of miscarriage. We'll run some tests, to be on the safe side, but, as far as I can tell, there's nothing wrong with the pregnancy."

"What's causing the pain, then?" asked Alric, frowning. "And you've seen the way she looks."

Again an easy look of dismissal. "It's nothing out of the ordinary, I can assure you. Sometimes stress can cause the muscles to constrict, or the baby might simply be kicking a bit hard. This is your wife's first pregnancy; it's not unusual for her to be feeling some discomfort." The doctor took Alric's arm as they began walking toward the hall closet. "As for her appearance," he continued, "I'll prescribe some additional nutritional supplements. I don't think she's been eating as well as she might. And we might check for anemia."

Alric looked up at the last words.

The doctor caught the look in the younger man's eyes and again smiled. "Also not uncommon among pregnant women," he reassured.

Alric nodded uncertainly.

"The important thing is not to overreact. Just let her relax; keep her off her feet for a few days. She'll be fine."

He set his bag down on a chair by the closet, and looked closely at Alric. "What else is bothering you, John?" he asked quietly.

Alric looked up. "What do you mean?"

"You look like hell."

Alric smiled weakly. "Nothing, really . . . I've had some things on my mind."

"Let me prescribe something for you. A mild sedative."

Alric shook his head resolutely.

"Your nerves look shot, John. Maybe it would be better if I did."

"No. Really. It's not necessary."

The doctor studied Alric's face for a moment, then shrugged. "At least try and get more rest," he said. "You can't be much help to Diana like that."

"I'll try," said Alric, helping the doctor into his coat. He held the front door open for him. "You're sure she'll be all right?"

Dr. Murray pressed Alric's arm firmly. "Your wife is a healthy young woman. She'll be just fine."

Alric smiled, nodding as the doctor exited.

But as the door closed behind the older man Alric's smile quickly faded. If only he could be as certain as the doctor. Or was it the certainty of ignorance? If only he could know. *"The pregnancy is normal. . . ."* How eerie the words had sounded to him, hollow and mechanical rather than comforting. Normal. He almost forced a grim smile at the irony, but could not; the memory of how she'd looked at him was too vivid.

236

Normal.

Suddenly he was struck by an image he had long suppressed: the memory of Ahmad, on their last day in the desert—and his final words to them, chilling in the intensity. In their warning.

Yes, Ahmad.

How long had it been since Alric had allowed himself to think of the man, or even internally voice the name? But he saw now that the memory was still fresh, sharp. It had been only hours before their departure, more an escape than a departing, amid the many conflicting plans, some hastened, others aborted. Now the scene played itself once again before his mind's eye.

And, again—Ahmad's final warning.

He shook his head in an effort to clear it, again going over all that the doctor had said, for it was a safe memory.

And perhaps, after all, there was no more to it than that. . . .

He walked to the bedroom door, turned the knob quietly, and stepped inside. Diana lay on the bed, sleeping peacefully, her hands clasped over her belly. Her breathing was deep, even; he found it comforting to watch, almost hypnotic in its regularity. Occasionally her head would twitch fractionally to one side, as if in an aborted effort to shake her head in the negative. Then she would relax again, and he would see the tension dissipate from her neck, and her body, which had stiffened slightly, would sink back into the mattress.

He stood watching her for several minutes, then pulled a chair over to the side of the bed and sat down, resting his chin thoughtfully on his palms. Through the open window a breeze played sporadically with the curtains, making them dance in sudden frantic bursts, then allowing them to fall back down to precarious tranquility. He watched them move about, fall, then move again. And he watched his wife's steady breathing.

And, gradually, he felt all thought leave his mind, expelled from the nerve fibers that energized his body, until all that was left was dark vacuum, and the fading red memory of warmth.

*

WHEN THE FIRST tests had proved negative, he had
been relieved; the doctor's words had seemed to
hold the strength of knowledge. For a while he
had even imagined that she was looking better, that
she seemed stronger. He would tell her of the latest
results and stand smiling before her, waiting for her
reaction. And she would smile weakly at his concern,
though she never really seemed to be listening; it
was as though it were a matter that only peripherally
concerned her. But now it was almost a month since
she had collapsed, and she was still bedridden. He
could no longer convince himself that she was im-
proving. And when he looked down at her while she
slept, listening to her shallow breaths, and imagining
that he could see the strength leaving her body like
heat from a dying coal; when her skin continued
to lose its color, until it had become a flat ashen
surface; when her eyes had become sunken globes
in her bony face; he began to realize that there was
nothing that would show up on any medical tests.
Nothing that *could* show up. But still there were
more tests, ordered by the specialists consulted by
Dr. Murray.

Alric had received the calls daily, always from
Dr. Murray, his soft voice each day revealing more
puzzlement, until puzzlement gave way to concern,
and concern to worry, as it became increasingly evi-

dent that he was at a loss to explain what was happening. Each day he had reported to Alric the results that should have been encouraging, but, with her weakening condition, only seemed to make a mockery of their efforts. EKG: within normal limits. Complete blood count: within normal limits. Electrolytes: within normal limits. Abdominal sonogram: findings consistent with duration of pregnancy; no abnormalities noted.

Normal.

And each day she grew weaker.

From her position on the bed she could see a small patch of sky through the window, above the top of the building across the street. For hours at a time she would stare out at the blue, watching an occasional plane or flight of birds, or waiting for an interesting cloud formation to break the monotony. She had given up on the stack of paperbacks on the chair by the bed, and the TV Alric had installed in the corner of the room had not been turned on in weeks. She merely lay there, gazing out the window. And thinking.

The pain wasn't so bad anymore—or perhaps she had simply been numbed by its constancy. But she was enervated, drained, as if something were sucking the life force from her: it had become a chore for her to brush back a strand of hair from her face.

And sometimes she felt close to giving up.

She couldn't say exactly at what point she had come to understand that there was nothing the doctors could do to help her, that it was beyond their knowledge. Perhaps it had been a gradual realization, growing slowly inside her until the early inklings had materialized to dark certainty. And now she could almost feel herself dying a little each day, her strength to fight abandoning her.

A sudden shrill chorus of birds caught her attention as a small flock passed her line of sight. Her eyes sharpened momentarily, watching a few stragglers following lazily. From the other room she could hear Alric walking around, quietly, so as not to disturb her. She stifled an impulse to cry, and again trained her eyes on the band of blue through the window. And even though the power of clear thought seemed to be leaving her, even though it would have been so easy to just close her eyes and shut everything out, she still would not let go, would not give in to whatever was killing her. Something inside continued to struggle.

She wondered, almost detachedly, for how long.

He watched the heat escape from a small bowl of broth in swirling gray clouds, quickly dissipating in the cool air from the open kitchen window. In a moment he set the bowl on a serving tray alongside a half-glass of orange juice. He shook his head at the pathetic meal. He wondered when she would stop eating entirely.

He entered the bedroom and walked around to her side of the bed. She looked up at him through filmed eyes and he braced himself for fear of betraying a reaction. She picked up her head a few inches from the pillow, her hair hanging in limp clumps.

He managed a smile. "Can you sit up?"

"I'm not hungry." It was a rasping sound from deep in her throat.

"You have to eat," he said patiently. He placed the tray on the bed.

"I'm going to die." It had been a simple statement, devoid of tone or expression.

He showed no reaction to her words, merely sat down beside her on the edge of the bed. He touched the glass of orange juice with a finger. "Why don't you try some? It's pretty good."

She looked up and caught his eye. "I'm going to die," she repeated.

He took his hand away from the tray. "You're

going to be all right," he said softly. "They'll find
out what's the matter, and then they'll—"

"You know what's the matter!"

He started at her outburst, her words chilling
him, echoing his own fears. He looked down into
her eyes and saw they were black with despair.
There was an oppressiveness in the room that
seemed to push against his lungs and make breathing
difficult. He reached down a hand to touch her
cheek; there was nothing he could say.

"Ahmad said we shouldn't leave, that we couldn't
run. . . ." Tears were streaming from her eyes. Her
thin hand came out from under the covers and
rested on his, pressing it close to her face. Her
fingers were like ice. "Oh, John, I'm scared," she
sobbed.

He looked down helplessly. He could no longer
pretend; he was beyond trying. He could no longer
convince himself that what was happening was
within the possible control of the doctors. They
knew nothing of what was at work here, just as he
knew nothing. Their antiseptic terms couldn't save
her—and if he told them, they wouldn't believe. He
was as blocked from them as they were from Diana: by the barrier between worlds. And therefore
he could no longer hope.

He could only hold her, press her body tightly
against him as if to squeeze the fear from both of
them. Because, deep inside, he knew that she was
right. That Ahmad had been right. And that an old
man who had stood among the ruins until he had become one with them had been right as well. Perhaps he had always known.

Now all he could do was hold his wife to keep her
from crying. And to keep himself from going insane.

*

ALRIC TRACED HIS usual path through the park, this time his steps preserved in the smooth overlay of a recent snow. The numbing white confines seemed to be his only comfort, his only retreat. Beyond the borders of the park, the streets of Manhattan were already clear, as they were within hours of all but the most furious of snowstorms, the city's harsh machine expirations melting most of the flakes before they could reach the ground. But inside the park the snow would remain until the next thaw. Alric walked quickly, though without destination, hands buried deep in his pockets, body hunched against the cold wind that seemed to be coming from all directions at once.

The scene at the apartment had been too much for him. He'd had to get away, if only for a little while. He'd needed the cold air to bite his skin, as if it could chill him awake to some new knowledge, for there *had* to be something more. She *couldn't* just die; it made no sense. He could not let it happen, though he had no idea what he *could* do.

He'd watched her as she lay in bed, twisting violently, sweat forming beads along her forehead that clung like small glass globes. Every so often she would lurch forward in a sudden spasm, shouting *no!* into her darkness.

He shuddered, not from the cold, but at the

thought of what she might be seeing; and he tried to drown in blackness the memory of his own vision, which still returned when his awareness slipped. With an internal chill he realized that it could always return, that it would never be farther from him than the closing of his eyes.

"She's going to have to be hospitalized," Dr. Murray had said, his long face gray with concern.

It had been a long moment before Alric had reacted, although the doctor's words had been anticipated.

"Are you going to induce labor?"

The doctor had shaken his head. "She's too weak." Then he'd looked closely at Alric. "We may have to do a cesarean."

The words had torn at Alric's belly, but his brain could no longer feel. He'd just nodded, and again asked if there was anything he could do.

If there was anything he could do . . . how pathetic it now sounded to him, the words of utter powerlessness. She had been scared and he had been unable to help her. Now he stood in a vast expanse of white, and he felt empty, drained. Helpless. He looked around as if to extract an answer from the air itself. His eyes burned in the light, his skin from the touch of the cold.

Alone.

He had grabbed the doctor's arm with a force that must have been painful, and had asked, for perhaps the thousandth time, "What's *wrong* with her, Doctor?"

And again the other man had shaken his head, gravely, his voice exhibiting the strain of the last few hours. "John, I just don't know." He'd given an aborted shrug, a gesture of helplessness, and his eyes had avoided contact with Alric's. "Physiologically, she appears normal—at least there's nothing that shows upon any of the tests. . . ."

He had paused, and then his eyes had risen to

meet Alric's. He had continued in a voice barely
above a whisper. "She's dying, John. And for the life
of me, I don't know why."

The ambulance was due to arrive in half an hour.
Until then it had been necessary for him to leave,
to escape, if only for a few minutes. He had needed
to walk, to let his body do the work: he had felt
no longer capable of thought. And he had needed
the harsh freedom of the cold. Dr. Murray had understood. He had nodded as Alric had exited. Then
he had turned and rejoined the nurse in the bedroom to watch over Diana. And wait.

From just up ahead, Alric could see the clash of
motion that signaled the end of the park and the
beginning of the city. Outside, traffic pushed forward
in its usual brief spurts, and the people had taken
to the streets for the lunch hour, walking briskly
against the cold. At Fifth Avenue and 59th Street he
left the park. He looked up to the sky for a moment,
as if trying to discern the next shift in weather, but
it told him nothing. A gray ceiling hung over the
tips of the highest skyscrapers, a featureless, dead
covering.

He started downtown along Fifth Avenue, taking
in the agitated motion of the crowds, the press of
traffic, the random movement that seemed to surge
from all directions. He could have drowned in the
eddies of motion—but the picture of Diana kept
coming back, of her tortured face; and the pale grave
face of Dr. Murray. Alric could anticipate the doctor's next words: *"We did all we could . . ."* He tried
to shake the image from his mind, but the words
would not leave him. *We did all we could. . . .*

But had *he* done all he could?

The city sounds drew away from him until all
became a dreamlike hum. He felt pressure building
behind his eyes, and turned his head upward to
allow the air to soothe his face. There was a small
fluttering movement from above, and he followed

245

intently the flight of a single snowflake against the
massive backdrop of New York. It coursed downward for a few feet, until, caught in a small updraft,
it hung suspended for an instant, then traced a
mazelike path, finally coming to rest on the sidewalk
before his feet.

He stood still, looking down at the snowflake,
imagining its internal configuration. And slowly it
seemed to magnify in his field of vision, becoming an
intricate webwork. He stood mesmerized by its com-
plexity, its shimmering beauty: light was reflected
and refracted inside it in myriad small spectral
beams, a mutating labyrinth. The inner walls sparkled, as pristine as the instant before Creation.

And it continued to grow, a planet of ice. . . .

—The cold hit him with a paralyzing pressure that
squeezed the breath from his lungs. He reeled sideways, as if caught in a raging blizzard spontaneously
generated in the air around him. He gasped painfully
for breath, feeling himself drowning, sinking into
white vacuum. He was blinded, his eyes burning in
an unending storm of white, and a tumult of the
wind crashed against his ears. He felt himself stumbling, falling, his arms flailing for balance. . . .

Until. . . .

Silence.

Absolute and deafening.

Vision returned with the tentative opening of his
eyes. And if he'd had the strength left to care he
would have closed them again, pressed them together until pain drowned sight.

He stood empty, mute. New York stretched before him, a maze of ruins, a jagged, three-dimensional framework of broken concrete and steel,
shrouded by the eternally lingering black smoke of
decay. The air was no longer cold, but heavy with
an acrid dust that burned his nostrils.

The smell of burning flesh.

And then he felt it.

Slowly, like melting ice, it drew along his back, and he wanted to scream, but had no voice. His eyes widened as he could see the blue-white of a corpse's hand; between his shoulder blades, along the ridge of his spine, the long, ragged fingernails tearing small bits of flesh from him, leaving behind stinging raw strips of skin.

And he remembered.

Walking into the living room that night. That ear-piercing sound, the scream of the pyramid. Looking from his window on a dead city, a city destroyed by time.

And the vague, rustling sound from behind.

And turning.

And—

An outline in black against the darkness of the room. Cowled, within the folds of shadow, a face, glowing with the pale light of a funeral shroud. The cruel gash of mouth, twisted hideously into a grin that burned itself indelibly into his memory: a grin that had smiled at the taste of charred human flesh, a mouth that had drunk hot, pumping blood. And the eyes, empty receding caverns. Yet not empty . . . not empty . . . within them a vision of squirming victims impaled on sacrificial stakes, their skin licked greedily by flames like dagger-points until melting to heavy misshapen beads that clung to the splintered ends of protruding bones, gouts of blood oozing like dark lava from the gaps, quickly vaporizing to a red mist around their heads . . . and the sharp *cracks* of heat-split bone . . . and the screams, the screams . . . and all the while that hideous mocking smile. Until a hand came out from within the shadow, leprous, black talons reaching out toward him, toward his eyes. . . .

And he was running, blindly, frantically, through the gutted ruins that had been his city moments ago. Above him the sky was a dead black cast, bloated and oppressive. Around him buildings had been reduced to twisted steel skeletons, rising precariously from beds of fragmented glass and concrete. What remained of Fifth Avenue stretched before him, a broken line crisscrossed by jagged cracks like the web of a spider gone mad. To either side, remnants of concrete walls rose several feet from the rubble, looking incongruously intact.

And he ran on.

In the ruins.

And in its whitening walls he saw Chandler's splattered brains, like some madman's graffiti.

He wanted to cry out.

Instead he fell.

His eyes closed with the shock of pain; he felt a warm liquid on his knees, running in slow rivulets down his calves.

He opened his eyes.

Looked up.

. . . Stillness and night.

Frozen calm.

All around him the carcasses of ancient structures rise up solid and dark against the faint glow of the night sky: the remnants of a forgotten civilization.

The ruins.

But these are ruins of stone: he can find no trace of the steel frameworks that were there an instant before.

And he realizes: these are the ruins within the walls of the Old City.

And before him, surrounded by long shadows resembling flat, angular night creatures, stands the Blind Man.

Alric watches the words fall from those ancient lips in slow motion, caught inside an endless four-dimensional spiral. . . .

"It began here. And it must end here."

It was an everyday occurrence: a man lying unconscious on the sidewalk. Around him, people continued toward their destinations, most paying no attention, a few shaking their heads. It was midday, and the business crowds were rushed. A light snow was falling.

The man's head twitched briefly: the cold, yes, the cold. . . . Darkness threatened his mind again, but the images would not leave him. And he remembered, in the deepest substrata of his body: yes, the cold, there can be salvation in the cold. Must find it.

One man stopped, about thirty years old, dressed in workclothes. He bent over the fallen man and reached down a hand.

Alric continued to fight for vision, for light, gradually finding consciousness in the small areas of exposed skin which burned in the cold air.

"Are you all right, buddy?" the man was asking. "Should I get a cop?"

The tingling reminders of life pushed through to deeper and deeper levels until his mind responded. He opened his eyes.

"Are you all right?"

A band of light, a soft glare. Slow resolution. Then: the colorless swatch of sky, an uneven pale stretch bordered by the gray stone of New York. A man's face. Soft white crystals falling around him, outlined in sudden clarity against the mottled backdrop of pedestrian traffic. Snow.

He nodded uncertainly, then reached up and took the man's hand. He rose unsteadily to his feet. "Yes. . . ." It was still tentative. Then, again, "Yes. Thank you."

"You sure, now?"

Alric nodded, then turned from the man.

He was stung with a sudden touch of clarity; he felt a blindness leave his mind, stunning him with the pain of nascent sight. As he moved he felt it in his body, in the fibers of his nervous system, an electric tingling. Knowledge. A course stretched before him, sure and immediate; and the once-familiar feeling of trust in himself came back with a heady surge.

He walked faster, feeling his blood pumping with a violence that rang a harsh cleansing chorus in his ears.

Alric walked brisky through the front door, tossing his overcoat onto the chair by the hall closet. His cheeks were red with the exhilaration of the cold.

Dr. Murray stood wearily from the sofa and looked over at Alric through tired red eyes. "I've reserved a room at Mount Sinai," he said hoarsely.

"Cancel it," said Alric, entering the living room.

"What . . . ?"

"Cancel the room," repeated Alric with quiet intensity. "She's not going."

"I don't understand," said the doctor, shaking his head briefly in confusion.

"She won't be going to the hospital." Alric's voice was emotionless.

The doctor approached him. "I don't know what you're saying. She'll die if we don't—"

"She's not going to die." Alric's eyes glowed with an intensity resembling religious fervor. Dr. Murray was startled by them.

Behind the two men, the bedroom door opened and the nurse, a middle-aged, overweight woman, entered, carrying a tray of medications. She stopped abruptly at the confrontation in the living room.

Alric looked at her, then back at the doctor. He spoke softly. "Thank you, Doctor. But there's nothing more you can do here." He went to the closet and removed the coats of the two visitors, draping them over his arm.

Dr. Murray walked over to him. "John, this is crazy," he said, his voice emphatic, yet almost whispering, as if he didn't want the nurse to overhear. "Without proper treatment she'll die. And the baby will die."

250

"She'll have treatment."

The doctor hesitated. "John, if you've brought in another man, I understand, but—"

Alric held out the doctor's coat. "Thank you, Doctor. Good-bye."

"Please, John, I ask you to consider your actions."

"Thank you, Doctor."

The nurse had put her tray on the dining table and come farther into the room. Her eyes flicked nervously back and forth between the two men as she tried vainly to assess the situation. The doctor motioned to her and she stepped over to the door, taking her coat from Alric. He held the door open as she exited.

Dr. Murray leaned closer to Alric. "I think you're making a grave mistake," he said, his voice dark with concern. When Alric did not react, the doctor took his coat and quietly left the apartment.

Alric closed the door behind them, then turned and walked quickly to the bedroom.

Diana was sleeping uneasily as he approached the bed, her breathing labored, her body twisting partially on one side, then the other, as if held down by invisible restraints. He looked down at her thin face, shadowed and slick with sweat. Her hair clung loosely to her temples and jawline, and her eyelids twitched violently, as if her eyes were in flight from unknown horrors. He reached down and held her hand, which moved slightly at his touch. The skin along the back of her hand was feverish, though her palm was like ice. His face softened at the sight of her.

"It'll be all right," he whispered. "You'll be just fine. I promise you." He replaced the hand by her side, realizing on another level that he felt a coolness and clarity of mind that he had not experienced since before he had begun work on the project.

He straightened abruptly and left the room, walking through the living room to the storage closet. He opened the door and stepped inside, wading into stores of half-filled cartons and stacks of yellowing paperbacks. In a moment he found what he was searching for: the narrow cardboard box containing the pieces of the model pyramid Tom Scott had brought over. He stepped out of the closet and sat on the floor, emptying the shiny steel rods onto the carpet. With a singleness of mind that had been absent for many months, he began assembling them.

When he had finished he sat still for a moment, studying the small pyramid—this strange, ancient key, all but forgotten by modern man until recently. Its slender gold-flecked steel arms shone like cylindrical mirrors, sending cold sparks of light into his eyes. But this time he stayed with it, fused to its core. How long ago had it been that he had first become involved with this enigma stretching back to the roots of man? He could no longer remember a time when the shape had meant no more to him than a species of geometrical form. It seemed to have always been with him, inside him; it went further back than memory. If only now he had learned to use it correctly. . . . He thought back to those early experiments, seemingly centuries ago, demonstrating the healing potential, the force for good, that the ancients had understood. The force they had known was somehow linked to the holy object, the holy shape that concentrated the forces of the cosmos. And he remembered the nightmare, which had also sprung from the secret, and the terror which would, perhaps, always be with him, not far below the surface, ready to erupt at any unguarded moment. And he knew that the two could not be separated.

Then he rose, cradling the pyramid in his arms. All hesitation was gone from him. He returned to the bedroom, gently placing the model beside Diana on the bed. He looked around the room briefly, his eyes stopping at the wooden serving tray used for her meals. He lifted it from the chair by the bed and positioned it over Diana's stomach, its legs just touching her sides. He then carefully placed the pyramid on top of it, so that the apex was directly above the center of her belly. She stirred briefly, turning her head to one side so that she now faced him; her eyes remained closed. For a moment he stood watching her, remembering how she had looked only a few months ago. Then he turned from the bed and walked back to the living room, seating himself by the phone. He lifted the receiver with one hand and reached for the directory with the other.

There were plans to be made.

It was a world without form, without dimension. A unity of senses. Colors moved, swirling alive, magic creatures within the field of his awareness, though he could not have put into words just how he perceived them. In fact, he had no words. No concepts. Only being. A sea of being. He had no eyes, but saw. No ears, but heard. And felt, though with a body not his own, a body without discrete boundary. Without name. And he remembered. The past, the future . . . all spun away from and toward him, though there was no direction. Only presence. And he understood: the visions of Plato, the parables of Jesus, the formulae of Einstein. All knowing is remembering, all being is return. *Time is the shortest distance between two points*. The universe reflected itself between infinite mirrors, infinite eyes, spiraling endlessly between microcosm and macrocosm. He swayed within the soft pressure of knowledge, vibrated within the space between two quantum levels, existed within two instants, two eternities. . . .

When Alric opened his eyes it was late afternoon; the deep colors of sunset entered through the open window with a cool rush of air. He'd been dozing in the chair beside Diana. Now he looked over at her. She lay peacefully under the apparatus he had erected, her body no longer in constant, agitated motion. In the weak light he could see the early traces of color returning to her cheeks, so faint that at first he thought he might be imagining it. But no, she *did* look different: the thick black bands under her eyes had faded considerably, looking now like old and healing bruises. And her skin was smooth and dry, her breathing unstrained and even. He resettled in his chair, clasping his hands in front of him.

Slowly her eyes opened, at first remote, then sharpening, and narrowing in curiosity at the model pyramid perched before her on the wooden tray. She turned to Alric. "John . . . ?" Her voice was weak, yet clear.

He smiled at her.

"How long have I been out?" She looked briefly around. "Where's Dr. Murray?"

"No longer needed."

"What's been—?" She cut herself short, then turned back to him. She stared vaguely for a few seconds, as if trying to formulate the next thought.

"I had the strangest dream. . . ." she said.

"How do you feel?" asked Alric softly.

(The morning air is chill, yet somehow comforting, as they exit the building. He looks up briefly to the sky, squinting slightly at its blue glare. He holds his wife tightly around the waist.

The taxi is double-parked in front of the building's entrance. The driver stands by the door, looks up as the couple approaches. He notices the woman's condition: she appears due imminently.

"What hospital?" he asks.)

She was silent for a moment, as if taking internal inventory. "Better," she said, finally. "And different." Then she paused, looking intently into his eyes.

("Kennedy Airport," says the man. His blue eyes are intense in the bright sunlight.

254

"*Kennedy?*" *The cabby eyes the couple curiously. He shrugs. "Whatever you say. Where's your luggage?*"

"*There is none.*"

The man opens the cab door and helps his wife inside.)

"We're going back, aren't we." It was not a question.

Alric studied her face for a moment, looking into her eyes.

"Yes," he said quietly.

He reached out to hold her hand.

Part Three

*

THE DARK, SLENDER man paced back and forth in the spill of light coming through the glass doors of the terminal, his hands alternately in and out of his pockets, his nostrils dilating with each intake of air. He glanced inside every few seconds, either at the door leading to Customs or at one of the many clocks behind the row of airline counters. How grudgingly those slender black arms seemed to give up each new minute. He could feel his body tensing, as if to sympathetically impart some energy to the progress of time. At any other time he would have chided himself for his impatience: it was not a trait common among his people, who had grown used to waiting. But this night he allowed himself this small frailty: it was other human weaknesses that concerned him now.

The call he had received last night had been expected; anything else would have been unthinkable. Still, he had greeted it with a transcendent relief that he had never known. It heightened his senses to their peak, and the agitation he now knew was a supreme dialectic of joy and pain. He watched the pieces come together, engaged in a primal dance.

The ancient game would begin.

The two men sat quietly in a parked car, twenty yards from the passenger terminal. They had been

259

waiting for some time, but neither grew restless. Behind the wheel, Inspector Yadin restoked his pipe, took a few coughing draws, then opened the window a few more inches to empty the spent tobacco. Beside him, Dan Michaels did not remove his eyes from the slender man who paced before the terminal entrance, except for an occasional downward look at his wristwatch. Suddenly his eyes sharpened. He nudged Yadin's side, nodding toward the entrance, where the two Americans emerged through the glass doors. The couple exchanged greetings with the Arab, then accompanied him to the parking lot.

Yadin nodded, closing his window against the chill night air. He reached his hand to the ignition key.

By the time Ahmad left the highway, turning onto the desert road, Alric's mind had achieved a state of calm, had become a protective envelope around him, a filter between him and the world. He felt prepared. As the jeep continued under the clear night sky, the events of the last few hours seemed to have grown distant, like the interminable highway lights that had flashed in and out of his field of vision as they had driven toward the desert. New York was already a fleshless memory; the time spent there had congealed to a point. There was only the present.

Alric did not know how long they had driven on this second paved stretch before the narrow dirt road appeared like a dry riverbed beginning and ending nowhere. Ahmad now swung the jeep deftly onto this new road, and Alric shortly realized, without knowing what had told him, that he had been here before.

He held Diana's hand as they drove on in the darkness, the headlight beams revealing nothing but a pale ellipse of packed sand. He had watched her closely on the plane and had been amazed at how she had seemed to improve with each passing minute, until even the last lingering traces of weakness had left her. She had asked few questions, had seemed to understand, in some ways, perhaps, better than he. But as the plane had touched down she had turned to him, reaching for his hand.

"What will we do when we get there?" she had asked.

"I spoke to Ahmad while you were sleeping. He's going to meet us at the airport."

She had looked at him, indicating that this was not what she had meant.

He had merely shaken his head.

Ahmad slowed the jeep, and Alric wondered what unseen landmarks the guide was using to judge distances, how he could find exactly the point along the road he was looking for. The jeep stopped, and Ahmad turned to them.

"There is no place that will be safe," he said softly. "Not until he is born." His eyes glittered in the weak yellow light from the dashboard. "But it must be done," he continued, "Here, where it began."

Alric said nothing. He glanced at Diana, then back at Ahmad. He nodded.

They pulled off the narrow road, the jeep kicking up small clouds of sand as it headed into the desert.

Yadin and Michaels had been driving without headlights since leaving the paved road. Even one other vehicle on this lonely dirt road stretching through the desert might have been cause for suspicion. Fortunately, it was a clear night; a plenary field of stars outlined the narrow road in a pale blue-white glow. And the two orange-red taillights up ahead had led the way, a few hundred yards distant. Once Yadin had been distressed to see the lights go out, as the other vehicle had curved around a slight rise in the terrain. For a moment he had feared that they, too, had decided to go on under cover of darkness. But he had kept his hands steady on the wheel, his foot applying even pressure to the gas pedal; he had reined himself to a single-minded concentration on the thin line of road ahead, waiting for the re-emergence of the two lights. And then they had reappeared, and he had exhaled deeply, only then allowing himself to acknowledge how concerned he had been. Michaels had not spoken a word.

Then the two lights ahead had grown suddenly brighter. Yadin's foot had reacted immediately, shifting to the brake pedal as the other vehicle had slowed; stopped. Yadin had braked the car to a crawl, then had traded glances with Michaels as the jeep had veered sharply to the right, indicating that it had been leaving the road.

The inspector and the government man drove slowly on to the point where the jeep had changed course. They, too, left the road, heading into the desert behind the twin stars of the jeep's taillights.

He could not have said exactly how long they had been traveling roadless in the desert, surrounded by little more than transitory curves of sand and an occasional outcropping of dark rock. Certainly it hadn't been more than a few minutes. He found the gentle rocking motion of the jeep soothing, and the crystal darkness of the night was like a protective womb. Though the terrain was without obvious features, it was familiar to Alric. He remembered the nights he'd spent walking in this desert, thinking of the future and the past. And he understood its power, like that of the cold night sky: the power of changelessness. Here past and future were one, the primal unity of an infinite present. Here the sun and moon danced at opposite ends of the firmament, one rising as the other set, as if connected by a giant lever with the earth as fulcrum, the reflection between them setting up a resonance. And in the gap: a world in perpetual creation.

The jeep approached a low hill, little more than a mound of sand, and Alric recognized it immediately. As they rounded the hummock a dark, angular shape appeared, like a flat inverted V, just where he had known it would be. There was a mild glitter from the apex: reflected starlight from the pyramid's gold capstone.

Ahmad stopped the jeep fifty yards from the structure and turned off the ignition. The engine died in a soft echo, and then there was complete silence.

Again the two red beacons up ahead had brightened. Yadin had braked in response, reaching his hand quickly to the ignition key. He'd killed the engine as soon as the taillights had died out, allowing the car to coast to a stop, partially blocked from view by the low hill. He had held his breath for a moment, hoping the occupants of the jeep hadn't heard his engine. Then he had relaxed, assured he'd been quick enough.

He and Michaels sat in silence, looking out through the windshield at the jeep parked near the pyramid.

They waited.

And watched, as the three figures emerged, clearly visible in the starlight.

It was a mild night, like many others he'd spent here during work on the excavation. The stars were brilliant points of light in the black fabric of the sky; the moon hung full and tumescent near the horizon. The air was still and clean, free of the fumes of the city, only a few miles away.

The pyramid was entirely revealed now, and the displaced sand deposited elsewhere in the desert. Alric realized with a mild shock that the project had gone on without him. And, as they stood before the pyramid, coldly majestic in the night, it was hard for him to appreciate that any time had passed. Or even that it was *possible* for time to pass, as though it were an unseen, unfelt current, omnipresent, reducing man to the role of spectator. He remembered his first glimpse of the ancient structure as if it had been an instant ago, its gold tip protruding from the sand like an unearthed time capsule, a cryptic message to mankind. Or, as he had sometimes felt, to him alone. How long ago had it been? There had been the news reports, followed by the inevitable papers written for the various journals, the new theories offered by certain scientists, the old ones others had felt were substantiated by this latest discovery. And his own theories, though he could no longer recall their substance. Just words. And now, so much had been revealed and yet so little. He still felt ignorant in the pyramid's presence, awed by its ultimate mystery. No matter how many layers he peeled back, there was always another level, a deeper uncertainty. . . . For a moment he imagined he could feel time moving in discrete jumps, the quantum grains of space. Then he smiled, realizing it was his pulse, throbbing steadily in his temples.

He and Diana looked at each other, simultaneously realizing that they were still wearing their heavy winter overcoats. They removed the garments, letting them fall to the ground.

Alric turned to Ahmad. "Where?" he asked.

"You'll know better than I," answered the guide.

Alric let go a deep breath. The throbbing in his temples grew, was reassuring. He took a last look at the pyramid, understanding that it had served its purpose, completed its role.

They began walking farther into the desert.

Yadin and Michaels exchanged puzzled glances as they watched the three figures begin to walk away from the jeep. They had not known what to expect, had had no real theories with which to work; but the latest actions of the three were unfathomable. The abrupt, apparently unplanned return of the two Americans, their airport meeting with the Arab guide—and now this nocturnal trek into the desert.

Yadin wanted to shake his head in confusion, his mind weary from turning over the few facts he'd gathered since the beginning of the investigation. He'd been pondering them for almost a year now, and still had come up with nothing he could call hard evidence, nothing he could allow himself to believe.

Michaels sat quietly beside him, clearly perplexed as well—by his own feelings as well as the bizarre activities of the three people in the desert. He somehow felt immensely tired, seemed to be looking through the eyes of an old man. And suddenly, for the first time, he had a powerful impulse to give it up, to let it end without him: he had the uneasy feeling that he was intruding on some kind of ancient religious rite.

Through the clear glass of the windshield, the two men watched the three dark silhouettes recede from them. Yadin motioned his head slightly toward the dashboard. "There are some binoculars in the glove compartment."

Michaels nodded, opening the compartment and removing the glasses. He looked through them for a few seconds, watching the three figures walking steadily away. He handed the binoculars to Yadin.

The silence was awesome, as broad and profound as the vast dome of sky. They had been walking for some minutes, and the desert calm seemed to have become a part of Alric, infusing him with a peace he had never known—or, perhaps, had merely forgotten; he understood, he accepted the darkness of the night, on his deepest level. And he wished it could go on. He blinked at the huge white globe of the moon, hanging directly before them. It shone with a strength that made him squint, as if looking into the eye of the sun.

When they stopped, he was not sure who had made the decision. They had just seemed to slow, incrementally, as one body, until they stood facing each other like the three points of an equilateral triangle. Between Ahmad and Diana, in the direction from which they had come, Alric thought he could discern the distant shapes of the two cities, Old and New, lying side by side like petrified angular twins. Then his eyes narrowed: slightly to the left, he had detected a small shadow, black against the horizon's faint glow. He touched Ahmad's arm, motioning toward the small darkness.

Ahmad turned his head, then nodded. "It begins."

Alric and Diana were silent.

"You'd better continue without me," said Ahmad. "The birth is all that matters."

Alric looked at Ahmad, then stretched out his arms, resting his palms on his guide's shoulders. He gripped the smaller man firmly.

Ahmad smiled, his eyes shining in the strong moonlight. There might have been the trace of a shrug.

For a brief moment Alric thought back to the first time he had seen the man.

Ahmad looked into his eyes. "Do you know yet?"

Alric hesitated. "Not for sure."

"Be careful," warned the dark man. "It can still go either way."

Alric nodded, then he and Diana turned from the guide and continued on in the darkness.

Ahmad watched for a moment as the two figures grew small in his sight.

Then he turned around.

And planted his feet.

Yadin had not said a word since lifting the binoculars to his eyes. He had simply watched as the three figures had walked farther into the desert, without apparent destination. They were still within range of the glasses, and he realized that only a few minutes had elapsed since they had left the jeep, perhaps no more than five—but, as he had watched, his sense of time had seemed to recede from him, as if somehow connected to the desert wanderers by an umbilical link. He had been mesmerized by the strange scene: the three slowly moving shadows, proceeding under the immense globe of the moon, for what purpose he could not imagine. It was an image he would not forget. And the utter silence of the night was disconcerting; it seemed unnatural. Then the figures had stopped. For a while they had remained stationary, apparently discussing something. They had been quite small in the field of the binoculars, but he'd been able to easily visualize their faces: intent, haunted, bathed in the blue-white of the moon, their eyes entranced, lit with something he could not comprehend. . . . And then he had to stop himself, give his head a brief shake. He was a policeman, not a mystic, and his imagination *had* to be reined to the probable. He had to regain himself, cling to his objectivity like a buoy in a maelstrom. But what *was* it about this case . . . ? And yes, he reminded himself—surprised that he needed reminding—this *was* just a case. Unlike any he had ever been on, but a case nonetheless: he had to hold that in the fore of his mind. It had to be a beacon in this new darkness. Finally he lowered the binoculars.

"They're splitting up," he said hoarsely. "I won't be able to keep them all in range." He strapped the glasses around his neck. "We'd better get out and follow."

Michaels nodded, reaching for the door lever and pressing it down. Then he looked back at Yadin. "It's stuck," he said.

Yadin looked at him uncomprehendingly.

"It won't open," said Michaels, twisting the handle several more times. He leaned his shoulder against the door and pushed. He shook his head.

Yadin reached for the handle on his side, flicking it up and down in rapid succession.

The door would not move.

He grabbed the window knob, attempted to lower the window. The knob would not turn, resisting his force with equal pressure until the skin along his knuckles whitened. "Try your window," he told Michaels.

But the other man was already struggling with the crank, as unsuccessful as Yadin in moving it. He turned back to Yadin. He shook his head, and his eyes met the inspector's in mutual bewilderment.

And then the bewilderment turned into an ill-defined fear, and Michaels brought his knees up against his chest, swiveling sideways in his seat. With both legs he kicked out at the jammed door.

They had reached a wide stretch of sand, rippled gently with long flat dunes, when Alric slowed, reaching out for Diana's hand. They stopped walking, and he sat down in the sand and began to remove his shoes, motioning her to do the same. When they had finished they stood simultaneously, and for a moment faced each other in silence. The moon was directly behind Diana, its light entering her dark hair in a diffuse glow, forming a muted nimbus around her face. He knew then that he could have stood there looking at her until the sun superseded the moon on the horizon and its harsher fire blinded him. It would have been so easy. . . . But he knew that these few seconds would have to last. He reached out and touched her face, and she pressed her cheek against his palm. He gave her a small smile, then turned from her, looking back in the direction from which they had come.

And he saw it.

No more than an indistinct blurring on the horizon, a bending of light. Or darkness. But he understood its meaning. And he understood Ahmad's words.

It begins.

Without turning, he pulled Diana to him, his eyes still off in the distance. He squinted into the darkness, his senses attuned to the subtlest traces.

Again, a flicker of motion.

This time the movement sparked reciprocal activity in his brain. He turned back to Diana and held her shoulders tightly. "Start running," he said quietly. "Straight ahead." He pointed in the direction in which they had been moving, toward the heart of the desert. "I won't be far behind."

He saw protest come alive in her eyes, but stopped it with a quick shake of his head. "Don't worry. I'll be right behind."

She gave an imperceptible nod, and stretched on her toes to kiss him briefly on the lips. Then she turned and ran deeper into the desert. . . .

And he was alone.

He looked up at the sky, in the desert an unending inverted bowl. It was dizzying in its remoteness, quelling his senses and compressing him to a point. Suddenly he was struck by a long-forgotten memory, recalling himself as a child, when he had first experienced intimations of the power of space. It had been in the dark of night in a lonely field, not far from his home, but it might as well have been on another planet. And he had felt the same then as now. Distilled to his essence, no longer a three-dimensional being, living in time, capable of feeling, but a point, a mathematical construct, a statistical probability, the finest wave of matter. And he had no longer been the observer—or even the observed—but the minutest reflection of the universe. And, yes, the books had said, an atom was like a tiny solar system, its electrons the planets of inner space, ever-spiraling within the field of dimensional continua. Where distance had no meaning, nor time any dominion. Where there is only presence, only—

No! He brought himself back with an effort of will. It took all his strength, for the memory was powerful, hypnotic. But he knew he could not let his attention slip or he was lost. Gradually, he managed to quiet his thoughts; letting them sleep again, so that he could remain awake. He took a few deep breaths, allowed himself a moment's peace. Then he readied himself. Only one thought would not leave him, and it tingled inside him like a bead of ice.

Alone.

And the desert, the night, seemed to become reflections of his solitude. The muted sounds that had grown unnoticeable in their constancy now became noticeable in their absence; even the itinerant flapping of an occasional bird, or the faintest soughing of wind, was gone. And the mild warmth of the night air had vanished as well, leaving behind what could have been a dead planet. He stared across the stark lunar-like landscape, hyperborean under the glacial white sphere of the moon. And the cold clawed at his back with jagged crystal shards.

He turned.

Waited. . . .

—And the stars disappeared in a stunning splash of lightning, leaving behind blackened holes, like spent cinders, in an unending field of white. He took an involuntary step backward, momentarily blinded. The breath tightened in his lungs: for, just before his senses had been overloaded, he had seen the dark figures outlined clearly on the unnatural white horizon.

Moving toward him.

By the time he had brought his hands up to shield his eyes from the glare of the sky, the gesture was

unnecessary. Night and stars had returned—briefly
—sheltering him in domed calm.

It was a moment before either Yadin or Michaels
could react. They just sat there, openmouthed, eyes
wide, stunned by the explosion of light that seemed
to incinerate the sky. Yadin's arm had swung
out reflexively to clutch Michaels's shoulder. The
smaller man sat motionless, sideways on the seat,
staring incredulously through the windshield.

And then it was dark again.

They finally looked at each other, speechless. For a
brief moment their eyes locked, passing messages
between them, collaborating on unspoken fears. Then
Michaels turned back in his seat, again thrusting
out his legs at the stuck door.

Again the sky erupted.

"What the hell—?" began Yadin.

The door flew open with the next thrust of
Michaels's legs. He slid quickly across the seat, turning briefly back to Yadin. "Let's go!" he shouted,
his right foot already on the sand.

And then it was upon him, scrabbling up the front
of his shirt, stinger upraised and ready to strike.
He hadn't seen it spring from the dashboard air
vent; there had merely been a peripheral blur and
the scorpion was on him. And he knew that he
would die. But his body was already in motion,
circumventing the brain's too-slow commands. He
arched backward as his hand swung out; the
scorpion fell free, scrambling for purchase on the
floor of the car. Michaels brought down his left foot,
missed; the scorpion lurched, practically jumped,
forward at his ankle, but he moved quickly. He
brought his foot down again, this time crushing the
thing with his heel. His breath escaped in a shudder
of relief. He slumped back in his seat, spent.

"My God!" whispered Yadin. "What *is* this?"

Michaels's face went expressionless for an instant,

271

his eyes half-closed and glazed, his skin as white as the sky had been. Yadin reached out a hand to him, fearing a delayed reaction of shock. Then Michaels's face contorted—by degrees, it seemed to Yadin, as if in slow motion—into a frightful mask, his mouth opening soundlessly into a wide circle. When the scream came out, agonized and disbelieving, Yadin fell back in his seat, stiffened with alarm. Then Michaels moved, slowly, as if moving in jelly: he gripped his right knee with both hands and pulled his leg back into the car. Yadin's breath stopped.

Attached to Michael's ankles was the long, writhing body of a desert viper, its two-inch fangs plunged to the bone.

Yadin's hand jumped reflexively under his coat and came out with his service revolver. He leaned over, prodding with the end of the weapon until he had it inserted between Michaels's leg and the snake's head. The creature squirmed, but held fast; Yadin thought he could hear the sound of tooth scraping bone. He steadied his grip on the revolver—

And hesitated.

The face of the snake. . . .

A hoarse gurgling sound came from deep in Michaels's throat. Yadin squeezed the trigger, and his ears erupted in pain as the explosion rocked the car. There was a thick cold spray of blood and bits of flesh. When he looked down, the snake lay headless at Michaels's feet. He reached down for the limp body and tossed it from the car, pulling the door closed. He leaned back against the window, taking deep breaths to relieve the pain across his chest.

Michaels stared blankly through the windshield, his face dotted with the snake's blood. Yadin reached up a hand to his own brow and it came away red and wet. He shifted in his seat, reaching for the ignition key.

"We'll have to get you to a hospital," he said,

though he knew the other man could not hear him.

A thud sounded against his left ear.

He flinched, turning to the window.

A blur of motion—and he snapped his head back violently as the desert cobra sprang for his face, smashing its head to a red pulp against the closed window. Yadin stared outside, incredulously, his mind racing. *What was happening?* The desert floor had been transformed into a living reptilian sea, Yadin's eyes blinded by silvery, darting bodies and the glint of venomous fangs—and he knew he had to be imagining it, it *had* to be a hallucination.

Or was it real?

He felt paralyzed by sudden waves of fear welling up cold inside him. His body was leaden and his skin burning. And he wanted to close his eyes to shut out the horror. But a part of him knew that he had to move. Had to act, or Michaels would die. Again he reached for the ignition key.

But no.

The face of the snake: he had glimpsed it for an instant.

He shook his head. It had to have been a trick of the senses.

A face of . . .

The sky was split by a blinding arc of light. Yadin shielded his eyes but could not keep out of the scathing brightness, as once more the sky erupted, soundlessly, becoming a burning white dome. Then black again. Then white, burning.

Finally his hand responded to the brain's interrupted command; the ignition key turned and the engine responded with a low roar.

Alric stood watching the sky.

He had no idea how long it had gone on, this awesome display of lights resembling a paradoxically silent electrical storm in a cloudless sky. But his eyes had grown used to the intensity, functioning well in this new realm. Again and again, blades of light slashed across the sky, forming intricate angular patterns, like unknown hieroglyphs. Or the stars and moon would disappear as the entire sky went white —and it was then that he could see them against the brilliant wall of light: the dark figures that had been distant moving shadows, like the skyline of a fluid city.

Again it went dark.

He spun quickly toward a noise that came from off to his left. He could see nothing.

"Ahmad . . . ?" he called out.

Silence.

Nightmare day again. Were the figures larger? *Closer?*

And then, exploding from inside him like poisonous aliment: the vision of evil, clear, before him, inside him, seen looking in the dead of the night . . . into its eyes, its eyes . . . victims impaled, sacrificed to the god of pain, burning, burning. . . .

He wanted to run; felt himself running; felt the familiar tension in his calf and thigh muscles, his breath quickening, his heart beating faster and stronger—but he knew his body was stationary, frozen to the spot: he could feel individual grains of sand with his toes. He could have counted them.

An explosion of noise circumvented his eardrums, jumping directly into his brain—an omnipresent thunder, convulsing his body and threatening to shatter his bones. He wanted to cry out in pain. . . . Or had he already? Had it been his own cry that deafened him?

He struggled to turn his head to look around, buffeted by a confusion of sensations: the noise, the light—and, suddenly, a wind that almost tore him from the ground. He braced, fighting to keep his balance. But the earth was shattering around him, splitting like a swollen sack. And above him, the insane maze of lightning. His brain erupted in mimicry of the sky, a searing rite of imitation—and he could see them, through the dimension of time: creatures of Eluth, grinding down human flesh as mortar for their edifice.

For the gods take notice of nothing less than human sacrifice.

The sky became an orange field of flames, a domed pyre, and the roar of the earth shook him. His muscles cried out in agony.

For an instant he wanted the dark comfort of unconsciousness . . .

. . . and the demons are upon him, grotesque shapes flowing unendingly from caves deep inside the earth, fingers curved into claws, teeth glinting in the fulgurating light, eyes glistening blood-red. His head turns in soundless shrieking prayer as the sky is torn like the curtain in the Temple of Jerusalem: a bloody corridor of time. And he can see the tiny grains, flitting like sand—

It sprang from beneath the sand like a steel trap. Alric cried out as the fangs sank deep into the flesh of his calf. He doubled over in agony, reaching down both hands to the head of the snake, his vision already clouding. An arc of pain pounded an unrelenting pulse between his leg and his brain, and he could barely make out the slender, undulating body, the strange small eyes. . . . He tore desperately at the head, finally wrapping his hands tightly around it. With his remaining strength, he pulled. His mind went black for an instant, then returned in a blinding field of pain. The snake came away in his hands, and he realized that the small pale bits in its viselike jaws had been his flesh. The creature thrashed about wildly, its mouth snapping open and shut in the air, twisting toward his fingers. His grip tightened until his knuckles went white. Suddenly the snake stopped its violent motion.

And he saw it.

He shook his head to clear the tears of pain from his eyes, but the sight would not leave him: the snake's head had changed; metamorphosed. He stared disbelievingly into the small white face, the black gash of mouth, the hollow eyes: the mocking feral grin of the Eluthi.

He hurled the creature from him with an unintelligible cry, and turned to run. But his leg buckled under him, and he fell to one knee. He reached down to his damaged calf, pressing at the wound to try to stop the bleeding. He stood again and took a hobbling step.

Fire seared his leg.

He stiffened in a new burst of pain—and looked down at the gnarled black hand that had sprung from under the sand like an unholy flower, clutching his ankle with the burning touch of dry ice. The fingers were talons, imbedding themselves deeper, deeper. . . . He fell forward, his momentum freeing him from the thing's grip. He staggered to his feet, stumbling away from the slender, elongated fingers that twisted a malefic dance in the air.

But now all around him they rose up from beneath the sand—and there was nowhere else to go. The pure black forms, the dead white faces, the clawed hands, reaching out toward him, reaching . . . and through the waves of pain clouding his consciousness he could see the dark blood rites that had taken place those many years ago, the summoning of these creatures to await the birth . . . and he wondered why the Powers of Light could not also be summoned. . . .

An agonized scream pierced the tumult.

Alric spun around and gazed into the darkness.

The thing was less than fifty yards away: an insane figure of shifting lines and curves resembling some malformed multilimbed beast, a mutant of nature. It seemed to be moving toward him, the lines separating, converging, separating again. He watched it uncomprehendingly.

Then the sky exploded again—and in its white glare he looked on in horror at the monster that had been his friend. Ahmad was covered with a web-work of writhing, twisting snakes, his clothes and hair glistening, slick and red, the sand at his feet a dark thick mud. He screamed again, and the sound boiled Alric's blood. He seemed to reach out a hand in Alric's direction, then went down.

The Eluthi fell upon him with an obscene wailing.

It was madness getting to the narrow dirt road leading to the highway. Many times Yadin had feared he'd lost his bearings, as he'd tried desperately to keep the car pointed toward where the road should have been. The desert had become a living primeval sea, the sky its chaotic reflection. And there had been vague glimpses of dark shapes, mutating. . . . The car had swerved wildly, as if buffeted by strong winds; several times it had threatened to overturn. But he managed to continue on, and gradually the insanity began to abate, as if they were in a boat approaching the edge of a storm. Finally the car lurched over a small rise, dropping heavily onto the dirt road.

Yadin slumped against the steering wheel in exhaustion, his heart and breath racing. He let himself relax for a few seconds, immensely comforted by the thin dark line of road stretching back toward civilization. Through the window he could see the tumult raging on, but now in the distance, the sky along the horizon continually split by sharp blades of light.

Beside him, Michaels sat glassy-eyed, his head lolling back and forth in semiconsciousness. But Yadin thought he would live if they could reach the hospital in time. He took a last look out at the unceasing frenzy in the distance, then swung the jeep around to face in the direction of the highway, pressing his foot evenly to the accelerator.

Night.

Stars and moon, field of black.

As abruptly as it had begun, the violence had ended, and a paradoxical calm prevailed. The sky and earth were again cold, silent. And the creatures were solid unmoving shadows, watching him. The atmosphere was charged; it tingled his skin. He had watched his friend fall, die; had watched them tear him apart. And he had been helpless. Now he stood motionless, waiting, a strange cold link between him and the creatures. They were all around him now, a crude circle. And he realized that he no longer felt *anything*. He was drained. Empty. He longer felt any fear. He could only look at the creatures with an indistinct, detached curiosity, wondering if they had ever been men. Or a part of man.

Eluthi. . . .

The circle closed.

And he watched them, as if from a distance, or another time. Watched as their cracked, leathery hands reached out. . . .

The circle. . . .

A glimmer in his brain, a burning spark like a bead of sun- or moonlight, intense, painful; the memory of a brilliantly glowing gold capstone—and he remembered.

Not words. Or a feeling.

But a knowledge.

The circle is complete.

And. . . .

The Eluthi seemed to hesitate.

He could feel their vile breath upon him like the putrescence of decaying flesh. He could taste the burning odor in the air, singeing his nostrils and leaving his tongue dry and stinging. And the hands moved out toward him. Claws like daggers, glistening in the moonlight.

And stopped.

Had he heard—?

He looked into the faces, the deep, hollow eyes. Had there been a strange flicker there, for just an instant? Again they moved toward him.

But, again, they hesitated.

And then he became aware of a sound, coming from farther in the desert, somewhere behind him. A strangely haunting sound, familiar, yet indefinable. He tried to attach a name to what he was hearing, but could not. Instead, four words echoed inside his head, over and over, until they became a part of him—and it was as though they were an ancient chant, a charm that seemed to keep the creatures away, seemed to protect him from them:

The circle is complete.

From behind him the sound grew louder, becoming a magnificent harmony to the words in his brain. And, suddenly, a feeling welled up from the center of his body, pounding through his limbs with each pulsebeat, each breath: a feeling of power. Of infinite possibilities. His teeth clenched tight and his mouth twisted into a cruel smile, as he lifted up his arm, slowly, his outstretched hand raised toward the creature nearest him. There was the slightest flicker of movement among the Eluthi—and he knew what was happening.

They had begun to back away from him.

The sound in the desert grew, seeming to come from all directions at once. And he could feel the strength inside him growing: the power of knowledge, clear and cold. The two seemed to merge—the sound outside with the feeling inside—feeding on each other, pyramiding to explosive fury . . . and at the apex of ever-spiraling energy—

All ceased, suspended for an eternal instant: he at

last recognized the sound. And it was a chorus in his ears.

A baby's cry.

For a while, there was nothing but the sound. . . .

An explosion shattered the air.

Alric was nearly thrown to the ground by the force, and looked out as the Eluthi nearest him burst in a flash of lightning as the sky erupted once again, shaking the earth. There was a cold black shower, and what remained of the creature fell, split and oozing gouts of a thick, dark liquid.

The Eluthi shrank from him like leaves from a flame.

Again a thunderous blast—and another of the creatures fell, incinerated to a smoldering deformity, an excrescence of the sand.

And the baby's crying grew louder.

A sick wailing arose among the Eluthi, a pathetic chant of the dead. Dark limbs drew up around them like reptilian wings, as if to block out the sound.

Suddenly, light became a sea around Alric; he almost fell back from its intensity.

The Eluthi drew farther away, huddling against the glare . . .

. . . as the sky is split, shattered into myriad crystalline fragments, burning . . . and from behind the broken facade, blades of light sweep forth, cauterizing waves, overwhelming the demon hordes, and tempting the man to flee as well. . . .

Sensation swelled around Alric, pushing in from all sides with crushing pressure: the noise, the acrid, burning air, and the light, the light . . . Time dilated as he saw himself, felt his senses reach the point of pain, surpass it, enter a new realm. Overloaded, his nerve circuits functioned in a new domain, distilling his mind from his body until all that was left was primal thought . . .

. . . as he felt himself propelled through the vortex

with the force of birth, spiraling down to the place of Beginning. . . .

End! his brain screamed, *God, end it!*

And the high-pitched crying shook his universe. . . .

. . . Gathered stone, the works of an ancient race, standing against time.

An old man with tattered robes and tangled hair emerged into the night: the man of the ruins. He turned his head, his closed, seeing eyes, toward the sky, reaching a hand up to his chest.

A smile flickered across his lips.

He staggered.

Fell . . .

. . . The Eluthi had shrunk from the sound, from him, had become huddling black form. Then the dark ring around him melted away quickly, a flesh-less shadow.

They were gone.

The sky was dark again, except for the stars' points of light, and the immense moon hanging behind him. A soft roll of thunder, like a final shuddering of the earth, spread across the desert floor, to expend itself at the horizons.

Alric turned, took a step. The thunder enveloped him in a heady miasma, sending him careening over the edge of a low sand dune, *falling as though in slow motion, from a great height: he can see the stars around him, a sphere inside his head, spinning in an ancient circular dance.* . . .

. . . Calm descended lightly on the stone remnants devoid of human life for millennia: the ruins.

A cool breeze stirred.

On the ground a mass of tattered rags shifted about, breaking apart in the air, turning to a fine dust.

Quietly, it scattered to the wind. . . .

. . . falling, so slowly, suspended in the instant, surrounded by eternity, seeing through its multi-dimensional funnel the image of a man, himself, standing against the pale backdrop of sky, words turned to stone in his brain, below and above him, the earth, spinning, so fast, dizzying, so slowly, hypnotic . . . until all is within him, all is outside him . . . there is nothing, there is all. . . .

Stars, electrons.

Can go either way.

Can always go either way.

Except for the possibility of a higher determinism.

The Will of Man-God.

,falling, a confluence of images impaled on his brain, no longer capable of concepts, but seeing: black on white on black, the field of stars, the sway of earth—finally superseded by a blazing triangle of gold, blossoming into a pyramid, and continuing on into a dimension for which he had neither name nor number, falling, arms outstretched and reaching for Earth, and gently landing, grateful at last to be returned to her firm grip.

He closed his eyes.

*

IT WAS MORNING when Alric awoke.

He opened his eyes, slowly, squinting slightly at the blue glare of the sky. For a few minutes he remained stationary, not rising from the desert floor. He allowed the quiet, the peace, to enter through his pores. A light breeze was stirring, fluttering his clothes and hair. The distant call of a bird in flight reached his ears. Finally he lifted his head a few inches from the sand, looking left and right in the barren expanse of desert. Then he stood slowly, brushing the sand from his hair and clothes. He took a deep breath, stretching to wake his body. The air had a dry, clean taste.

He began walking along a narrow trail that led through the sand, a slender thread of footprints. The huge red sphere of the sun was directly ahead of him, a few degrees above the horizon. The easy motion of his walking warmed him.

And without struggle, without pain, he remembered.

The project of the Wisemen. The project that would span the experience of man, that would see untold civilizations grow and decay, and the lives of their people interweave a four-dimensional arras that only the gods could fathom.

And he remembered his central role.

His understanding was the merest spark. But it set his mind on fire.

His vision was complete, fulfilled and complemented by its twin pole: Knowledge.

Fresh morning light, pristine and clear; the street below his feet is smooth and flawless, the marble buildings to either side appear carved in a crystal atmosphere.

It is the Center.

He looks straight ahead to the end of the broad avenue.

A hundred yards distant is the gold-topped pyramid, the project of the Wisemen, to carry the spark of their civilization into the future.

For their world is dying.

He approaches the pyramid.

The Wiseman standing before the structure looks up at him, smiles.

Alric nods.

Alric stopped walking, attuning his ears to the silence of the desert. And in a moment he was sure: there was a muffled sound coming from somewhere up ahead.

He continued walking, the bright sunlight bathing him in replenishing warmth.

The Wiseman places his hand on Alric's shoulder, a warm, familiar touch. His eyes speak. And Alric knows that they haven't much longer: perhaps only long enough to see the pyramid safely buried. But his son. . . .

His son will live.

It was coming from just above the next dune, a soft rustle, barely audible over the low sound of the wind.

Her footprints led up the slope.

Alric nods, understanding.

Knowledge flows from the Wiseman's eyes, a soft, redolent music, telling Alric of the future, of the turning points, the junctures where the currents of time will be turned against one another. Telling him of the existences he will know. . . .

284

And Alric understands that when a time comes
that needs the wisdom of this age, a time when
history again threatens to end, when again the
Powers struggle: then the pyramid will be discovered.

Then his son will be born.

Alric returns the Wiseman's gaze, then looks over
at the pyramid. A soft glint of reflected sunlight
sparks from the gold capstone to his eye. . . .

He Knows.

— Alric climbed the low mound of sand and looked
down its shallow slope.

Diana looked up at him and smiled. The infant in
her arms was sleeping.

Alric remained on top of the dune, transfixed.

Diana's eyes glowed. "Come down and look at
your son," she called to him.

Alric descended slowly, and sat down beside his
wife and child.

The baby felt the pressure of their touching bodies
and awoke. And, for the first time, he opened his
eyes to the blue dome of the sky. . . .

Knowing eyes, blinking at the sun, returning its
celestial fire with the burning spark of their own
tiny star of gold.

AN **EXPERIENCE IN HORROR**
YOU MAY TRY TO FORGET . . .
AND TRY . . . AND TRY . . .

COLD MOON OVER BABYLON

BY MICHAEL McDOWELL
AUTHOR OF *THE AMULET*

Terror grows in Babylon, a typical sleepy Southern town
with its throbbing sun and fog-shrouded swamps.

Margaret Larkin has been robbed of her innocence—
and her life. Her killer is rich and powerful,
beyond the grasp of earthly law.

Now, in the murky depths of the local river,
a shifting, almost human shape slowly takes form.
Night after night it will pursue the murderer.
It will watch him from the trees.
And in the chill waters of the river,
it will claim him in the ultimate embrace.

 AVON 48660/$2.50

CMO 2-80